THE BLUE AND THE GRAY SERIES

ON THE BLOCKADE

BY

OLIVER OPTIC

MULGRUM AND THE ENGINEER

The BLUE AND THE GRAY SERIES

BY OLIVER OPTIC

ON THE BLOCKADE

THE

BLUE and the GRAY SERIES

By Oliver Optic

TAKEN BY THE ENEMY
WITHIN THE ENEMY'S LINES
ON THE BLOCKADE
STAND BY THE UNION
FIGHTING FOR THE RIGHT
A VICTORIOUS UNION

THE BLUE AND THE GRAY SERIES

ON THE BLOCKADE

BY

OLIVER OPTIC

Author of
The Army and Navy Series, Young America Abroad, The Great Western Series, The Woodville Stories, The Starry-Flag Series, The Boat-Club Stories, The Onward and Upward Series, The Yacht-Club Series, The Lake-Shore Series, The Riverdale Series, The Boat-Builder Series, Etc.

With Illustrations by L. Bridgman

LOST CLASSICS BOOK COMPANY
PUBLISHER
LAKE WALES
FLORIDA

PUBLISHER'S NOTE

—♦—

Recognizing the need to return to more traditional principles in education, Lost Classics Book Company is republishing forgotten late 19th and early 20th century literature and textbooks to aid parents in the education of their children.

This edition of *On the Blockade* was reprinted from the 1894 copyright edition. The text has been updated and edited only where necessary. Some of the quotes and expressions in the book reflect the attitudes of their time and do not necessarily reflect today's attitudes. We have left these passages intact in order to give an accurate portrayal of the times.

We have included a Build-Your-Vocabulary Glossary of more than 290 words at the end of the book to encourage children to look up words they don't know. While these definitions are not a substitute for dictionary definitions, they do provide a quick lookup to give children the meaning of their use in this story.

We have also included two maps, created specially for this edition, to enhance this book's usefulness as a teaching tool.

COVER IMAGES

GRAND ARMY OF THE REPUBLIC VETERANS' BADGE
Photo provided with kind permission of
Mr. George William Contant, Dover, DE (*left*)

LEE CAMP CONFEDERATE VETERANS' BADGE
Photo provided with kind permission of
The Museum of the Confederacy, Richmond, VA
Photography by Katherine Wetzel (*right*)

Background image is from *Campfire and Battlefield* by Rossiter
Johnson, LL.D., published by Knight & Brown, about 1900

Oliver Optic

William Taylor Adams, American author, better known and loved by boys and girls through his pseudonym "Oliver Optic," was born July 30, 1822, in the town of Medway, Norfolk County, Massachusetts, about twenty-five miles from Boston. For twenty years he was a teacher in the Public Schools of Boston, where he came in close contact with boy life. These twenty years taught him how to reach the boy's heart and interest as the popularity of his books attest.

His story writing began in 1850 when he was twenty-eight years old and his first book was published in 1853. He also edited *The Oliver Optic Magazine*, *The Student and Schoolmate*, and *Our Little Ones*.

In 1865, Mr. Adams began writing full time and completed in all about 125 books and more than 1000 stories, always using a pseudonym. Most of his books were published in series. He was a prolific writer and his stories often led their heroes through eccentric yet educational adventures.

In 1869, Mr. Adams served one term in the Massachusetts legislature; he declined a renomination.

William Taylor Adams died at the age of seventy-five, in Boston, March 27, 1897.

To my son-in-law,

SOL SMITH RUSSELL

of the United States of America,

though residing in Minneapolis, Minnesota,

who is always

"On the Blockade" Against Melancholy, "The Blues,"

and all similar maladies

This Volume

Is Affectionately Dedicated.

——+——

ON THE BLOCKADE is the third of *The Blue and the Gray Series*. Like the first and second volumes its incidents are dated back to the War of the Rebellion, and located in the midst of its most stirring scenes on the Southern coast, where the naval operations of the United States contributed their full share to the final result.

The writer begs to remind his readers again that he has not felt called upon to invest his story with the dignity of history, or in all cases to mingle fiction with actual historic occurrences. He believes that all the scenes of the story are not only possible, but probable, and that just such events as he has narrated really and frequently occurred in the days of the Rebellion.

The historian is forbidden to make his work more palatable or more interesting by the intermixture of fiction with fact, while the story-writer, though required to be reasonably consistent with the spirit and the truth of history, may wander from veritable details, and use his imagination in the creation of incidents upon which the grand result is reached. It would not be allowable to make the Rebellion a success, if the writer so desired, even on the pages of romance; and it would not be fair or just to ignore the bravery, the self-sacrifice, and the heroic endurance of the Southern people in a cause they believed to be holy and patriotic, as almost universally admitted at the present time, any more than it would be to lose sight of the magnificent spirit, the heroism, the courage, and the persistence, of the Northern people in accomplishing what they believed then, and still believe, was a holy and patriotic duty in the preservation of the Union.

Incidents not inconsistent with the final result, or with the spirit of the people on either side in the great conflict are of comparatively little consequence. That General Lee or General Grant turned this or that corner in reaching Appomattox may be important, but the grand historical tableau is the Christian hero, noble in the midst of defeat, disaster, and ruin, formally rendering his sword to the impassible but magnanimous conqueror as the crowning event of a long and bloody war. The details are historically important, though overshadowed by the mighty result of the great conflict.

Many of the personages of the preceding volumes have been introduced in the present one, and the central figure remains the same. The writer is willing to admit that his hero is an ideal character, though his lofty tone and patriotic spirit were fully paralleled by veritable individuals during the war; and he is not prepared to apologize for the abundant success which attended the career of Christy Passford. Those who really struggled as earnestly and faithfully deserved his good fortune, though they did not always obtain it.

Dorchester

April 24, 1890

Contents

——+——

(Map Illustrations by Michael Fitterling, 1999)

On the Blockade

Chapter I

"She is a fine little steamer, Father, without the possibility of a doubt," said Lieutenant Passford, who was seated at the table with his father in the captain's cabin on board of the *Bronx*. "I don't feel quite at home here, and I don't quite like the idea of being taken out of the *Bellevite*."

"You are not going to sea for the fun of it, my son," replied Captain Passford. "You are not setting out on a yachting excursion, but on the most serious business in the world."

"I know and feel all that, Father, but I have spent so many pleasant days, hours, weeks, and months on board of the *Bellevite* that I am very sorry to leave her," added Christy Passford, who had put on his new uniform, which was that of master in the United States Navy, and he was as becoming to the uniform as the uniform was to him.

"You cannot well help having some regrets at leaving the *Bellevite*, but you must remember that your life on board of her was mostly in the capacity of a pleasure seeker, though you made a good use of your time and of your opportunities for improvement, and that is the reason why you have made such remarkable progress in your present profession."

"I shall miss my friends on board of the *Bellevite*. I have sailed with all her officers, and Paul Vapoor and I have been cronies for years," continued Christy, with a shade of gloom on his bright face.

"You will probably see them occasionally, and if your life is spared you may again find yourself an officer of the *Bellevite*. But I think you have no occasion to indulge in any regrets," said Captain Passford, imparting a cheerful expression to his dignified countenance. "Allow me to call your attention to the fact that you are the commander of this fine little steamer. Here you are in your own cabin, and you are still nothing but a boy, hardly eighteen years old."

"If I have not earned my rank, it is not my fault that I have it," answered Christy, hardly knowing whether to be glad or sorry for his rapid advancement. "I have never asked for anything; I did not ask or expect to be promoted. I was satisfied with my rank as a midshipman."

"I did not ask for your promotion, though I could probably have procured for you the rank of master when you entered the navy. I do not like to ask favors for a member of my own family. I have wished you to feel that you were in the service of your country because it needs you, and not for glory or profit."

"And I have tried to feel so, Father."

"I think you have felt so, my son, and I am prouder of the fact that you are a disinterested patriot than of the rank you have nobly and bravely won," said Captain Passford as he took some letters from his pocket, from which he selected one bearing an English postage stamp. "I have a letter from one of my agents in England, which, I think, contains valuable information. I have called the attention of the government to these employees of mine, and they will soon pass from my service to that of the naval department. The information sent me has sometimes been very important."

"I know that myself, for the information that came from that source enabled the *Bellevite* to capture the *Killbright*," added Christy.

"The contents of the letter in my hand have been sent to the Secretary of the Navy, but it will do no harm for you to possess the information given to me," continued Captain Passford, as he opened the letter. "But I see a man at work at the foot of the companionway, and I don't care to post the whole ship's company on this subject."

"That is Pink Mulgrum," said Christy with a smile on his face. "He is deaf and dumb, and he cannot make any use of what you say."

"Don't be sure of anything, Christy, except your religion and your patriotism, in these times," added Captain Passford, as he rose and closed the door of the cabin.

"I don't think there is much danger from a deaf mute, Father," said the young commander of the *Bronx,* laughing.

"Perhaps not, but when you have war intelligence to communicate, it is best to believe that every person has ears and that every door has a keyhole. I learn from this letter that the *Scotian* sailed from Glasgow, and the *Arran* from Leith. The agent is of the opinion that both these steamers are fitted out by the same owners, who have formed a company, apparently to furnish the South with gunboats for its navy, as well as with needed supplies. In his letter my correspondent gives me the reason for this belief on his part."

"Does your agent give you any description of the vessels, Father?" asked Christy, his eyes sparkling with the interest he felt in the information.

"Not a very full description, my son, for no strangers were allowed on board of either of them, for very obvious reasons, but they are both of less than five hundred tons burthen, are of precisely the same model and build, evidently constructed in the same yard. Both had been pleasure yachts, though owned by different gentlemen. Both sailed on the same day, the *Scotian* from Greenock and the *Arran* from Leith, March 3."

Christy opened his pocket diary and put his finger on the date mentioned, counting up the days that had elapsed from that time to the present. Captain Passford could not help smiling at the interest his son manifested in the intelligence he had brought to him. The acting commander of the *Bronx* went over his calculation again.

"It is fourteen days since these vessels sailed," said he, looking at his father. "I doubt if your information will be of any value to me, for I suppose the steamers were selected on account of their great speed, as is the case with all blockade runners."

"Undoubtedly they were chosen for their speed, for a slow vessel does not amount to much in this sort of service," replied Captain Passford. "I received my letter day before yesterday, when the two vessels had been out twelve days."

"If they are fast steamers, they ought to be approaching the Southern coast by this time," suggested Christy.

"This is a windy month, and a vessel bound to the westward would encounter strong westerly gales, so that she could hardly make a quick passage. Then these steamers will almost certainly put in at Nassau or the Bermudas, if not for coal and supplies, at least to obtain the latest intelligence from the blockaded coast, and to pick up a pilot for the port to which they are bound. The agent thinks it is possible that the *Scotian* and *Arran* will meet some vessel to the southward of the Isle of Wight that will put an armament on board of them. He had written to another of my agents at Southampton to look up this matter. It is a quick mail from the latter city to New York, and I may get another letter on this subject before you sail, Christy."

"My orders may come off to me today," added the acting commander. "I am all ready to sail, and I am only waiting for them."

"If these two steamers sail in company, as they are likely to do if they are about equal in speed, and if they take on board an armament, it will hardly be prudent for you to meddle with them," said Captain Passford with a smile, though he had as much confidence in the prudence as in the bravery of his son.

"What shall I do, Father, run away from them?" asked Christy, opening his eyes very wide.

"Certainly, my son. There is as much patriotism in running away from a superior force as there is in fighting an equal, for if the government should lose your vessel and lose you and your ship's company, it would be a disaster of more or less consequence to your country."

"I hardly think I shall fall in with the *Scotian* and the *Arran*, so I will not consider the question of running away from them," said Christy, laughing.

"You have not received your orders yet, but they will probably require you to report at once to the flag officer in the Gulf, and perhaps they will not permit you to look up blockade runners on the high seas," suggested Captain Passford. "These vessels may be fully armed and manned, in charge of Confederate naval officers, and doubtless they will be as glad to pick up the *Bronx* as you would be to pick up the *Scotian* or the *Arran*. You don't know yet whether they will come as simple blockade runners, or as naval vessels flying the Confederate flag. Whatever your orders, Christy, don't allow yourself to be carried away by any Quixotic enthusiasm."

"I don't think I have any more than half as much audacity as Captain Breaker said I had. As I look upon it, my first duty is to deliver my ship over to the flag officer in the Gulf, and I suppose I shall be instructed to pick up a Confederate cruiser or a blockade runner, if one should cross my course."

"Obey your orders, Christy, whatever they may be. Now, I should like to look over the *Bronx* before I go on shore," said Captain Passford. "I think you said she was of about two hundred tons."

"That was what they said down south, but she is about three hundred tons," replied Christy, as he proceeded to show his father the cabin in which the conversation had taken place.

The captain's cabin was in the stern of the vessel, according to the orthodox rule in naval vessels. Of course it was small, though it seemed large to Christy, who had spent so much of his leisure time in the cabin of the *Florence*, his sailboat on the Hudson. It was substantially fitted up, with little superfluous ornamentation, but it was a complete parlor, as a landsman would regard it. From it, on the port side, opened the captain's stateroom, which was quite ample for a vessel no larger than the *Bronx*. Between it and the pantry on the starboard side was a gangway leading from the foot of the companionway, by which the captain's cabin and the wardroom were accessible from the quarterdeck.

Crossing the gangway at the foot of the steps, Christy led the way into the wardroom, where the principal officers were accommodated. It contained four berths, with *portières* in front of them, which could be drawn out so as to enclose each one in a temporary stateroom. The forward berth on the starboard side was occupied by the first lieutenant, and the after one by the second lieutenant, according to the custom in the navy. On the port side, the forward berth belonged to the chief engineer, and the after one to the surgeon. Forward of this was the steerage, in which the boatswain, gunner, carpenter, the assistant engineers, and the steward were berthed. Each of these apartments was provided with a table upon which the meals were served to the officers occupying it. The etiquette of a man-of-war is even more exacting than that of a drawing room on shore.

Captain Passford was then conducted to the deck where he found the officers and seamen engaged in their various duties. Besides his son, the former owner of the *Bellevite* was acquainted with only two persons on board of the *Bronx*: Sampson, the engineer, and Flint, the acting first lieutenant, both of whom had served on board of the steam yacht. Christy's father gave them a hearty greeting, and both were as glad to see him as he was to greet them. Captain Passford then looked over the rest of the ship's company with a deeper interest than he cared to manifest, for they were to some extent bound up with the immediate future of his son. It was not such a ship's company as that which manned the *Bellevite*, though composed of much good material. The captain shook hands with his son and went on board of his boat. Two hours later he came on board again.

Chapter II

A Dinner for the Confederacy

Christy Passford was not a little surprised to see his father so soon after his former visit, and he was confident that he had some good reason for coming. He conducted him at once to his cabin, where Captain Passford immediately seated himself at the table, and drew from his pocket a telegram.

"I found this on my desk when I went to my office," said he, opening a cable message and placing it before Christy.

" 'Mutton, three veal, four sea chickens,'" Christy read from the paper placed before him, laughing all the time as he thought it was a joke of some sort. "Signed 'Warnock.' It looks as though somebody was going to have a dinner, Father. Mutton, veal, and four sea chickens seem to form the substantials of the feast, though I never ate any sea chickens."

"Perhaps somebody will have a dinner, but I hope

it will prove to be indigestible to those for whom it is provided," added Captain Passford, amused at the comments of his son.

"The message is signed by Warnock. I don't happen to have the pleasure of his acquaintance, and I don't see why he has taken the trouble to send you this bill of fare," chuckled the commander of the *Bronx*.

"This bill of fare is of more importance to me, and especially to you, than you seem to understand."

"It is all Greek to me, and I wonder why Warnock, whoever he may be, has spent his money in sending you such a message, though I suppose you know who is to eat this dinner."

"The expense of sending the cablegram is charged to me, though the dinner is prepared for the Confederate States of America. Of course I understand it, for if I could not, it would not have been sent to me," replied Captain Passford, assuming a very serious expression. "You know Warnock, for he has often been at Bonnydale, though not under the name he signs to this message. My three agents, one in the north, one in the south, and one in the west of England, have each an assumed name. They are Otis, Barnes, and Wilson, and you know them all. They have been captains or mates in my employ, and they know all about a vessel when they see it."

"I know them all very well, and they are all good friends of mine," added Christy.

"Warnock is Captain Barnes, and this message comes from him. Captain Otis signs himself Bixwell in his letters and cablegrams, and Mr. Wilson, who was formerly mate of the *Manhattan*, uses the name of Fleetley."

"I begin to see into your system, Father, and I suppose the government will carry out your plan."

"Very likely; for it would hardly be proper to send such information as these men have to transmit in plain English, for there may be spies or operators bribed by Confederate agents to suppress such matter."

"I see. I understand the system very well, Father," said Christy.

"It is simple enough," added his father, as he took a paper from his pocket-book.

"If you only understand it, it is simple enough."

"I can interpret the language of this message, and there is not another person on the western continent that can do so. Now, look at the cablegram, Christy," continued Captain Passford, as he opened the paper he held in his hand. "What is the first word?"

"Mutton," replied the commander.

"'Mutton' means armed; that is to say the *Scotian* and the *Arran* took an armament on board at some point south of England, as indicated by the fact that the intelligence comes from Warnock. In about a week the mail will bring me a letter from him in which he will explain how he obtained this information."

"He must have chartered a steamer and cruised off the Isle of Wight to pick it up," suggested Christy.

"He is instructed to do that when necessary. What is the next word?"

"'Three,'" replied Christy.

"'One' means large, 'two' medium, and 'three' small," explained his father. "'Three' what, does it say?"

"'Three veal.'"

"'Veal' means ship's company, or crew."

"Putting the pieces together, then, 'three veal' means that the *Scotian* and the *Arran* have small crews," said Christy, intensely interested in the information.

"Precisely so. Read the rest of the message," added Captain Passford.

" 'Four sea chickens,'" the commander read.

" 'Four' means some, a few, no great number; in other words, rather indefinite. Very likely Warnock could not obtain exact information. 'C' stands for Confederate, and 'sea' is written instead of the letter. 'Chickens' means officers. 'Four sea chickens,' translated means 'some Confederate officers.'"

Christy had written down on a piece of paper the solution of the enigma as interpreted by his father, though not the symbol words of the cablegram. He continued to write for a little longer time, amplifying and filling in the wanting parts of the message. Then he read what he had written, as follows: "'The *Scotian* and the *Arran* are armed; there are some Confederate officers on board, but their ship's companies are small.' Is that it, Father?"

"That is the substance of it," replied Captain Passford, as he restored the key of the cipher to his pocket-book and rose from his seat. "Now you know all that can be known on this side of the Atlantic in regard to the two steamers. The important information is that they are armed, and even with small crews they may be able to sink the *Bronx*, if you should happen to fall in with them, or if your orders required you to be on the lookout for them. There is a knock at the door."

Christy opened the door and found a naval officer waiting to see him. He handed him a formidable looking envelope with a great seal upon it. The young commander looked at its address and saw that it came from the Navy Department. With it was a letter, which he opened. It was an order for the immediate sailing of the *Bronx*, the sealed orders to be opened when she reached latitude 38° N. The messenger spoke some pleasant words and then took his leave. Christy returned to the cabin and showed the ponderous envelope to his father.

"Sealed orders, as I supposed you would have," said Captain Passford.

"And this is my order to sail immediately on receipt of it," added Christy.

"Then I must leave you, my son, and may the blessing of God go with you wherever your duty calls you!" exclaimed the father, not a little shaken by his paternal feelings. "Be brave, be watchful, but be prudent under all circumstances. Bravery and Prudence ought to be twin sisters, and I hope you will always have one of them on each side of you. I am not afraid that you will be a poltroon, a coward, but I do fear that your enthusiasm may carry you farther than you ought to go."

"I hope not, Father, and your last words to me shall be remembered. When I am about to engage in any important enterprise, I will recall your admonition and ask myself if I am heeding it."

"That satisfies me. I wish you had such a ship's company as we had on board of the *Bellevite*, but you have a great deal of good material, and I am confident that you will make the best use of it. Remember that you are fighting for your country and the best government God ever gave to the nations of the earth. Be brave, be prudent, but be a Christian, and let no mean, cruel, or unworthy action stain your record."

Captain Passford took the hand of his son, and though neither of them wept, both of them were under the influence of the strongest emotions. Christy accompanied his father to the accommodation ladder and shook hands with him again as he embarked in his boat. His mother and his sister had been on board that day, and the young commander had parted from them with quite as much emotion as on the present occasion. The members of the family were devotedly attached to each other, and in some respects the event seemed like a funeral to all of them, and not less to Christy than to the others, though he was entering upon a very exalted duty for one of his years.

"Pass the word for Mr. Flint," said Christy, after he had watched the receding boat that bore away his father for a few minutes.

"On duty, Captain Passford," said the first lieutenant, touching his cap to him a few minutes later.

"Heave short the anchor, and make ready to get under way," added the commander.

"Heave short, sir," replied Mr. Flint, as he touched his cap and retired. "Pass the word for Mr. Giblock."

Mr. Giblock was the boatswain of the ship, though he had only the rank of a boatswain's mate. He was an old sailor, as salt as a barrel of pickled pork, and knew his duty from keel to truck. In a few moments his pipe was heard, and the seamen began to walk around the capstan.

"Cable up and down, sir," said the boatswain, reporting to the second lieutenant on the forecastle.

Mr. Lillyworth was the acting second lieutenant, though he was not to be attached to the *Bronx* after she reached her destination in the Gulf. He repeated the report from the boatswain to the first lieutenant. The steamer was rigged as a topsail schooner, but the wind was contrary, and no sail was set before getting under way. The capstan was manned again, and as soon as the report came from the second lieutenant that the anchor was aweigh, the first lieutenant gave the order to strike one bell, which meant that the steamer was to go "ahead slow."

The *Bronx* had actually started on her mission,

and the heart of Christy swelled in his bosom as he looked over the vessel and realized that he was in command, though not for more than a week or two. All the courtesies and ceremonies were duly attended to, and the steamer, as soon as the anchor had been catted and fished, at the stroke of four bells, went ahead at full speed, though, as the fires had been banked in the furnaces, the engine was not working up to its capacity. In a couple of hours more she was outside of Sandy Hook and on the broad ocean. The ship's company had been drilled to their duties, and everything worked to the entire satisfaction of the young commander.

The wind was ahead and light. All hands had been stationed, and at four in the afternoon, the first dog watch was on duty, and there was not much that could be called work for anyone to do. Mr. Lillyworth, the second lieutenant, had the deck, and Christy had retired to his cabin to think over the events of the day, especially those relating to the *Scotian* and the *Arran*. He had not yet read his orders, and he could not decide what he should do, even if he discovered the two steamers in his track. He sat in his arm chair with the door of the cabin open, and when he saw the first lieutenant on his way to the wardroom, he called him in.

"Well, Mr. Flint, what do you think of our crew?" asked the captain, after he had seated his guest.

"I have hardly seen enough of the men to be able to form an opinion," replied Flint. "I am afraid we have some hard material on board, though there are a good many first-class fellows among them."

"Of course we cannot expect to get such a crew as we had in the *Bellevite*. How do you like Mr. Lillyworth?" asked the commander, looking sharply into the eye of his subordinate.

"I don't like him," replied Flint bluntly. "You and I have been in some tight places together, and it is best to speak our minds squarely."

"That's right, Mr. Flint. We will talk of him another time. I have another matter on my mind just now," added Christy.

He proceeded to tell the first lieutenant something about the two steamers.

Chapter III

Before he said anything about the *Scotian* and the *Arran*, Christy, mindful of the injunction of his father, had closed the cabin door, the *portière* remaining drawn as it was before. When he had taken this precaution, he related some of the particulars which had been given to him earlier in the day.

"It is hardly worthwhile to talk about the matter yet awhile," added Christy. "I have my sealed orders, and I cannot open the envelope until we are in latitude 38, and that will be sometime tomorrow forenoon."

"I don't think that Captain Folkner, who expected to be in command of the *Teaser*, as she was called before we put our hands upon her, overestimated her speed," replied Lieutenant Flint, consulting his watch. "We are making fifteen knots an hour just now, and Mr. Sampson is not hurrying her. I have been watching her very closely since we left Sandy Hook, and I really believe she will make eighteen knots with a little crowding."

"What makes you think so, Flint?" asked Christy, much interested in the statement of the first lieutenant.

"I suppose it is natural for a sailor to fall in love with his ship, and that is my condition in regard to the *Bronx*," replied Flint, with a smile which was intended as a mild apology for his weakness. "I used to be in love with the coasting schooner I owned and commanded, and I almost cried when I had to sell her."

"I don't think you need to be ashamed of this sentiment, or that an inanimate structure should call it into being," said the young commander. "I am sure I have not ceased to love the *Bellevite*, and in my eyes she is handsomer than any young lady I ever saw. I have not been able to transfer my affections to the *Bronx* as yet, and she will have to do something very remarkable before I do so. But about the speed of our ship?"

"I have noticed particularly how easily and gracefully she makes her way through the water when she is going fifteen knots. Why that is faster than most of the ocean passenger steamers travel."

"Very true, but like many of these blockade runners and other vessels which the Confederate government and rich men at the South have purchased in the United Kingdom, she was doubtless built on the Clyde. Not a few of them have been constructed for private yachts, and I have no doubt, from what I have seen, that the *Bronx* is one of the number. The *Scotian* and the *Arran* belonged to wealthy Britishers, and of course they were built in the very best manner and were intended to attain the very highest rate of speed."

"I shall count on eighteen knots at least on the part of the *Bronx* when the situation shall require her to do her best. By the way, Captain Passford, don't you think that a rather queer name has been given to our steamer? *Bronx*! I am willing to confess that I don't know what the word means, or whether it is fish, flesh or fowl," continued Flint.

"It is not fish, flesh, or fowl," replied Christy, laughing. "My father suggested the name to the department, and it was adopted. He talked with me about a name, as he thought I had some interest in her, for the reason that I had done something in picking her up."

"Done something? I should say that you had done it all," added Flint.

"I did my share. The vessels of the navy have generally been named after a system, though it has often been varied. Besides the names of states and cities, the names of rivers have been given to vessels. The *Bronx* is the name of a small stream, hardly more than a brook, in West Chester County, New York. When I was a small boy, my father had a country place on its banks, and I did my first paddling in the water in the *Bronx*. I liked the name, and my father recommended it."

"I don't object to the name, though somehow it makes me think of a walnut cracked in your teeth when I hear it pronounced," added Flint. "Now that I know what it is and what it means, I shall take more kindly to it, though I am afraid we shall get to calling her the *Bronxy* before we have done with her, especially if she gets to be a pet, for the name seems to need another syllable."

"Young men fall in love with girls without regard to their names."

"That's so. A friend of mine in our town in Maine fell in love with a young lady by the name of Leatherbee, but she was a very pretty girl and her name was all the objection I had to her," said Flint, chuckling.

"But that was an objection which your friend evidently intended to remove at no very distant day," suggested Christy.

"Very true, and he did remove it some years ago. What was that noise?" asked the first lieutenant, suddenly rising from his seat.

Christy heard the sounds at the same moment. He and his companion in the cabin had been talking about the *Scotian* and the *Arran*, and what his father had said to him about prudence in speaking of his movements came to his mind. The noise was continued, and he hastened to the door of his stateroom and threw it open. In the room, he found Dave hard at work on the furniture; he had taken out the berth sack and was brushing out the inside of the berth. The noise had been made by the shaking of the slats on which the mattress rested. Davis Talbot, the cabin steward of the *Bronx*, had been captured in the vessel when she was run out of Pensacola Bay some months before. As he was a very intelligent colored man, or rather mulatto, though they were all the same at the South, the young commander had selected him for his present service, and he never had occasion to regret the choice. Dave had passed his time since the *Teaser* arrived at New York at Bonnydale, and he had become a great favorite, not only with Christy, but with all the members of the family.

"What are you about, Dave?" demanded Christy, not a little astonished to find the steward in his room.

"I am putting the room in order for the captain, sir," replied Dave with a cheerful smile, such as he always wore in the presence of his superiors. "I found something in this berth I did not like to see about a bed in which a gentleman is to sleep, and I have been through it with poison and a feather; and I will give you the whole southern Confederacy if you find a single redback in the berth after this."

"I am very glad you have attended to this matter at once, Dave."

"Yes, sir; Captain Folkner never let me attend to it properly, for he was afraid I would read some of his papers on the desk. He was willing to sleep six in a bed with redbacks," chuckled Dave.

"Well, I am not, or even two in a bed with such companions. How long have you been in my room, Dave?" added Christy.

"More than two hours, I think, and I have been mighty busy too."

"Did you hear me when I came into the cabin?"

"No, sir, I did not, but I heard you talking with somebody a while ago."

"What did I say to the other person?"

"I don't know, sir; I could not make out a word, and I didn't stop in my work to listen. I have been very busy, Captain Passford," answered Dave, beginning to think he had been doing something that was not altogether regular.

"Don't you know what we were talking about, Dave?"

"No, sir; I did not make out a single word you said," protested the steward, really troubled to find that he had done something wrong, though he had not the least idea what it was. "I did not mean to do anything out of the way, Captain Passford."

"I have no fault to find this time, Dave."

"I should hope not, sir," added Dave, looking as solemn as a sleepy owl. I would jump overboard before I would offend you, Massa Christy."

"You need not jump overboard just yet," replied the captain with a pleasant smile intended to remove the fears of the steward. "But I want to make a new rule for you, Dave."

"Thank you, sir; if you sit up nights to make rules for me, I will obey all of them, and I would give you the whole state of Florida before I would break one of them on purpose, Massa Christy."

"Massa Christy!" exclaimed the captain, laughing.

"Massa Captain Passford!" shouted Dave, hastening to correct his over familiarity.

"I don't object to your calling me Christy when we are alone, for I look upon you as my friend, and I have tried to treat you as a gentleman, though you are a subordinate. But are you going to be a nigger again, and call white men 'Massa?' I told you not to use that word."

"I done forget it when I got excited because I was afraid I had offended you," pleaded the steward.

"Your education is vastly superior to most people of your class, and you should not belittle yourself. This is my cabin, and I shall sometimes have occasion to talk confidentially with my officers. Do you understand what I mean, Dave?"

"Perfectly, Captain Passford; I know what it is to talk confidently and what it is to talk confidentially, and you do both, sir," replied the steward.

"But I am sometimes more confidential than confident. Now you must do all your work in my stateroom when I am not in the cabin, and this is the new rule," said Christy, as he went out of the room. "I know that I can trust you, Dave, but when I tell a secret, I want to know to how many persons

I am telling it. You may finish your work now," and he closed the door.

Christy could not have explained why he did so if it had been required of him, but he went directly to the door leading out into the companionway and suddenly threw it wide open, drawing the *portière* aside at the same time. Not a little to his surprise, for he had not expected it, he found a man there, and the intruder was down on his knees, as if in position to place his ear at the keyhole. This time the young commander was indignant, and without stopping to consider as long as the precepts of his father required, he seized the man by the collar and dragged him into the cabin.

"What are you doing there?" demanded Christy in the heat of his indignation.

The intruder, who was a rather stout man, began to shake his head with all his might, and to put the fore finger of his right hand on his mouth and one of his ears. He was big enough to have given the young commander a deal of trouble if he had chosen to resist the force used upon him, but he appeared to be tame and submissive. He did not speak, but he seemed to be exerting himself to the utmost to make himself understood. Flint had resumed his seat at the table, facing the door, and in spite of himself, apparently, he began to laugh.

"That is Pink Mulgrum, Captain Passford," said he, evidently to prevent his superior from misinterpreting the lightness of his conduct. "As you are aware, he is deaf and dumb."

"I see who he is now," replied Christy, who had just identified the man. "He may be deaf and dumb, but he seems to have a great deal of business at the door of my cabin."

"I have no doubt he is as deaf as the keel of the ship, and I have not yet heard him speak a word," added the first lieutenant. "But he is a stout fellow, very patriotic, and willing to work."

"All that may be, but I have found him once before hanging around that door today."

At this moment Mulgrum took from his pocket a tablet of paper and a pencil and wrote upon it, "I am a deaf mute, and I don't know what you are talking about." Christy read it and then wrote, "What were you doing at the door?" He replied that he had been sent by Mr. Lillyworth to clean the brasses on the door. He was then dismissed.

MULGRUM AT THE CAPTAIN'S DOOR

CHAPTER IV

A DEAF AND DUMB MYSTERY

As he dismissed Mulgrum, Christy tore off the leaf from the tablet on which both of them had written before he handed it back to the owner. For a few moments he said nothing, and had his attention fixed on the paper in his hand, which he seemed to be studying for some reason of his own.

"That man writes a very good hand for one in his position," said he, looking at the first lieutenant.

"I had noticed that before," replied Flint, as the commander handed him the paper, which he looked over with interest. "I had some talk with him on his tablet the day he came on board. He strikes me as a very intelligent and well-educated man."

"Was he born a deaf mute?" asked Christy.

"I did not think to ask him that question, but I judged from the language he used and his rapid

writing that he was well educated.   There is
character in his handwriting too, and that is hardly
to be expected from a deaf mute," replied Flint.

"Being a deaf mute, he can not have been shipped
as a seaman, or even as an ordinary steward,"
suggested the captain.

"Of course not; he was employed as a sort of
scullion to be worked wherever he could make
himself useful. Mr. Nawood engaged him on the
recommendation of Mr. Lillyworth," added Flint with
something like a frown on his brow, as though he
had just sounded a new idea.

"Have you asked Mr. Lillyworth anything about
him?"

"I have not, for somehow Mr. Lillyworth and I
don't seem to be very affectionate towards each
other, though we get along very well together. But
Mulgrum wrote out for me that he was born in
Cherryfield, Maine, and obtained his education as
a deaf mute in Hartford. I learned the deaf and
dumb alphabet when I was a schoolmaster, as a
pastime, and I had some practice with it in the house
where I boarded."

"Then you can talk in that way with Mulgrum."

"Not a bit of it; he knows nothing at all about
the deaf and dumb alphabet, and could not spell out

a single word I gave him."

"That is very odd," added the captain musing.

"So I thought, but he explained it by saying that at the school they were changing this method of communication for that of actually speaking and understanding what was said by observing the vocal organs. He had not remained long enough to master this method; in fact, he had done all his talking with his tablets."

"It is a little strange that he should not have learned either method of communication."

"I thought so myself, and said as much to him, but he told me that he had inherited considerable property at the death of his father, and he was not inclined to learn new tricks," said Flint. "He is intensely patriotic, and said that he was willing to give himself and all his property for the salvation of his country. He had endeavored to obtain a position as Captain's clerk, or something of that sort, in the navy, but failing of this, he had been willing to go to the war as a scullion. He says he shall fight, whatever his situation, when he has the opportunity, and that is all I know about him."

Christy looked on the floor, and seemed to be considering the facts he had just learned. He had twice discovered Mulgrum at the door of his cabin, though his presence there had been satisfactorily explained, or at least a reason had been given. This man had been brought on board by the influence of Mr. Lillyworth, who had been ordered to the Gulf for duty, and was on board as a substitute for Mr. Flint, who was acting in Christy's place, as the latter was in that of Mr. Blowitt, who outranked them all. Flint had not been favorably impressed with the acting second lieutenant, and he had not hesitated to speak his mind in regard to him to the captain. Though Christy had been more reserved in speech, he had the feeling that Mr. Lillyworth must establish a reputation for patriotism and fidelity to the government before he could trust him as he did the first lieutenant, though he was determined to manifest nothing like suspicion in regard to him.

At this stage of the war, that is to say in the earlier years of it, the government was obliged to accept such men as it could obtain for officers, for the number in demand greatly exceeded the supply of regularly educated naval officers. There were a great many applicants for positions, and candidates were examined in regard to their professional qualifications rather than their motives for entering the service. If a man desired to enter the army or the navy, the simple wish was regarded as a sufficient guarantee of his patriotism, especially in connection with his oath of allegiance. With the deaf mute's leaf in his hand, Christy was thinking over this matter of the motives of officers. He was not satisfied in regard to either Lillyworth or Mulgrum, and besides the regular quota of officers and seamen permanently attached to the *Bronx*, there were eighteen seamen and petty officers berthed forward who were really passengers, though they were doing duty.

"Where did you say this man Mulgrum was born, Mr. Flint?" asked the captain after he had mused for quite a time.

"In Cherryfield, Maine," replied the first lieutenant, and he could not help feeling that the commander had not been silent so long for nothing.

"You are a Maine man, Flint; were you ever in this town?"

"I have been; I taught school there for six months, and it was the last place I filled before I went to sea."

"I am glad to hear it, for it will save me from looking any farther for the man I want just now. If this deaf mute was born and brought up in Cherryfield, he must know something about the place," added Christy as he touched a bell on his table, to which Dave instantly responded.

"Do you know Mulgrum, Dave?" asked the captain.

"No, sir; never heard of him before," replied the steward.

"You don't know him! The man who has been cleaning the brass work on the doors?" exclaimed Christy.

"Oh! Pink, we all call him," said the steward.

"His name is Pinkney Mulgrum," Flint explained.

"Yes, sir; I know him, though we never had any long talks together," added Dave with a rich smile on his face.

"Go on deck and tell Mulgrum to come into my cabin," said Christy.

"If I tell him that, he won't hear me," suggested Dave.

"Show him this paper," interposed the first lieutenant, handing him a card on which he had written the order.

Dave left the cabin to deliver the message, and the captain immediately instructed Flint to question the man in regard to the localities and other matters in Cherryfield, suggesting that he should conduct his examination so as not to excite any suspicion. Pink Mulgrum appeared promptly and was placed at the table where both of the officers could observe his expression. Then Flint began to write on a sheet of paper, and passed his first question to the man. It was: "Don't you remember me?" Mulgrum wrote that he did not. Then the inquisitor asked when he had left Cherryfield to attend the school at Hartford, and the date he gave placed him there at the very time when Flint had been the master of the school for four months. On the question of locality, he could place the church, the schoolhouse and the hotel, and he seemed to have no further knowledge of the town. When asked where his father lived, he described a white house next to the church, but Flint knew that this had been owned and occupied by the minister for many years.

"This man is a humbug," was the next sentence the first lieutenant wrote, but he passed it to the captain. Christy wrote under it: "Tell him that we are perfectly satisfied with his replies, and thank him for his attendance," which was done at once, and the captain smiled upon him as though he had conducted himself with distinguished ability.

"Mulgrum has been in Cherryfield, but he could not have remained there more than a day or two," said Flint when the door had closed behind the deaf mute.

The captain made a gesture to impose silence upon his companion.

"Mulgrum is all right in every respect," said he in a loud tone, so that if the subject of the examination had stopped at the keyhole of the door, he would not be made any the wiser for what he heard there.

"He knows Cherryfield as well as he knows the deck of the *Bronx*, and as you say, Captain Passford, he is all right in every respect," added the first lieutenant in the same loud tone. "Mulgrum is a well educated man, Captain, and you will have a great deal of writing to do: I suggest that you bring him into your cabin and make him your clerk."

"That is a capital idea, Mr. Flint, and I shall consider it," returned the commander, making sure that the man at the door should hear him, if Mulgrum lingered there. "I have a number of letters sent over from England relating to blockade runners that I wish to have copied for the use of any naval officers with whom I may fall in, and I have not the time to do it myself."

"Mulgrum writes a very handsome hand, and no one could do the work any better than he."

Christy thought enough had been said to satisfy the curiosity of Mulgrum if he was still active in seeking information, and both of the officers were silent. The captain had enough to think of to last

him a long while. The result of the inquiry into the
auditory and vocal powers of the scullion, as Flint
called him, had convinced him that the deaf mute
was a fraud. He had no doubt that he could both
speak and hear as well as the rest of the ship's
company. But the puzzling question was in relation
to the reason why he pretended to be deaf and
dumb. If he was desirous of serving his country in
the navy, and especially in the *Bronx*, it was not
necessary to pretend to be deaf and dumb in order
to obtain a fighting berth on board of her. It looked
like a first class mystery to the young commander,
but he was satisfied that the presence of Mulgrum
meant mischief. He could not determine at once
what it was best to do to solve the mystery, but he
decided that the most extreme watchfulness was
required of him and his first lieutenant. This was
all he could do, and he touched his bell again.

"Dave," said he, when the cabin steward
presented himself before him, "go on deck and ask
Mr. Lillyworth to report to me the log and the
weather."

"The log and the weather, sir," replied Dave, as
he hastened out of the cabin.

Christy watched him closely as he went out at
the door, and he was satisfied that Mulgrum was not

in the passage, if he had stopped there at all. His present purpose was to disarm all the suspicions of the subject of the mystery, but he would have been glad to know whether or not the man had lingered at the door to hear what was said in regard to him. He was not anxious in regard to the weather, or even the log, and he sent Dave on his errand in order to make sure that Mulgrum was not still doing duty as a listener.

"Wind south south west, log last time fifteen knots and a half," reported Dave, as he came in after knocking at the door.

"I cannot imagine why that man pretended to be deaf and dumb in order to get a position on board of the *Bronx*. He is plainly a fraud," said the captain when Dave had gone back to his work in the stateroom.

"I don't believe he pretended to be a deaf mute in order to get a place on board, for that would ordinarily be enough to prevent him from getting it. I should put it that he had obtained his place in spite of being deaf and dumb. But the mystery exists just the same."

The captain went on deck, and the first lieutenant to the wardroom.

Chapter V

A Confidential Steward

The wind still came from the southward, and it was very light. The sea was comparatively smooth, and the *Bronx* continued on her course. At the last bi-hourly heaving of the log, she was making sixteen knots an hour. The captain went into the engine room, where he found Mr. Gawl, one of the chief's two assistants, on duty. This officer informed him that no effort had been made to increase the speed of the steamer, and that she was under no strain whatever. The engine had been thoroughly overhauled, as well as every other part of the vessel, and every improvement that talent and experience suggested had been made. It now appeared that the engine had been greatly benefited by whatever changes had been made. These improvements had been explained to the commander by Mr. Sampson the day before, but Christy had not given much attention to the matter, for he preferred to let the speed of the vessel speak for itself; and this was what it appeared to be doing at the present time.

Christy walked the deck for some time, observing everything that presented itself, and taking especial notice of the working of the vessel. Though he made no claims to any superior skill, he was really an expert, and the many days and months he had passed in the companionship of Paul Vapoor in studying the movements of engines and hulls had made him wiser and more skillful than it had even been suspected that he was. He was fully competent for the position he was temporarily filling, but he had made himself so by years of study and practice.

Christy had not yet obtained all the experience he required as a naval officer, and he was fully aware that this was what he needed to enable him to discharge his duty in the best manner. He was in command of a small steamer, a position of responsibility which he had not coveted in this early stage of his career, though it was only for a week or less, as the present speed of the *Bronx* indicated. He had ambition enough to hope that he should be able to distinguish himself in this brief period, for it might be years before he again obtained such an opportunity. His youth was against him, and he was aware that he had been selected to take the steamer to the Gulf because there was a scarcity of officers of the proper grade, and his rank gave him the position.

The motion of the *Bronx* exactly suited him, and he judged that in a heavy sea she would behave very well. He had made one voyage in her from the Gulf to New York, and the steamer had done very well, though she had been greatly improved at the navy yard. Certainly her motion was better, and the connection between the engine and the inert material of which the steamer was constructed seemed to be made without any straining or jerking. There was very little shaking and trembling as the powerful machinery drove her ahead over the quiet sea. There had been no very severe weather during his first cruise in the *Bronx*, and she had not been tested in a storm under his management, though she had doubtless encountered severe gales in crossing the Atlantic in a breezy season of the year.

While Christy was planking the deck, four bells were struck on the ship's great bell on the top-gallant forecastle. It was the beginning of the second dog watch, or six o'clock in the afternoon, and the watch which had been on duty since four o'clock was relieved. Mr. Flint ascended the bridge and took the place of Mr. Lillyworth, the second lieutenant. Under this bridge was the pilothouse, and in spite of her small size, the steamer was steered by steam. The ship had been at sea but a few hours, and the crew were not inclined to leave the deck. The number of men on board was nearly doubled by the addition of those sent down to fill vacancies in other vessels on the blockade. Christy went on the bridge soon after, more to take a survey inboard than for any other purpose.

Mr. Lillyworth had gone aft, but when he met Mulgrum coming up from the galley, he stopped and looked around him. With the exception of himself, nearly the whole ship's company were forward. The commander watched him with interest when he stopped in the vicinity of the deaf mute, who also halted in the presence of the second lieutenant. Then they walked together towards the companionway, and disappeared behind the mainmast. Christy had not before noticed any intercourse between the lieutenant and the scullion, though he thought it a little odd that the officer should set the man at work cleaning the brasses about the door of the captain's cabin, a matter that belonged to the steward's department. He had learned from Flint that Mulgrum had been recommended to the chief steward by Lillyworth, so that it was evident enough that they had been acquainted before either of them came on board. But he could not see them behind the mast, and he desired very much to know what they were doing.

Flint had taken his supper before he went on duty on the bridge, and the table was waiting for the other wardroom officers who had just been relieved. It was time for Lillyworth to go to the meal, but he did not go, and he seemed to be otherwise engaged. After a while, Christy looked at his watch and found that a quarter of an hour had elapsed since the second lieutenant had left the bridge, and he had spent nearly all this time abaft the mainmast with the scullion. The commander had become absolutely absorbed in his efforts to fathom the deaf and dumb mystery, and fortunately there was nothing else to occupy his attention, for Flint had drilled the crew, including the men for other vessels, and had billeted and stationed them during the several days he had been on board. Everything was working as though the *Bronx* had been at sea a month instead of less than half a day.

Christy was exceedingly anxious to ascertain what, if anything, was passing between Lillyworth and Mulgrum, but he could see no way to obtain any information on the subject. He had no doubt he was watched as closely as he was watching the second lieutenant. If he went aft, that would at once end the conference, if one was in progress. He could not call upon a seaman to report on such a delicate question without betraying himself, and he had not yet learned whom to trust in such a matter, and it was hardly proper to call upon a foremast hand to watch one of his officers.

The only person on board besides the first lieutenant in whom he felt that he could repose entire confidence was Dave. He knew him thoroughly, and his color was almost enough to guarantee his loyalty to the country and his officers, and especially to himself, for the steward possessed a rather extravagant admiration for the one who had "brought him out of bondage," as he expressed it, and had treated him like a gentleman from first to last. He could trust Dave even on the most delicate mission, but Dave was attending to the table in the wardroom, and he did not care to call him from his duty.

At the end of another five minutes, Christy saw Mulgrum come from abaft the mainmast, and descend the ladder to the galley. He saw no more of Lillyworth, and he concluded that, keeping himself in the shadow of the mast, he had gone below. He remained on the bridge a while longer considering what he should do. He said nothing to Flint, for he did not like to take up the attention of any officer on duty. The commander thought that Dave could render him the assistance he required better than any other person on board, for being only a steward and a colored man at that, less notice would be taken of him than of one in a higher position. He was about to descend from the bridge when Flint spoke to him in regard to the weather, though he could have guessed to a point what the captain was thinking about, perhaps because the same subject occupied his own thoughts.

"I think we shall have a change of weather before morning, Captain Passford. The wind is drawing a little more to the southward, and we are likely to have wind and rain," said the first lieutenant.

"Wind and rain will not trouble us, and I am more afraid that we shall be bothered with fog on this cruise," added Christy as he descended the ladder to the main deck.

He walked about the deck for a few minutes, observing the various occupations of the men, who were generally engaged in amusing themselves, or in "reeling off sea yarns." Then he went below. At the foot of the stairs in the companionway, the door of the wardroom was open, and he saw that Lillyworth was seated at the table. He sat at the foot of it, the head being the place of the first lieutenant, and the captain could see only his back. He was slightly bald at the apex of his head, for he was an older man than either the captain or the first lieutenant, but inferior to them in rank, though all of them were masters, and seniority depended upon the date of the commissions, and even a single day settled the degree in these days of multiplied appointments. Christy went into his cabin, where the table was set for his own supper.

The commander looked at his barometer, and his reading of it assured him that Flint was correct in regard to his prognostics of the weather. But the young officer had faced the winter gales of the Atlantic, and the approach of any ordinary storm did not disturb him in the least degree. On the contrary, he rather liked a lively sea, for it was less monotonous than a calm. He did not brood over a storm, therefore, but continued to consider the subject which had so deeply interested him since he discovered Mulgrum on his knees at the door, with a rag and a saucer of rottenstone in his hands. He had a curiosity to examine the brass knob of his door at that moment, and it did not appear to have been very severely rubbed.

"Quarter of seven, sir," said Dave, presenting himself at the door while Christy was still musing over the incidents already detailed.

"All right, Dave; I will have my supper now," replied Christy indifferently, for though he was generally blessed with a good appetite, the mystery was too absorbing to permit the necessary duty of eating to drive it out of his mind.

Dave retired and soon brought in a tray from the galley, the dishes from which he arranged on the table. It was an excellent supper, though he had not given any special orders in regard to its preparation. He seated himself and began to eat in a rather mechanical manner, and no one who saw him would have mistaken him for an epicure. Dave stationed himself in front of the commander, so that he was between the table and the door. He watched Christy, keeping his eyes fixed on him without intermitting his gaze for a single instant. Once in a while he tendered a dish to him at the table, but there was but one object in existence for Christy at that moment.

"Dave," said the captain, after he had disposed of a portion of his supper.

"Here, sir, on duty," replied the steward.

"Open the door behind you, quick!"

Dave obeyed instantly, and threw the door back so that it was wide open, though he seemed to be amazed at the strangeness of the order.

"All right, Dave; close it," added Christy, when he saw there was no one in the passage, and he concluded that Mulgrum was not likely to be practicing his vocation when there was no one in the cabin but himself and the steward.

Dave obeyed the order like a machine, and then renewed his gaze at the commander.

"Are you a Freemason, Dave?" asked Christy.

"No, sir," replied the steward with a magnificent smile.

"A Knight of Pythias, of Pythagoras, or anything of that sort?"

"No, sir; nothing of the sort."

"Then you can't keep a secret?"

"Yes, sir, I can. If I have a secret to keep, I will give the whole Alabama River to anyone that can get it out of me."

Christy felt sure of his man without this protestation.

CHAPTER VI

A MISSION UP THE FOREMAST

Christy spent some time in delivering a lecture on naval etiquette to his single auditor. Probably he was not the highest authority on the subject of his discourse, but he was sufficiently learned to meet the requirements of the present occasion.

"You say you can keep a secret, Dave?" continued the commander.

"I don't take any secrets to keep from everybody, Captain Passford, and I don't much like to carry them about with me," replied the steward, looking a little more grave than usual, though he still wore a cheerful smile.

"Then you don't wish me to confide a secret to you?"

"I don't say that, Captain Passford. I don't want any man's secrets, and I don't run after them, except for the good of the service. I was a slave once, but

I know what I am working for now. If you have a secret I ought to know, Captain Passford, I will take it in and bury it away down at the bottom of my bosom, and I will give the whole state of Louisiana to anyone that will dig it out of me."

"That's enough, Dave, and I am willing to trust you without any oath on the Bible, and without even a Quaker's affirmation. I believe you will be prudent, discreet, and silent for my sake."

"Certainly I will be all that, Captain Passford, for I think you are a bigger man than Jeff Davis," protested Dave.

"That is because you do not know the president of the Confederate states, and you do know me, but Mr. Davis is a man of transcendent ability, and I am only sorry that he is engaged in a bad cause, though he believes with all his heart and soul that it is a good cause."

"He never treated me like a gentleman, as you have, sir."

"And he never treated you unkindly, I am very sure."

"He never treated me any way, for I never saw him, and I would not walk a hundred miles barefooted to see him, either. I am no gentleman or anything of that sort, Massa—Captain Passford, but if I ever go back on you by the breadth of a hair, then the Alabama River will run up hill."

"I am satisfied with you, Dave, and here is my hand," added Christy, extending it to the steward, who shook it warmly, displaying a good deal of emotion as he did so. "Now, Dave, you know Mulgrum, or Pink, as you call him?"

"Well, sir, I know him as I do the rest of the people on board, but we are not sworn friends yet," replied Dave, rather puzzled to know what duty was required of him in connection with the scullion.

"You know him; that is enough. What do you think of him?"

"I haven't had any long talks with him, sir, and I don't know what to think of him."

"You know that he is dumb?"

"I expect he is, sir, but he never said anything to me about it," replied Dave. "He never told me he couldn't speak, and I never heard him speak to anyone on board."

"Did you ever speak to him?"

"Yes, sir; I spoke to him when he first came on board, but he didn't answer me, or take any notice of me when I spoke to him, and I got tired of it."

"Open that door quickly, Dave," said the captain suddenly.

The steward promptly obeyed the order, and Christy saw that there was no one in the passage. He told his companion to close the door, and Dave was puzzled to know what this movement could mean.

"I beg your pardon, Captain Passford, and I have no right to ask any question, but I should like to know why you make me open that door two or three times for nothing," said Dave, in the humblest of tones.

"I told you to open it so that I could see if there was anybody at the door. This is my secret, Dave. I have twice found Mulgrum at that door while I was talking to the first lieutenant. He pretended to be cleaning the brass work."

"What was he there for? When a man is as deaf as the foremast of the ship what would he be doing at the door?"

"He was down on his knees, and his ear was not a great way from the keyhole of the door."

"But he could not hear anything."

"I don't know; that is what I want to find out. The mission I have for you, Dave, is to watch Mulgrum. In a word, I have my doubts in regard to his deafness and his dumbness."

"You don't believe he is deaf and dumb, Captain Passford!" exclaimed the steward, opening his eyes very wide and looking as though an earthquake had just shaken him up.

"I don't say that, my man. I am in doubt. He may be a deaf mute, as he represents himself to be. I wish you to ascertain whether or not he can speak and hear. You are a shrewd fellow, Dave, I discovered some time ago; in fact, the first time I ever saw you. You may do this job in any manner you please, but remember that your mission is my secret, and you must not betray it to Mulgrum, or to any other person."

"Be sure I won't do that, Captain Passford."

"If you obtain any satisfactory information, convey it to me immediately. You must be very careful not to let anyone suspect that you are watching him, and least of all to let Mulgrum know it. Do you understand me perfectly, Dave?"

"Yes, sir; perfectly. Nobody takes any notice of me but you, and it won't be a hard job. I think I can manage it without any trouble. I am nothing but a nigger, and of no account."

"I have chosen you for this mission because you can do it better than any other person, Dave. Don't call yourself a nigger; I don't like the word, and you are ninety degrees in the shade above the lower class of Negroes in the South."

"Thank you, sir," replied the steward with an expansive smile.

"There is one thing I wish you to understand particularly, Dave. I have not set you to watch any officer of the ship," said Christy impressively.

"No, sir; I reckon Pink Mulgrum is not an officer any more than I am."

"But you may discover, if you find that Mulgrum can speak and hear, that he is talking to an officer," added the captain in a low tone.

"What officer, Captain Passford?" asked the steward, opening his eyes to their utmost capacity and looking as bewildered as an owl in the gaslight.

"I repeat that I do not set you to watch an officer, and I leave it to you to ascertain with whom Mulgrum has any talk, if with anyone. Now I warn you that, if you accomplish anything in this mission, you will do it at night and not in the daytime. That is all that need be said at the present time, Dave, and you will attend to your duty as usual. If you lose much sleep, you may make it up in the forenoon watch."

"I don't care for the sleep, Captain Passford, and I can keep awake all night."

"One thing more, Dave; between eight bells and eight bells tonight, during the first watch, you may get at something, but you must keep out of sight as much as you can," added Christy, as he rose from his armchair and went into his stateroom.

Dave busied himself in clearing the table, but he was in a very thoughtful mood all the time. Loading up his tray with dishes, he carried them through the steerage to the galley, where he found Mulgrum engaged in washing those from the wardroom, which he had brought out some time before. The steward looked at the deaf mute with more interest than he had regarded him before. He was a supernumerary on board, and anyone who had anything to do called Pink to do it. Another waiter was greatly needed, and Mr. Nawood, the chief steward, had engaged one, but he had failed to come on board before the steamer sailed. Pink had been pressed into service for the steerage, but he was of little use, and the work seemed very distasteful, if not disgusting, to him. He carried in the food, but that was about all he was good for.

Dave watched him for a few minutes as he washed and wiped the dishes, and saw that he was very awkward at it; it was plain to him that he was not an experienced hand at the business. But he was doing the steward's work, and Dave took hold and helped him. Pink was as solemn as an owl, and did his work in a very mechanical manner and without the slightest interest in it. The cabin steward had a mission, and he was profoundly interested in its execution.

By the side of the galley, or range, was a sink at which they were at work. Dave thought he might as well begin then and there to test the hearing powers of his companion. Picking up one of the large blowers of the range, he placed himself so that Pink could not see what he was about, and then banged the sheet iron against the cast iron of the great stove. He kept his eye fixed all the time on the scullion. The noise was enough for the big midship gun on deck, or even for a small earthquake. Pink was evidently startled by the prodigious sound, and turned towards the steward, who was satisfied that he had heard it, but the fellow was cunning, and realizing that he had committed himself, he picked up one of his feet, and began to rub it as though he had been hit by the falling blower. At the same time, he pretended to be very angry, and demonstrated very earnestly against his companion.

Dave felt that he had made a point, and he did not carry his investigation of the auditory capacity of the scullion any farther that night. He finished his work below, and then went on deck. He lounged about in a very careless manner till eight bells were struck. Mr. Flint on the bridge was relieved by Mr. Lillyworth, and the port watch came on duty for the next four hours, or until midnight. This was the time the captain had indicated to Dave as a favorable one for the discharge of his special duty. Taking advantage of the absence of any person from the vicinity of the foremast, he adroitly curled himself up in the folds of the foresail, which was brailed up to the mast. He had his head in such a position that he could see without being seen by any casual passer-by.

He waited in this position over an hour, and during that time Pink went back and forth several times, and seemed to be looking up at the bridge, which was just forward of the foremast. On the top-gallant forecastle were two men on the lookout; in the waist was a quartermaster, who was doing the duty that belonged to the third lieutenant, if the scarcity of officers had permitted the *Bronx* to have one. The body of the port watch were spinning yarns on the forecastle, and none of them were very near the foremast. After a while, as Pink was approaching the forecastle, Dave saw the second lieutenant gesticulating to him very earnestly to come on the bridge. The supernumerary ascended the ladder, and the officer set him at work to lace on the sailcloth to the railing of the bridge, to shelter those on duty there from the force of the sea blast.

Dave listened with all his ears for any sound from the bridge, but he soon realized that if there was any, he was too far off to hear it. With the aid of the lashings of the foresail, he succeeded in climbing up on the mast to a point on a level with the bridge, and at the same time to make the mast conceal him from the eyes of Mr. Lillyworth and the scullion. The latter pretended to be at work, and occasionally the second lieutenant "jawed" at him for his clumsiness in lacing the sailcloth. Between these growls, they spoke together in a low tone, but Dave was near enough to hear what they said. Though he had never heard the voice of Pink Mulgrum before, he knew that of the second lieutenant, and he was in no danger of confounding the two. Pink used excellent language, as the steward was capable of judging, and it was plain enough that he was not what he had appeared to be.

Lillyworth and Mulgrum on the Bridge

Chapter VII

Although Mr. Lillyworth knew very well that Pink Mulgrum was deaf and dumb, he "jawed" at him as though his hearing was as perfect as his own, doubtless forgetting for the moment his infirmity.

"Draw up the bight, and lace it tighter," exclaimed the second lieutenant, intermixing an expletive at each end of the sentence. "Oh, you can't hear me!" he shouted, as though the fact that the scullion could not hear him had suddenly come to his mind. "Well, it is a nice thing to talk to a deaf man!"

Dave could see that Mulgrum also seemed to forget that his ears were closed to all sounds, for he redoubled his efforts to haul the screen into its place.

81

"I could not hear anything that was of any consequence," the steward heard the deaf mute say in a lower tone than his companion used.

"Couldn't you hear anything?" asked Mr. Lillyworth making a spring at the canvas as though he was disgusted with the operations of his companion on the bridge.

"Only what I have just told you," replied Mulgrum.

"But you were at the door when the captain and the first lieutenant were talking together in the cabin," continued the officer in a low tone.

"But they were talking about me, as I told you before," answered the scullion, rather impatiently, as though he too had a mind of his own.

"Wasn't anything said about the operations of the future?" demanded Mr. Lillyworth.

"Not a word, but you know as well as I do that the captain has sealed orders which he will not see before tomorrow. I heard him tell his father that he was to open the envelope in latitude 38," said the supernumerary.

"You must contrive some way to hear the captain when he reads his orders," continued the second lieutenant. "He will be likely to have Mr. Flint with him when he opens the envelope."

"It will be difficult," replied Mulgrum, and Dave could imagine that he saw him shake his head. "The captain has found me cleaning the brasses on his door twice, and it will hardly do to be found at the door again."

"Isn't there any place in his cabin where you can conceal yourself?" inquired Mr. Lillyworth.

"I don't know of any place, unless it is his stateroom, and the cabin steward has been at work there almost all the time since we got under way. Dave seems to be a sort of confidant of the captain," suggested Mulgrum, and it looked as though the deaf mute had not held his tongue and kept his ears open for nothing, but the steward could not understand how he had got this idea into his head, for he had received his instructions while the commander was at supper, and he was sure, as he had thrown the door open several times, that the scullion was not on the other side of it.

"A Negro for his confidant!" exclaimed the second lieutenant, as he interpolated a little jaw for the benefit of the seamen and petty officers within earshot of him. "What can we expect when a mere boy is put in command of a steamer like this one?"

"I think you need not complain, Pawcett, for you are on board of this vessel, and so am I, because she is under the command of a boy. But he is a tremendous smart boy, and he is older than many men of double his age," added Mulgrum.

Dave realized that the supernumerary was well informed in regard to current history in connection with naval matters, and he was willing to believe that he was quite as shrewd as the officer at his side.

"The boy is well enough, though he is abominably overrated, as you will see before I have done with him," said Mr. Lillyworth contemptuously. "It is galling for one who has seen some service to touch his cap to this boy and call him Captain."

"I hope you are not forgetting yourself, Pawcett—"

"Don't mention my name on board of this vessel, Hungerford," interposed the officer.

"And you will not mention mine," added the scullion promptly. "We are both careless in this matter, and we must do better. I think I ought to caution you not to neglect any outside tokens of respect to the captain. You can have your own opinions, but I think you do not treat him with sufficient deference."

"Perhaps I don't, for it is not an easy thing to do," replied the second lieutenant. "But I think the captain has no cause to complain of me. We must find out something about these orders, and you must be on the lookout for your chances at meridian tomorrow. If you can stow yourself away under the captain's berth in his stateroom, you may be able to hear him read them to the first lieutenant, as he will be sure to do."

"I don't believe in doing that," replied Mulgrum. "If I am discovered, no explanation could be made as to why I was concealed there."

"But we must take some risks," persisted Mr. Lillyworth. "After what you told me in the first of our talk, it may not be necessary to conceal yourself. I shall say something to the captain on the subject at which you hinted as soon as I get a chance. You may be in a situation to hear all that is said without danger."

Dave wondered what could be meant by this remark, for he had not heard the conversation between the captain and the first lieutenant which was intended as a "blind" to the listener, known to be at the door.

"I am willing to take any risk that will not ruin our enterprise," Mulgrum responded to the remark of his companion.

"At noon tomorrow, I shall come on deck in charge,

and the first lieutenant will be relieved, so that he will be at liberty to visit the captain in his cabin. That will be your time, and you must improve it."

"But I shall meet you again tomorrow, and I will look about me and see what can be done," said Mulgrum, as he made a new demonstration at the canvas screen.

"I will keep my eyes open, and you must do the same. How is it with our men forward?" asked the officer.

"I have had no chance to speak with any of them, for they are all the time in the midst of the rest of the seamen," replied the deaf mute. "But I have no doubt they are all right."

"But you must have some way to communicate with them, or they might as well be on shore. As there are six of them, I should say you might get a chance to speak to one of them whenever you desire."

"I have had nothing to say to them so far, and I have not considered the matter of communicating with them."

"It is time to know how you can do so."

"I can manage it in some way when the time comes," replied Mulgrum confidently. "I am sure the captain and the first lieutenant have no suspicion that I am not what I seem to be. The executive officer put me through a full examination, especially in regard to Cherryfield, where I told him I used to live. I came off with flying colors, and I am certain that I am all right now."

Dave knew nothing about the examination to which Mr. Flint had subjected the deaf mute. It is evident that Mulgrum took an entirely different view of the result of the test from that taken by the examiner and the captain; but both of the latter had taken extreme pains to conceal their opinion from the subject of the test.

"I think we had better not say anything more tonight, and you have been on the bridge long enough," said Mr. Lillyworth, walking to the windward end of the bridge and peering out into the gloom of the night.

He had hardly looked in the direction of the deaf mute while he was on the bridge, but had busied himself with the lashing of the screen, and done everything he could to make it appear that he was not talking to his companion. Mulgrum, overhauling the screen as he proceeded, made his way to the steps by the side of the foremast. But he did not go down, as he had evidently intended to do, and waited till the second lieutenant came over to the lee side of the vessel.

"Perhaps the man at the wheel has been listening to our conversation," said the deaf mute, plainly alarmed at the situation. "I did not think of him."

"I did," replied Mr. Lillyworth; "but it is all right, and the man at the wheel is Spoors, one of our number."

"All right," added Mulgrum, and he descended the steps.

Dave kept his place in the folds of the foresail, and hardly breathed as the scullion passed him. With the greatest caution, and after he had satisfied himself that no one was near enough to see him, he descended to the deck. He wandered about for a while, and saw that the supernumerary went to the galley, where, in the scarcity of accommodations for the extra persons on board, he was obliged to sleep on the floor. He was not likely to extend his operations any farther that night, and Dave went to the companionway, descended the steps, and knocked at the door of the captain's cabin.

"Come in," called the occupant, who had been writing at his desk in the stateroom, though the door was open.

Dave presented himself before the commander, who was very glad to see him. Christy wiped the perspiration from his forehead, for he had evidently been working very hard all the evening. Four bells had just struck, indicating that it was ten o'clock in the evening. Flint's prediction in regard to the weather seemed to be in the way of fulfillment, for the *Bronx* had been leaping mildly on a head sea for the last hour. But everything was going well, and the motion of the vessel was as satisfactory to the commander in rough water as it had been in a smooth sea.

"I am glad to see you, Dave," said Christy, as the steward presented himself at the door of the stateroom. "I suppose from your coming tonight that you have something to tell me."

"Yes, sir; I have, and I will give you the whole Gulf of Mexico if it isn't a big thing," replied Dave with his most expansive smile.

"You done got into a hornet's nest, Captain Passford."

"Not so bad as that, I hope," replied Christy, laughing.

"Bad enough, sir, at any rate," added Dave. "Pink Mulgrum has been talking and listening to the second lieutenant all the evening."

"Then he is not a deaf mute, I take it."

"Not a bit of it; he can talk faster than I can, and he knows all about his grammar and dictionary.

You have just eight traitors on board of the *Bronx*, Captain Passford," said Dave very impressively.

"Only eight?"

"That's all I know about, and I think that is enough for one cruise in a Yankee ship."

"Eight will do very well, Dave, but who are they?" asked the captain with interest.

"I know just three of them. One is the second lieutenant; Pink Mulgrum is another; and Spoors, one of the quartermasters, is the third. They didn't mention any more of them."

"All right, Dave; now sit down on that stool, and tell me the whole story," said Christy, pointing to the seat.

The steward, believing that he had done a "big thing" that evening, did not hesitate to seat himself in the presence of the commander, and proceeded at once to relate all that he had done and all that he had seen and heard on the bridge. When Dave had finished his story and answered the questions put to him, the commander was willing to believe that he had done a big thing; though he said nothing beyond a few words of general commendation to the steward. Then he dismissed him, and, locking his desk, he went on deck. After taking an observation of the weather he mounted the bridge.

CHAPTER VIII

IMPORTANT INFORMATION, IF TRUE

"Good evening, Mr. Lillyworth," said Captain Passford, when he reached the bridge.

"Good evening, Captain Passford," replied the second lieutenant, as he touched his cap to his superior, galling as the act was, according to his own statement.

"It looks as though we should have some wind," added the captain.

"Yes, sir, and we shall have a nasty time of it across the Gulf Stream."

"If there is any decided change in the weather during your watch, you will oblige me by having me called," added the captain. "I think I am tired enough to turn in, for I have been very busy all the evening copying letters and papers. I think I need a clerk almost as much as the captain of a frigate."

"I think you ought to have one, sir," added Mr. Lillyworth, manifesting a deep interest in this matter.

"As the matter now stands, I have to use a good deal of my time in copying documents. By the way, if we fall in with any United States man-of-war, I wish to communicate with her."

"Of course I shall report to you, sir, if one comes in sight during my watch," replied the second lieutenant with a greater manifestation of zeal than he had before displayed in his relations with his commander, evidently profiting by the suggestion made to him by Pink Mulgrum.

"But I hope we shall not fall in with one before day after tomorrow, for I have not copied all the letters I desire to use if such an occasion offers," said Captain Passford, who was really playing out a baited hook for the benefit of the second lieutenant, in regard to whose intentions he had no doubt since the revelations of the steward.

"By the way, Captain Passford, what you say in regard to the amount of writing imposed upon you reminds me that there is a man on board who might afford you some relief from this drudgery. Possibly you may have noticed this man, though he is doing duty as a mere scullion."

"Do you mean the man I have seen cleaning brass

work about the cabin?" asked Christy, glad to have the other take hold of the baited hook.

"That is the one; he is deaf and dumb, but he has received a good education, and writes a good hand, and is rapid about it," added the second lieutenant with some eagerness in his manner, though he tried to conceal it.

"But my writing is of a confidential nature," replied the captain.

"I have known this man, whose name is Pink Mulgrum, for some time. He is deaf and dumb, and you must have noticed him."

"Oh, yes; I have seen him, and he had an interview with Mr. Flint in my presence. I observed that he wrote a good hand, and wrote very rapidly."

"I am very confident that you can trust him with your papers, Captain Passford. He could not go into the service as a soldier or a sailor on account of his infirmity, but he desired to do something for his country. He was determined to go to the war, as he called it, in any capacity, even if it was as a scullion. He wrote me a letter to this effect, and Mr. Nawood consented to take him as a man of all work. If he ever gets into an action, you will find that he is a fighting character."

"That is the kind of men we want, and at the present time, when we are hardly in a fighting latitude, perhaps I can use him as a copyist, if he will agree to make no use whatever of any information he may obtain in that capacity. I will speak to Mr. Nawood about the matter."

"Thank you, Captain Passford. Mulgrum is a very worthy man, patriotic in every fiber of his frame and in every drop of his blood. I should be glad to obtain some permanent occupation for him in the service of his country, for nothing else will suit him in the present exciting times. Perhaps when you have tested his qualifications, this will make an opening for him."

"I will consider the subject tomorrow," said Christy, as he descended from the bridge.

The commander was satisfied that the portion of the conversation which had taken place between the aspirant for the position of captain's clerk and the second lieutenant, and which had been finished before the steward had reached his perch on the foremast, related to this matter. Mulgrum had heard the conversation between the first lieutenant and himself, which was intended to blind the listener, and he had reported it to his confederate. It was only another confirmation, if any were needed, in regard to the character of the conspirators.

Christy had no doubt in regard to the disloyalty of these two men, but nothing in respect to their ultimate intentions had yet been revealed. They had brought six seamen on board with them, and they appeared to have influence enough in some quarter to have had these men drafted into the *Bronx*. Eight men, even if two of them were officers, was an insignificant force, though he was willing to believe that they intended to obtain possession of the vessel in some manner. The captain returned to his cabin and resumed his work in the stateroom.

Though Christy had spent seven hours at his desk, he had really produced but a single letter, and had not yet finished it. When he heard eight bells strike, he left his stateroom and seated himself at the table in the middle of his cabin. The door was open into the companionway. Mr. Flint presently appeared and went on deck to relieve the second lieutenant, who came below a few minutes later, though the captain did not allow himself to be seen by him. Then he closed the cabin door and turned in, for he began to realize that he needed some rest. He went to sleep at once, and he did not wake till four bells struck in the morning. The *Bronx* was pitching heavily, though she still maintained her reputation as an easy-going ship in spite of the head sea. He dressed himself, and seated himself at his desk at once, devoting himself to the letter upon which he had been engaged the evening before. The second lieutenant was on duty at this time and the first was doubtless asleep in his berth, but he had been below six hours during the night, and, calling Dave with his bell, he sent him for Mr. Flint, who presented himself a few minutes later.

"Good morning, Captain Passford; you have turned out early, sir," said the first lieutenant.

"Not very early, and I am sorry to wake you so soon. I did not turn in till after you had gone on deck to take the midwatch. I have been very busy since we parted, and I need your advice and assistance," replied the commander. "I have got at something."

"Indeed! I am glad to hear it," added Mr. Flint.

Without the loss of any time, the captain called Dave, who was at work in the wardroom, and told him to see that no one came near the door of his cabin. The steward understood him perfectly, and Christy resumed his place at the table with the executive officer, and proceeded to detail to him as briefly as he could all the information he had obtained through Dave, and the manner of obtaining it. It required some time to do this, and the first lieutenant was intensely interested in the narrative.

"I am not greatly surprised so far as Lillyworth is concerned, for there has been something about him that I could not fathom since both of us came on board," said Mr. Flint.

"Of course, these men are on board for a purpose, though I acknowledge that I cannot fathom this purpose, unless it be treason in a general sense, but I am inclined to believe that they have some specific object," added the captain. "Of course, you will be willing to believe that both of these men are sailing under false colors."

"Undoubtedly. It has occurred to me that the second lieutenant invented the name that represents him on the ship's books. Lillyworth is a little strained; if he had called himself Smith or Brown, it would have been less suspicious."

"In the conversation to which Dave listened on the bridge, both of them blundered and let out their real names, though each of them reproved the other for doing so. The second lieutenant's real name is Pawcett, and that of the deaf mute is Hungerford."

"The last is decidedly a Southern name, and the other may be for aught I know. Hungerford,

Hungerford," said Mr. Flint, repeating the name several times. "It means something to me, but I can't make it out yet."

The first lieutenant cudgeled his brains for a minute or two as though he was trying to connect the name with some event in the past. The captain waited for him to sound his memory, but it was done in vain; Flint could not place him. He was confident, however, that the connection would be made in his mind at some other moment.

"The interesting question to us just now is to determine why these men, eight in number, are on board of the *Bronx* at all, and why they are on board at the present time," said the captain. "I happen to know that Lillyworth was offered a better position than the one he now fills temporarily, but my father says he insisted on going in the *Bronx*."

"Certainly he is not here on a fool's errand. He has business on board of this particular steamer," replied Flint, speaking out of his musing mind. "Ah! now I have it!" he suddenly exclaimed. "Hungerford was the executive officer of the *Killbright*, or the *Yazoo*, as they called her afterwards. I had a very slight inkling that I had seen the face of the deaf mute before, but he has shaved off his beard and stained his face, so that it is no wonder I did not identify him, but the name satisfies me that he was the first officer of the *Yazoo*."

"That means then that he is a regular officer of the Confederate navy," suggested the captain, "and probably Lillyworth is also. The only other name Dave was able to obtain was that of Spoors, one of the quartermasters, and very likely he is also another."

"We have almost a double crew on board, Captain Passford, and what can eight men do to capture this vessel?" asked Flint.

"I don't know what they intend to do, and I must give it up. Now I want to read a letter to you that I have written, and you can tell me what you think of it." The commander then read as follows from the sheet in his hand, upon which appeared no end of changes and corrections:

"To the Commander of any United States Ship of War, Sir:—The undersigned, master in the United States Navy, in temporary command of the United States Steamer *Bronx*, bound to the Gulf of Mexico, respectfully informs you that he has information, just received, of the approach to the coast of the Southern states of two steamers, the *Scotian* and the *Arran*, believed to be fitted out as cruisers for the Confederate navy. They will be due in these waters about March 17. They are of about five hundred tons each. A letter from the confidential agent of my father, Captain Horatio Passford, an agent in whom he has perfect confidence, both on account of his loyalty to his country undivided, and because of his skill as a shipmaster, contains this statement, which is submitted to you for your guidance: 'I have put twelve loyal American seamen, with an officer, on board of each of the steamers mentioned above; and they comprise about one-half of the crew of each vessel; and they will take possession of each of the two steamers when supported by any United States man-of-war. WARNOCK.'

Respectfully yours,

CHRISTOPHER PASSFORD,

Master Commanding."

"I beg your pardon, Captain Passford, but what under the canopy is that letter for?" asked Flint, not a little excited.

"It is for Pink Mulgrum to copy," replied the captain. "That is all the use I intend to make of it."

Flint leaned back in his chair and laughed heartily, and the commander could not help joining him.

Chapter IX

A Volunteer Captain's Clerk

Mr. Flint was really amused at the plan of the commander of the *Bronx*, as indicated in the letter he had just read, and he was not laughing out of mere compliment to his superior officer, as some subordinates feel obliged to do even when they feel more like weeping. Perhaps no one knew Christy Passford so well as his executive officer, not even his own father, for Flint had been with him in the most difficult and trying ordeals of his life. He had been the young leader's second in command in the capture of the *Teaser*, whose cabin they now occupied, and they had been prisoners together. He had been amazed at his young companion's audacity, but he had always justified his actions in the end. They had become excellent friends as well as associates in the navy, and there was a hearty sympathy between them.

Christy laughed almost in spite of himself, for he had been giving very serious attention to the situation on board of the *Bronx*. In the ship's company were at least two officers on the other side of the great question of the day, both of them doubtless men of great experience in their profession, more mature in years than their opponent on this chessboard of fate, and they had come on board of the steamer to accomplish some important purpose. The game at which they were engaged had already become quite exciting, especially as it looked as if the final result was to be determined by strategy rather than hard fighting, for Pawcett and Hungerford could hardly expect to capture the *Bronx* with only a force of eight men.

"Mulgrum is to copy this letter," said Flint, suppressing his laughter.

"I have written the letter in order to have something for him to copy, and at the same time to give him and his confederate something to think about," replied Christy, and he could hardly help chuckling when he thought of the effect the contents of the letter would produce in the minds of those for whom the missive was really intended.

"Do you think they will swallow this fiction, Captain Passford?" asked the first lieutenant.

"Why shouldn't they swallow it, hook, bait, and sinker? They are Confederate agents beyond the possibility of a doubt, and they are looking for a ship in which they intend to ravage the commerce of the United States," replied Christy, and the question had done something to stimulate his reasoning powers. "They want a vessel, and the *Bronx* would suit them very well."

"But they will not attempt to capture her under present circumstances, I am very confident. They know that we have about twenty seamen extra on board."

"They know that certainly, but possibly they know some things in this connection that we do not know," added Christy, as he put his hand on his forehead and leaned over the table, as though his mind were strongly exercised by some serious question he was unable to answer satisfactorily to himself.

"What can they know that we don't know in regard to this vessel?" demanded Flint, looking quite as serious as the commander.

"Whether our extra men are loyal or not," answered Christy, dropping his hand and looking his companion full in the face.

"Do you think there is any doubt in regard to them?"

"I confess that I have not had a doubt till this moment," said the captain, wiping the perspiration from his brow, for the terrible possibility that any considerable portion of the extra men were in the employ of the two Confederates had almost overcome him.

For a few moments he was silent as he thought of this tremendous idea. It was appalling to think of going into action with the *Scotian* or the *Arran*, or both of them, and have a part of his own force turn against him on his own deck. This was possible, but he could hardly believe it was probable. Dave had reported very faithfully to him all the details of the conversation between the Confederates, and they had claimed only six men. If they had any hold on the extra men on board, they would have been likely to say so, or at least to speak more indefinitely than they had of their expectations.

"Have you any friends on board, Mr. Flint, among the crew?" asked Christy suddenly, as though a solution of the difficult question of the loyalty of the men had suggested itself to him.

"I have at least half a dozen whom I worked hard to have drafted into the *Bronx*, for I know that they are good and true men, though they may not be able to pass the technical examination of the naval officers," replied the first lieutenant promptly. "I can trust every one of them as far as I could trust myself. One of them was the mate of my vessel at the time I sold her, and he has since been in command of her."

"Who is he?"

"His name is Baskirk, and he is a quartermaster now. I wrote to him and promised to do the best I could to advance him. He is not a graduate of a college, but he is a well-informed man, well read, sober, honest, and a man of good common sense."

"The others?"

"McSpindle was a classmate of mine in college, and he is a capital fellow. Unfortunately, he got into the habit of drinking more than was good for him, and spoiled his immediate future. He has made two foreign voyages, and he is a good seaman. He came home second mate of an Indiaman, promoted on his merit. He is also a quartermaster," said Flint, who was evidently very deeply interested in the persons he described.

"Any more?"

"Luffard is a quartermaster, for I selected the best men I had for these positions. He is a young fellow, and the son of a rich man in Portland. He is a regular water bird, though he is not over eighteen years old."

"His age is no objection," added Christy with a smile.

"I suppose not, but I have taken Luffard on his bright promise rather than for anything he has ever done, though I have seen him sail a forty-footer in a race and win the first prize. The other men I happen to think of just now have been sailors on board of my coaster. They are good men, and I can vouch for their loyalty, though not for their education. They are all petty officers."

"I have a mission for your men, to be undertaken at once, and I shall be likely to want the first three you named for important positions, if my orders do not fetter me too closely," said Christy. "As the matter stands just now, Mr. Flint, it would hardly be expedient for us to capture a schooner running the blockade for the want of an officer to act as prize master."

"The three quartermasters I named are competent for this duty, for they are navigators, and all of them have handled a vessel."

"I am glad to hear it; we are better off than I supposed we were. My father told me that several vessels had been sent to the South short of officers, and we are no worse off than some others, though what you say makes us all right."

"I can find three officers on board who are as competent as I am, though that is not saying much," added Flint.

"I can ask no better officers, then. But to return to this letter. I have spent a considerable part of my time at Bonnydale in talking with my father. He is in the confidence of the naval department."

"He ought to be, for he gave to the navy one of its best steamers, to say the least."

"I don't want to brag of my father," suggested Christy laughing, "I only wanted to show that he is posted. Coming to the point at once, putting this and that together of what I learned on shore, and of what I have discovered on board of the *Bronx*, I am inclined to believe that Pawcett and Hungerford have their mission on board of this steamer in connection with the *Scotian* and the *Arran*. I will not stop now to explain why I have this idea, for I shall obtain more evidence as we proceed. At any rate, I thought I would put the ghost of a stumbling block in the path of these conspirators, and this is the reason why I have put thirteen American seamen on board of each of the expected steamers. If my conjectures are wrong, the stumbling block will be nothing but a ghost; if I am right, it will make our men somewhat cautious as to what they do if we should be so fortunate as to fall in with the two vessels."

"I understand you perfectly, Captain Passford. You said that you had something for my men to do at once, but you did not explain what this duty was," said Flint. "If you require their services at once, I will instruct them."

"I did not explain, for I have so many irons in the fire that I am afraid I am getting them mixed, and I forgot to tell you what they were to do. But I shall leave the details to be settled in your own way. I want to know who are loyal men and who are not. There are at least six men, according to the report of Dave, who are followers of Pawcett and Hungerford. We don't know who they are, but doubtless they have been selected for their shrewdness. Probably they will be looking for information among the men. Spoors is one of them, and by watching him some clue may be obtained to the others."

"I am confident my men can find out all you want to know," added the first lieutenant.

"It should be done as soon as possible," replied the commander.

"Not a moment shall be lost. I have the deck at eight this morning, and one of the quartermasters will be at the wheel. I will begin with him."

Mr. Flint left the cabin, for his breakfast was waiting for him in the wardroom. Christy walked through to the steerage, where he found Mulgrum attending to the wants of the warrant officers as well as he could. He looked at this man with vastly more interest than before he had listened to Dave's report. It was easy to see that he was not an ordinary man such as one would find in menial positions, but it was not prudent for him to make a study of the man, for his quick eye was taking in everything that occurred near him.

Eight bells struck, and Mr. Flint hastened on deck to relieve the second lieutenant. Christy took his morning meal at a later hour, and when he had finished it, he sent for Pink Mulgrum. Of course the conversation had to be written, and the captain placed the scullion opposite himself at the table.

"I learn from Mr. Lillyworth that you are a good writer, and that you are well educated," Christy wrote on a piece of paper, passing it to the deaf mute.

Mulgrum read the sentence and nodded his head with something like a smile. If Christy was a judge of his expression, he was certainly pleased, evidently to find that his confederate's plan was working well.

"I have a letter of which I desire several copies. Can I trust you to make these copies?" Christy wrote.

The man read and nodded his head eagerly.

"Will you promise on your honor as a man that you will not reveal what you write to any person whatever?" Christy proceeded. Mulgrum read, and nodded his head earnestly several times.

The commander procured paper and other writing materials for him and placed them before him. Then he seated himself again opposite the copyist and fixed his gaze upon him; unfolding the letter, of which he had made a fair copy himself, he placed it under the eyes of the deaf mute. Mulgrum had retained his smile till this moment. He had arranged his paper and taken a pen in his hand. Then he began to read; as he proceeded, the smile deserted his face. He was plainly startled.

CHAPTER X

THE UNEXPECTED ORDERS

Christy sat for some minutes watching the expression of Mulgrum as he read the letter he was to copy. Like a careful man, he was evidently taking a glance at it as a whole. The interested observer could see that he fixed his gaze upon the last part of the letter, the extract from the missive of Warnock, relating to the twelve loyal American seamen and their officer. In fact, he seemed to be paralyzed by what he read.

The commander was satisfied with what he had seen, and he rose from his chair. His movement seemed to restore the self-possession of the deaf mute, and he began to write very rapidly. Christy went into his stateroom, where he kept all his important papers in his desk. He gave himself up to a consideration of the situation in which he was placed. He had partly closed the door. But he had not been in the room half an hour before he heard a knock.

"Come in," said he, supposing the caller was Dave.

The door was pushed open, and Mulgrum came in with his tablet in his hand. The deaf mute had certainly heard his reply to the knock, for he had heeded it instantly, and he smiled at the manner in which the conspirator had "given himself away." The scullion presented his tablet to the captain with a very deferential bow.

"There is an error in the copy of the letter you gave me—in the extract. If you will give me the original letter from Mr. Warnock, I will correct the mistake," Christy read on the tablet. It was not impossible that he had made a mistake in copying his letter, but the object of Mulgrum in desiring to see the original of the letter from England was sufficiently apparent. "Bring me my copy of the letter," he wrote on the tablet, and handed it back to the owner.

The captain took from his desk a bundle of letters and selected one, which he opened and laid on the table, though not where his copyist could see it. Mulgrum returned and presented him the letter, pointing out the mistake he had discovered. He looked at the blind letter, and then at the other. There was certainly an error, for his letter said "and they comprise about one of crew of each vessel." This was nonsense, for he had accidentally omitted the word "half" after "one." He inserted the word above the line in its proper place and gave it back to the copyist. It was clear enough that Mulgrum was disappointed in the result of this interview, but he took the letter and returned to the table.

At the end of another quarter of an hour, he brought the first copy of the letter. He knocked as before, and though Christy told him in a loud tone to come in, he did not do so. He repeated the words, but the conspirator, possibly aware of the blunder he had made before, did not make it again. Then he wrote on his tablet, after the captain had approved his work, that he found the table very uncomfortable to write upon while the ship was pitching so smartly, and suggested that he should be allowed to make the rest of the copies on the desk in the stateroom, if the captain did not desire to use it himself. Unfortunately for the writer, he did desire to use it himself, and he could not help smiling at the enterprise of the deaf mute in his attempt to obtain an opportunity to forage among the papers in his drawers.

Mulgrum certainly did his work nicely and expeditiously, for he had finished it at three bells in the forenoon watch. He was dismissed then, for his presence was not particularly agreeable to the commander. Christy locked his desk and all the drawers that contained papers, not as against a thief or a burglar, but against one who would scorn to appropriate anything of value that did not belong to him, for he had no doubt now that Mulgrum was a gentleman who was trying to serve what he regarded as his country, though it was nothing but a fraction of it.

In fact, inheriting, as it were, the broad and generous policy of his father, Christy had no personal prejudices against this enemy of his country, and he felt just as he would if he had been sailing a boat against him, or playing a game of whist with him. He was determined to beat him if he could. But he was not satisfied with locking his papers up; he called Dave and set him as a watch over them. If the conspirator overhauled his papers, he would have been more concerned about what he did not find than in relation to what he did find, for the absence of the original of Warnock's letter would go far to convince him that the extract from it was an invention.

When he had taken these precautions he went on deck. The wind was blowing a moderate gale, but the *Bronx* was doing exceedingly well, lifting herself very lightly over the foaming billows and conveying to one walking her deck the impression of solidity and strength. The captain went to the bridge after a while, though not till he had noticed that something was going on among the crew, but he was not disposed to inquire into the matter, possibly regarding it as beneath the dignity of a commander to do so.

Christy mounted the steps to the bridge. This structure is hardly a man-of-war appendage. It had been there, and it had been permitted to remain. The first shot in action might carry it away, and this contingency had been provided for, as she was provided with a duplicate steam-steering apparatus, as well as a hand wheel at the stern. The proper position of the officer of the watch, who is practically in command for the time being, is on the quarterdeck, though he is required during his watch to visit all parts of the deck. On board of the *Bronx* this officer was placed on the bridge, where he could overlook all parts of the ship.

The first lieutenant, who had the forenoon watch, saluted him, but there was nothing of interest to report. Christy asked the meaning of the movement he had observed among the seamen and petty officers, and was told that Baskirk was getting up an association on board, the first requirement to which was for all who wished to become members to sign the oath of allegiance to the United States government, "as represented by and presided over by the president at Washington." It was to be a secret society, and Flint added that it was really a branch of the Union League. Christy did not think it wise to ask any more questions, but he understood that this was really a movement to ascertain the sentiments of the members of the ship's company as to the extent of their duty in supporting the government.

"Mr. Flint, I am not a little dissatisfied with the manner in which we are compelled to carry on our duty on board of the *Bronx*, though no blame is to be attached to the naval department on account of it," said Christy, after he had walked the bridge for a time.

"Is anything going wrong, Captain Passford?" asked the first lieutenant anxiously.

"Oh, no; I have no fault to find with anyone, and least of all with you," added the captain promptly. "The trouble is that we are short of officers, though all that could be spared for this vessel were sent on board of her. As the matter now stands, Dr. Spokeley and I are the only idlers on board in the cabin and wardroom. The first lieutenant has to keep a watch, which is not at all regular, and I foresee that this arrangement will be a very great disadvantage to me. It could not be helped, and the *Bronx* was evidently regarded as of no great importance, for she is little more than a storeship just now, though the flag officer in the Gulf will doubtless make something more of her."

"We have a big crew for this vessel, but we are short of officers," added Flint.

"From the best calculations I have been able to make, with my father to help me, we ought to fall in with the *Scotian* and the *Arran*, and in view of such an event, I propose to prepare for the emergency by appointing a temporary third lieutenant."

"I think that would be a very wise step to take," added Flint very cordially.

"Of the men you mentioned to me, who is the best one for this position?" asked Christy.

"I have no hesitation in saying that Baskirk is the right man for the position."

"Very well; he shall be appointed," added Christy, as he left the bridge. But in a few minutes he returned and handed an order to the first lieutenant.

Baskirk was sent for, and the captain had a long talk with him. He found that the candidate had more knowledge of naval discipline than he had supposed, and he was pleased with the man. He was the leading quartermaster in rank, having been appointed first. After another talk with Flint, the latter gave the order to pass the word for Mr. Giblock, who was the acting boatswain, though in rank he was only a boatswain's mate. He was directed to call all hands. When the ship's company were assembled on the forward deck, though this is not the usual place for such a gathering, the first lieutenant read the order of the commander appointing George Baskirk as acting third lieutenant of the *Bronx*, and directing that he should be respected and obeyed as such. A smart cheer followed the announcement, though the second lieutenant, who had taken a place on the bridge, looked as though he did not approve the step the captain had taken. The officer of the deck next appointed Thomas McLinn a quartermaster. The ship's company were then dismissed.

Just before noon by the clocks, Lieutenant Baskirk appeared on the bridge, dressed in a brand new uniform, with a sextant in his hands. Christy, who did not depend upon his pay for the extent of his wardrobe, had not less than three new suits, and he had presented one of them to the newly appointed officer, for there was no material difference in the size of the two persons. All the officers who kept watches were required to "take the sun," and at the moment the meridian was crossed, the captain gave the word to "make it noon," and the great bell sounded out eight bells. The officers proceeded to figure up the results of the observations. The longitude and latitude were entered on the log slate, to be transferred to the log book. Baskirk was directed to take the starboard watch, and he was formally presented to the second lieutenant by the captain, and whatever his feeling or opinions in regard to the step which had just been taken, he accepted the hand of the new officer and treated him with proper courtesy.

"Latitude 37° 52′," said the captain significantly, as he led the way down from the bridge, attended by the first and third lieutenants.

They followed him to the captain's cabin. Christy gave them seats at the table and then went into his stateroom for the ponderous envelope which contained his orders. He seated himself between his two officers, but before he broke the great seal, he discovered Dave in the passageway making energetic signs to him. He hastened to him and followed him into the wardroom.

"Pink is under your berth in the stateroom," whispered the steward in the most impressive manner.

"All right, Dave; you have been faithful to your duty," said Christy, as he hastened back into his cabin.

Resuming his place at the table, he broke the seal of the huge envelope. He unfolded the enclosed instructions and ran over them without speaking a word.

"We have nothing to do on this cruise," said he, apparently taking his idea from the paper in his hand. "I will read the material parts of it," he continued in a much louder tone than the size of the cabin and the nearness of his auditors seemed to demand. " 'You will proceed with all reasonable dispatch to the Gulf of Mexico and report to the flag officer, or his representative, of the eastern Gulf Squadron. You will attempt no operations on your passage, and if an enemy appears, you will avoid her if possible with honor.' That's all, gentlemen."

The two listeners seemed to be utterly confounded.

Chapter XI

Another Reading of the Sealed Orders

Christy finished the reading of the orders, folded up the document, and put it in his pocket. But he immediately took it out and unfolded it again, as though a new thought had struck him. Flint watched him with the utmost attention, and he realized that the bearing of the commander was quite different from his usual manner, but he attributed it to the very unexpected nature of the orders he had just read. He was distinctly directed to attempt no operations on the passage, and to proceed to the destination indicated with all reasonable dispatch.

The wording of the order was rather peculiar and somewhat clumsy, Flint thought, but then he had been a schoolmaster, and perhaps he was inclined to be over critical. But the meaning of the first clause could not be mistaken, however, though the word "operations" seemed to indicate something on a grander scale and more prolonged than an encounter with a blockade-runner or a Confederate man-of-war; something in the nature of a campaign on shore or a thorough scouring of the ocean in search of the vessels of the enemy.

But any such interpretation of the order was rendered impossible by what followed. The commander was distinctly forbidden to engage the enemy if such an encounter could be avoided "with honor." The first lieutenant knew that a combat could be easily avoided simply by not following up any suspicious craft, unless a fully manned and armed Confederate cruiser presented herself, and then it might be honorable to run away from her. There was no mistaking the meaning of the orders, and there was no chance to strain a point and fall upon one or both of the expected steamers.

The captain was strictly enjoined from meddling with them, even if they came in his way. If they chased the *Bronx*, she would be justified in defending herself under the orders, and that was the most she could do. Flint was terribly disappointed, and he regarded the commander with the deepest interest to learn what interpretation he would give to the orders, though there seemed to him to be no room even to take advantage of any fortunate circumstance.

The appearance of the commander did not throw any new light upon the contents of the document. After he had finished the reading of the paper, Christy sat in his chair, apparently still looking it over, as though he did not fully comprehend its meaning. But he made no sign and indulged in no remark of any kind, and in a few moments folded the order and put it back into his pocket. Undoubtedly he was thinking very energetically of something, but he did not reveal the nature of his reflections.

Flint concluded that he was utterly dissatisfied with his orders, and even regarded them as a slight upon himself as the commander of the steamer for the time being. It was not customary to direct captains to avoid the enemy under all circumstances that were likely to be presented. The first lieutenant began to realize the disadvantage of sailing with a captain so young, for it looked to him as though the strange order had been issued on account of the youth of the commander.

When Christy had restored the paper to his pocket, he rose from his seat, and thus indicated that there was to be no consultation with the officers in regard to the unusual instructions. The two officers rose at the same time and closely observed the face of the commander, but this time Flint could find nothing there as serious as he had observed before; in fact, there was a twinkle in his eye that looked promising.

"Gentlemen, it is dinner time in the wardroom, and I will not detain you any longer," said Christy, as politely as he usually spoke to his officers, though the opera of *Pinafore* had not been written at that time.

Flint bowed to his captain and left the cabin, and his example was followed by Baskirk. Christy certainly did not look as though he were embarrassed by his orders, or as if he were disappointed at the restrictions they imposed upon him. He left the cabin so that Dave could prepare his table for dinner as he had the time to do so. He left the cabin, but in the passage he called the steward to him and whispered a brief sentence to him.

He then ascended to the deck and proceeded to take a "constitutional" on the windward side of the quarterdeck. The gale had moderated very sensibly, though the wind was still from the southward. The sea was still quite rough, though it was likely to subside very soon. After the captain had walked as long as he cared to do, he mounted the bridge.

"What do you think of the weather, Mr. Lillyworth?" he asked of the officer of the deck, after he had politely returned his salute.

"I don't believe we shall have any more wind today," replied the second lieutenant, as he looked wisely at the weather indications the sky presented. "But it don't look much like fairing off, and I shall look for fog as long as the wind holds where it is."

"I have been expecting to be buried in fog," added the captain, as he took a survey of the deck beneath him. "I see by the log slate that we are making fifteen knots an hour, and we certainly are not driving her."

"There can be no doubt that this is a very fast vessel," said Mr. Lillyworth. "Well, she ought to be, for I understand that she was built for a nobleman's yacht, and such men want speed and are willing to pay for it."

"By tomorrow, we shall be in the latitude of the Bermudas, and most of the blockade runners put in there, or some more southern port, to get the news and obtain a pilot, if they don't happen to have one on board."

"That seems to be the way they do it."

"This fog is favorable to blockade runners if they

have a skillful pilot on board, and they all contrive to have such a one," added the captain, as he moved towards the steps to the deck.

"I suppose you have opened your sealed orders, Captain Passford," said the second lieutenant, who seemed to be interested in this subject. "We have crossed the thirty-eighth parallel."

"Yes; I have opened the envelope and found the orders very peculiar and very disappointing," replied the captain as he took a step on the ladder. "But you will excuse me now from speaking of them, for I have another matter on my mind."

Christy thought Pink Mulgrum might as well tell him about the orders, and he could at least save his breath if he had no other motive for leaving the second lieutenant in the dark for the present. He went to the deck and then down into the cabin. His breakfast was ready, but Dave was not there, and he walked forward into the wardroom, from which he saw Mulgrum replenishing the table in the steerage. He had evacuated his place under the berth in the stateroom, and the captain went to his breakfast in his cabin. Dave soon appeared with the hot dishes from the galley, for he had seen Christy take his place at the table.

"What's the news, Dave?" asked the captain.

"No news, sir, except that I gave Pink a chance to get out of that stateroom," replied the steward, spreading out his broadest smile. "I spoke out loud just like I was calling to some one in the wardroom, 'No, sir, I can't go now; I have to go to the galley for the dishes.' Then I left the cabin and went forward; when I came back, I looked under your berth, sir, and Pink wasn't there then."

"How did you know he was under the berth in the first place, Dave?"

"Just before eight bells I saw him cleaning the brasses on the door. I think he will wear those door knobs all out before the cruise is up. I knew he was up to something, and I just watched him. He went out of sight, and I did not know where he was. Then I took the feather duster and worked about the cabin, but I couldn't find him. Then I dusted the stateroom, and then I did find him."

"You have rendered good service, Dave, and I shall not forget it," added Christy. "Where are Mr. Flint and Mr. Baskirk?"

"In the wardroom, sir."

"Give my compliments to them, and say that I wish to see them in my cabin in about ten minutes," continued the captain.

Dave left the cabin, and Christy devoted himself

Dave Finds Mulgrum under the Berth

to his breakfast, and in his haste to meet the officers indicated, he hurried the meal more than was prudent for the digestion. The steward reported that he had delivered the message, and Christy finished his hasty collation.

The table was hurriedly cleared by the steward, and the captain paid a visit to his stateroom, during which he did not fail to look under his berth. He had a trunk there, and he saw that it had been moved to the front of the space, so that there was room enough for the conspirator to conceal his body behind it, though his was a good-sized body. Returning to the cabin, he took his usual seat at the table, facing the door. In a few minutes more, Mr. Flint and Mr. Baskirk came to the door and were invited to come in. Dave had returned from the galley, and he was instructed to watch that door as he was told to close it.

Flint took the seat assigned to him, and Baskirk was placed opposite to him. The first lieutenant appeared to be a great deal more dissatisfied than the captain, but then he was a poor man, and next to his duty to his country, he was as anxious as the average officer to make all the money he could out of the prizes captured by his ship. It looked to him as though all his chances had slipped beyond his reach for the present.

Flint had taken no little stock in the two steamers that were expected on the coast at this time, and, in spite of the treachery anticipated, he had counted upon a share in at least one of them. He knew very well that the commander, from sharp experience at his side some months before, would not pass by an opportunity to strike a blow, even in the face of any reasonable risk. But now, as he looked at it, the wings of the young captain had been clipped by the authorities at Washington, in the sealed orders.

"I am glad to meet you again, gentlemen; indeed, I may say that I am particularly glad to see you," said Christy in his most cheerful tones, as he looked about the cabin, and especially at the ports, to see if there was a spy looking in at one of them.

The thought came to him then and there that it was possible for a man to hang over the rail and place one of his ears at an opening and listen to what was going on, and besides there were, besides Mulgrum, six others who were capable of doing such a thing. He sent Mr. Baskirk on deck to see that no man was at work over the side. He returned and reported that no one was in a position to hear what was said in the cabin.

Flint did not seem to be as much interested in the proceedings as on former occasions, for he had had time to consider the effect of the orders, and he saw no way to evade them. They might pick up some cotton schooners, but no such prizes as the *Scotian* and the *Arran* were likely to be taken when the steamer reached her station, wherever it might be, and the whole squadron shared the proceeds of the captures.

"You listened to the orders I read this noon," began Christy with a pronounced twinkling of his eyes.

"Yes, sir, and, Captain Passford, I have felt as if the gates of honor and profit had been closed against the *Bronx*," added Flint.

"Perhaps a second reading of the orders will put a different aspect on the gates," said the captain with a significant smile, the force of which, however, the first lieutenant failed to comprehend.

"Under these orders there seems to be no alternative but to hasten to the Gulf of Mexico and run away from any blockade runner we may happen to see," growled Flint.

"You are not as amiable as usual, Mr. Flint."

"How can one be amiable under such orders?" added Flint, trying to smile.

"I will read them over again, now that we have not as many auditors as before," said the captain.

Christy proceeded to read the document as it was written.

CHAPTER XII

Before Captain Passford had read two lines of the document in his hands, a noise as of a scuffle was heard in the passageway to the wardroom. Mr. Baskirk was sent to ascertain the cause of the disturbance, and he threw the door wide open. Dave was there, blocking the passageway, and Pink Mulgrum was trying to force his way towards the cabin door. The steward declared that no one must go to the cabin; it was the order of the captain himself. Mulgrum found it convenient not to hear on this occasion. The moment Baskirk appeared, the deaf mute exhibited a paper, which he passed to the new lieutenant, evidently satisfied that he could get no nearer to the door. When he had delivered the paper, he hastened up the ladder to the deck. Dave came into the cabin and explained that Mulgrum had tried to force him out of the way, and he had resisted. The intruder did not exhibit any paper till the third lieutenant appeared at the door.

"That man is very persevering in his efforts to procure information," said Christy, as he unfolded the paper. " 'The fog is very dense ahead, and we shall soon be shut in by it,' " he read from the paper. "Mr. Lillyworth might have found a man that could speak for his messenger," he continued, "but of course he wanted to assist his confederate to obtain more information."

"I don't see what he wants to know now, for Mulgrum has told him the contents of the sealed envelope before this time, and he knows that the gates are closed against us," added Flint. "It is plain enough that they have had their heads together."

"Certainly they have, but Mr. Lillyworth may not be any better satisfied with his information than you are, Mr. Flint," replied the captain with an expressive smile, though he felt that his fellow officer had been tantalized long enough by the circumstances. "I have read and studied my orders very attentively. They direct me to proceed with all reasonable dispatch to the Gulf of Mexico, and report to the flag officer of the Eastern Gulf Squadron, or his representative.

" 'But information has been received,' " continued Christy, reading what he had not read before, "'that two steamers, probably fitted out for service in the Confederate navy, are approaching the coast of the Southern States, and it is very important that they should be intercepted. Both of these vessels are reported to have small crews, but they are said to be fast. The department regrets that it has not a suitable steamer available to send in search of these two vessels, but relying upon your well-known patriotism and the excellent record you have already made, you are instructed to intercept them, even if you are delayed a week or more by any hopeful circumstances.' That is the material portion of my orders," added Christy, as he read the last sentence. "But I beg you to bear in mind that I did not write the commendatory expressions in the paper."

"But they are as true as the holy Gospels!" exclaimed Flint, springing out of his chair in the heat of the excitement which the new reading of the orders produced in his mind. "But I thought you had read the sealed orders to us before, Captain Passford."

"I read but a very small part of them before, and as I had to improvise the greater part of what I read, or rather did not read but simply uttered, the language was not all well chosen," replied Christy, laughing in spite of all his attempts to maintain his dignity. "The fact is, Mr. Flint, I had too many listeners when I read the paper before."

"There was no one in the cabin but Mr. Baskirk and myself, and Dave had been stationed at the door, or at least he was there, for he beckoned you out into the gangway just as you were beginning to read the orders," argued Flint. "Possibly I should have understood the first reading better if I had not seen for myself that you had taken all precautions against any listener. You went out when Dave called you, but you were not gone half a minute, and that was not long enough for the steward to spin any long yarn."

"But it was long enough for Dave to tell me that Pink Mulgrum was under my berth, with the stateroom door open," replied Christy.

"Just so; I comprehend the whole matter now," said Flint, joining the captain in the laugh.

"Now you know what my instructions are, gentlemen," continued the commander, "and I hope and believe that Mr. Lillyworth and his right hand man do not know them. I think you have been already posted, Mr. Baskirk, in regard to the anomalous state of affairs on board of the *Bronx*," added the captain.

"Not fully, Captain Passford, but Mr. Flint has told me something about the situation," replied the third lieutenant.

"It may not be necessary, gentlemen, that I should say it, but not a word of what passes in my cabin is to be repeated in any other part of the ship; not even in the wardroom when you believe you are entirely alone," said the captain very earnestly and impressively. "If the doors and keyholes do not have ears, there may be ears behind them, as some of us have learned to our entire satisfaction."

"Not a word from me, Captain Passford," added Baskirk.

"And not one from me," repeated Flint.

"Unquestionably the curiosity of Mr. Lillyworth and his confederate are and will continue to be excited to the highest pitch," continued Christy. "I shall have occasion to change the course of the ship and head her more to the eastward. Of course the second lieutenant will observe this, and will understand that I am not following the orders reported to him by Mulgrum. You are my only confidants on board, and it will be necessary for you to refer Mr. Lillyworth to me when he asks for further information."

"Perfectly understood," replied Flint, who was

now in most excellent humor.

"Now, gentlemen, I will leave you in my cabin that Mr. Baskirk may be more fully instructed in regard to the matters which have passed between Mr. Flint and myself. I have great expectations in regard to you, Mr. Baskirk, and I am confident that you will realize them."

Saying this, Christy bowed to his companions and left the cabin, retiring to his stateroom and closing the door. He had on board a full supply of charts and nautical instruments of his own, in addition to those belonging to the ship. Spreading out the chart of the South Atlantic on the desk, he went to work with his dividers and parallel rule. He made his figures on a piece of paper, and then laid off a course on the chart with a pencil, to be deepened in red ink at another time.

Writing "southeast by east" on a slip of paper, he restored his charts and instruments to their places and left the stateroom. The two lieutenants were still in his cabin, but he did not disturb them and went on deck. Before he reached the bridge, six bells struck, or three o'clock in the afternoon. He then ascended the ladder to the bridge. The fog which the second lieutenant had predicted had not yet enveloped the ship; on the contrary, it looked more like clearing off, and some patches of blue sky could be seen.

"Mr. Lillyworth, you will make the course southeast by east," said Christy, looking at the officer of the deck.

"Southeast by east!" exclaimed the second lieutenant, and his remark needed an exclamation point after it, for though it was customary to repeat an order to make sure that it was understood, he did so in such a tone and in such a manner as to manifest very clearly his astonishment at the nature of the order. The former course had been south by west.

One thing was fully evident from this surprise— that the officer of the deck gave full faith to the bogus instructions which had been imparted to him by Mulgrum. He believed that the *Bronx* was to hasten to the Gulf, as the former course indicated. It was plain enough to Lillyworth that the captain was disregarding his instructions, but his lips were sealed in regard to this disobedience, for he could not indicate in any manner that he knew the purport of the sealed orders, and doubtless it did not occur to him that the deaf mute had been blinded, in addition to his other infirmities. The course was given out to the quartermaster at the wheel. The steamer promptly fell off and began to ride quartering over the smart billows, brought out by the wind from the south-southwest, as it had blown for the last hour or more.

Christy believed that he had put everything in train for accomplishing the mission of the *Bronx* on the new course he had just ordered. There were no more orders to be read, and he did not see that the conspirators could do anything more to derange the plans of the loyal officers and seamen on board. All they had attempted so far was to obtain information in regard to the movements of the vessel, and Christy had taken care that they should receive all the information they wanted, though not as reliable as it might have been. He was satisfied with the situation as it must remain till some decided event should call for energetic action.

The captain and the two wardroom officers in his confidence were obliged to conduct themselves with the utmost caution and discretion in order not to undo anything which had been done in blinding the eyes of the conspirators. Christy had an abundance of writing to do, and it was of a kind that would not betray any of his secrets; he called upon Mulgrum to do this work, in order to keep up appearances. He did not call any more conferences with his friends in the cabin, for there was no need of any, and entire silence was the more prudent.

The *Bronx* proceeded on the course the captain had given out until the twentieth of the month, when the steamer was a little to the southward of the Bermudas. She had not been near enough to the islands to be made out from the shore. On this day, when the *Bronx* was three days from Sandy Hook, the fog which Mr. Lillyworth had been predicting settled down on the steamer, not as dense as it might be, but thick enough to prevent those on board of her from seeing anything at any great distance from her. The second lieutenant, in charge of the deck, suggested to the captain that the whistle should be blown, but Christy answered very emphatically that no whistles were to be blown; though he ordered the lookouts to be doubled, and the steamer to proceed at half speed.

In the middle of the second dog watch, in charge of Mr. Baskirk, the lookout on the topsail yard made himself heard, and the others aloft repeated the call.

"Sail on the starboard bow, sir!" said the first lookout from the yard, hailing the bridge.

Captain Passford heard the hail from aloft, for he was planking the deck with the first lieutenant.

Both of them rushed forward at a pace rather undignified for a commander.

"Silence, aloft!" shouted the captain. "We have made her out. Mr. Flint, you will take the deck, and call all hands without any unnecessary noise."

This order was given to Giblock, the boatswain, and in a minute or two every man on board was in his station. The first lieutenant remained on the bridge, but the second took his place in the waist, and the third forward, though this arrangement of the officers was not sanctioned by ancient usage. Silence was commanded, and the engine, working at half speed, made hardly any noise. The captain had spoken to Sampson, the chief engineer, and he had done his best to avoid all noise in his department.

The captain and the first lieutenant remained on the bridge, anxiously sighting in the direction in which the sail had been reported to be. As the captain had instructed the engineer to do, he had caused the fires to be reduced and a change of fuel used so that the smokestack of the *Bronx* was just beginning to send up volumes of black smoke. The bunkers contained a small portion of soft coal for this purpose.

CHAPTER XIII

THE STEAMER IN THE FOG

The *Bronx* was slowly approaching the steamer in the fog, which appeared to have stopped her propeller, and to be resting motionless on the long swells, hardly disturbed by a breath of air. By this time the smokestack of the *Bronx* was vomiting forth dense clouds of black smoke. The steamers of the navy used anthracite coal, which burns without any great volume of smoke, and blockade runners had already begun to lay in whatever stock of it they were able to procure to be used as they approached the coast where they were to steal through the national fleet. The attention of the naval department of the United States had already been given to this subject, and the first steps had been taken to prevent the sale of this comparatively smokeless coal where it could be obtained by the blockade runners.

Christy had been on the blockade, and he had been in action with a steamer from the other side of the ocean, and he knew that this black smoke of the soft coal, exclusively used by English steamers, was a telltale in regard to such vessels. It had been an idea of his own to take in a supply of this kind of fuel, for while its smoke betrayed the character of vessels intending to run the blockade, the absence of it betrayed the loyalty of the national steamers to the blockade runners. It was a poor rule that would not work both ways, and the commander of the *Bronx* had determined to adopt the scheme he had now put in force on board of his vessel. Although the craft on the starboard bow could hardly be distinguished in the fog, Christy had sent a trusty seaman aloft to report on the color of the smoke that issued from her funnel.

This man had reported by swinging his cap in the air, as the captain had instructed him to do if he found that the smoke was that of soft coal. If there was no black smoke, he was to return to the deck without making any sign. The moment, therefore, that the man had been able to see the quality of the smoke, the commander was made as wise as though he had seen it himself. The information left him no doubt that the steamer was intended to run the blockade, but whether or not she was one of the expected pair, of course he could form no opinion, for already this part of the ocean had begun to swarm with vessels in this service.

"I am beginning to make her out a little better," said Flint, who had been straining his eyes to the utmost capacity, as everybody else on board was doing, to obtain the best and earliest information in regard to the stranger on the starboard bow.

"What do you make out, Mr. Flint?" asked Christy, who was too busily employed in watching the movements of the officers and seamen on his own deck to give especial attention to the character of the other steamer.

"I can't see well enough yet to say anything in regard to details," replied the first lieutenant. "I can only make out her form and size, and she seems to be as nearly like the *Bronx* as one pea is like another, though I should say that she was longer."

"Is she in motion?" asked the captain with interest.

"She appears to be at rest, though it is possible that she is moving very slowly, but if she has not stopped her screw, she is not going more than four knots."

"You say that she is built like the *Bronx*, Mr. Flint?" asked Christy anxiously.

"Just like her; I should say that both hulls came out of the same mould."

"That very nearly settles the question in my mind. Probably she was designed by the same naval architect, and constructed by the same builders, as the *Bronx*," replied Christy, gazing intently at the dim outlines of the steamer in the fog. "When a designer has made a great reputation for fast ships, men with piles of money, like the former owners of the *Bronx*, the *Scotian*, and the *Arran*, employ him to furnish the plans for their steam yachts. From what we have learned so far, though it is very little indeed, I feel reasonably sure that this steamer ahead of us is the *Scotian* or the *Arran*, and I don't care much which it is. But why has she stopped her screw, or reduced her speed to four knots?"

"That is a question that can only be answered an hour or two hence, if ever," replied the first lieutenant.

"But it is a very important question all the same," added Christy.

"I doubt if the *Bronx* is making four knots at the present moment," said Flint, as he went to the end of the bridge and looked down into the water.

"In changing the fires in the furnaces, Mr. Sampson had been obliged to clear them out in part, and that has reduced the pressure of steam, but we shall soon have the usual head," said Christy, as he went to the speaking tube and communicated with the chief engineer.

He was informed that his explanation was correct in regard to the coal, and that in a very short time the boilers would have a full head of steam. Christy spent the next few minutes in an earnest study of the scarcely perceptible outline of the steamer in the fog. He was hardly wiser when he had finished his examination than before. The hull and lower masts of the vessel could be indistinctly made out, and that was all. Sampson informed him that he had not been using all the steam he had, and that the screw was hardly turning at all. He ordered him to stop it entirely.

Impatient as he was to follow up the discovery that had been made, he realized that it would be very imprudent to expose his ship to possible danger when he had not steam enough to work her to the best advantage. He could only wait, but he was satisfied that he had done the best possible thing in changing the coal, for the black smoke would effectually blind the officers of the other vessel. They were not engaged in a chase, and the exciting question could be settled a few hours hence as well as at the present time.

"If the steamer ahead is the *Scotian* or the *Arran*, as I fully believe she is, probably her consort is somewhere in these waters," said the commander.

"Probably she lost sight of her in this fog," added Flint. "But, Captain Passford, we are in the face of something, though we do not yet know precisely what. I suppose you have your eye on Mr. Lillyworth?"

"I have kept him in sight all the time. He is on the quarterdeck now, as he has been since all hands were called," replied Christy, who had not failed to look at him for a full minute since the discovery of the sail on the starboard. "He seems to be perplexed by the situation, and his time for action, if he intends to act, has not yet come."

"I don't see Pink Mulgrum anywhere about the deck."

"I saw him a few minutes since," added Christy. "He passed several times quite near Mr. Lillyworth, and very likely something was said between them, but they had no long talk."

Christy had charged Dave to watch Mulgrum if he went below, and to follow him up closely, but the deaf mute had been on deck most of the time. There was nothing that he could do, and nothing that the second lieutenant could do, to embarrass the operations of the ship while she remained at rest. The captain then descended to the deck and personally looked into the condition of everything. In the course of his round he came to the quarterdeck where the second lieutenant was stationed. He could see that he was nervous and uneasy about something, and it was not difficult to divine what perplexed him. He could hardly see the black smoke from the funnel of the steamer in the fog, for his place on the deck did not permit him to obtain as good a view of her as could be had from the bridge, and especially from aloft.

"Do you make out what that vessel is, Captain Passford?" asked Lillyworth, as Christy passed near him.

"Not yet, Mr. Lillyworth," replied the captain, not caring to converse with the conspirator.

"The fog does not seem to be very dense, and I should think the vessel might be made out from aloft," added the second lieutenant, evidently very anxious to know more about the sail ahead.

"Not very clearly," replied Christy, as he went forward to the engine hatch.

He descended to the engine room, and while he was listening to the roar of the flames in the furnaces, so different from the action of anthracite coal, Sampson came up from the fire room.

"We shall have a sufficient head of steam in a few minutes to justify you in going ahead, Captain Passford," said the engineer without waiting to be questioned.

"I am glad to hear it, though we are in no special hurry at present, in spite of our impatience to know what is before us," replied the captain. "Do you know the man who passes under the name of Mulgrum, Mr. Sampson?"

"You mean Pink, the deaf mute? Mr. Nawood pointed him out to me, and I have seen him about the deck or in the steerage several times."

"Has he been in the engine room at any time since we sailed?" asked Christy.

"He may have been, but I have not noticed him anywhere in my department," replied Sampson.

"You will not allow him in the engine or fire room," continued the captain. "Send him out, drive him out, if necessary, at once."

"Being deaf and dumb, I should suppose he were harmless wherever he happened to be. Is he—"

"Never mind what he is just now, Mr. Sampson," interposed Christy. "Be very particular to obey my order in regard to him to the letter; that's all now. Inform me at once when you are ready to go ahead, and I shall be on the bridge."

The order which Christy had just given to the engineer was the result of his reflection since he came down from the bridge. He had been cudgeling his brains to determine what the conspirators could possibly do when the decisive moment came, if it should happen to come as he neared the steamer in the fog, to derange the operations on board. It seemed to him before that all they could do was to leap on board of the enemy, if it came to boarding her, and reinforce her crew. He had talked over this matter with Flint and Baskirk, and there were three who would be ready to shoot either of them the instant their treachery should be apparent.

Before it would be possible to board, a man as intelligent as Mulgrum, who had served as executive officer, could easily disable the engine. This idea had but just come to the commander, who thought before that he had closed every opening against the conspirators. He went on deck as soon as he had settled this matter. The fog seemed to be rather more dense than before, and when he went on the bridge, it was reported that the stranger could no longer be made out.

"I have just received the roster of the '*Bronx* Association,' " said Flint, as the captain joined him. "It is signed by every man on board, including the supernumeraries forward, except Spoors, Blocker, Veering, Packer, Pickford, and Runyon. I inquired why these men would not join, but could not learn that they had any reason except that they did not wish to be members. I have seen Mr. Lillyworth talking to all of these men, and I think we can be certain now who is white and who is black."

"On the bridge!" came from the speaking tube at this moment, and the captain was near enough to hear it. Mr. Sampson reported that he had steam enough to make at least ten knots an hour.

The commander then instructed the first lieutenant to see that both divisions of boarders were armed with cutlass and revolver, in readiness for action. The second lieutenant was to attend to the working of the broadside guns, Mr. Baskirk was to lead the first division of boarders, and Mr. Giblock, the boatswain, the second. Flint went below to the deck to execute his orders, and the captain ordered the quartermaster to ring one bell.

CHAPTER XIV

THE CONFEDERATE STEAMER *SCOTIAN*

One bell sounded on the gong in the engine room, and the *Bronx* began to go ahead. Christy felt that the most tremendous hour of his lifetime had come, and he struggled to keep down the excitement which agitated him, and he succeeded so far that he appeared to be the coolest man on board of the ship. When Flint came in the vicinity of the bridge, he called to him to join him. The men were procuring their revolvers and cutlasses, and he had a moment to spare. The captain instructed him to conceal the boarders so that they could not be seen on board the steamer in the fog when the *Bronx* came up with her. He added some other details to his orders.

"If possible, I wish you to keep as near Lillyworth as you can," continued Christy, "for I shall not have the opportunity to watch him. This war cannot be

153

conducted on peace principles, and if that man attempts to defeat my orders in any manner, don't hesitate to put a ball from your revolver through his heart. Use reasonable care, Mr. Flint, but bear in mind that I am not to be defeated in the capture of that steamer, if she proves to be what I suppose she is, by the treachery of one who accepted a position as an officer on board of the *Bronx*." The commander was firm and decided in his manner, and Flint had served with him enough to know that he meant what he said.

"I will obey your orders to the letter, Captain Passford, using all reasonable precautions in the discharge of my duty," replied Flint. "Mr. Lillyworth was in a state of mutiny just now, and spoke to me."

"What did he say?"

"He declared that he was second lieutenant of the ship, and it was his right to command the first division of boarders. He wouldn't stand it. I told him he was to be in command of the guns. He insisted that you did not intend to fire a gun if you could help it. I replied that we should not board the vessel either if we could help it. But I had no time to argue with him, and referred him to the captain. Then he moved towards the ladder of the bridge, and I forbade him to leave his station. That is the whole of it. I have seen him speak to each of the six men we now know to be his friends, to say nothing of Mulgrum. I left him then."

"All right so far, Mr. Flint. Return to the deck, if you please, and be sure that the boarders are kept out of sight from this moment," added Christy. "Quartermaster, ring four bells," he added, turning to the pilothouse.

"Four bells, sir," repeated McSpindle, who was at the wheel.

The *Bronx* soon began to feel the effect of this order, and the smoke poured out in increased volume from the smokestack, affected by the stronger draught produced by the additional speed.

"On the topsail yard!" called the captain, directing his speaking trumpet aloft.

"On the bridge, sir!" replied the man.

"Can you make out the steamer?"

"No, sir; only her topmasts and fore rigging."

"How does she lie from the *Bronx*?"

"Still on the starboard bow, sir."

"Port the helm, quartermaster," added the captain.

"Port, sir," replied McSpindle.

For about five minutes more the *Bronx* went ahead at full speed, and Christy was confident that she was again making fifteen knots.

"On the bridge, sir!" called the man on the foreyard.

"Aloft!"

"I make her out now; she has the Confederate flag at the peak."

"All right!" exclaimed Christy to himself, though he spoke out loud.

The steamer had set her colors, and there was no longer any doubt in regard to her character. The flag also indicated that she was not a blockade runner in the ordinary sense of the word, but a Confederate man-of-war. Warnock reported that she had taken her armament on board from another vessel at some point south of England, and the colors also assured Christy that the steamer was one of the pair expected.

Still the *Bronx* went ahead at full speed, and presently a gun was heard from the direction in which she lay, though the captain was unable to decide what it meant. It might be a signal of distress, but the man on the yard had not reported the colors as union down, and it might be simply a defiance. It was probable that the *Scotian* and *Arran* had put in at St. George, and it was more than possible that they had shipped a reinforcement to her reported small crew.

"Aloft!" called the captain again.

"On the bridge, sir!" replied the lookout,

"Is the steamer under way?"

"I think not, sir, but I can't make out her wake, it is so low."

"Starboard a little, quartermaster."

"Starboard, sir."

Christy heard, or thought he heard, for he was not sure about it, the sound of a bell. A minute later the quartermaster in the pilothouse struck seven bells, which was repeated on the topgallant forecastle of the *Bronx*, and he was confident this was what he had heard on board of the stranger.

"Quartermaster, strike one bell," he added.

"One bell, sir," and the gong resounded from the engine room, and the speed of the *Bronx* was immediately reduced.

A minute later Christy obtained a full view of the steamer. She was headed to the southwest, and her propeller was not in motion. As the lookout had reported, she was the counterpart of the *Bronx*, though she was a larger vessel. He gave some further orders to the quartermaster at the wheel, for he had decided to board the steamer on her port side. The boarders had been concealed in proper places under this arrangement, and the captain had directed the course of the *Bronx* so that a shot from her could hardly do any harm, if she took it into her head to fire one.

"*Arran*, ahoy!" shouted a hoarse voice through a speaking trumpet from the steamer.

"On board the *Scotian!*" replied Christy through his trumpet.

After the vessel had hailed the *Arran*, the captain had no difficulty in deciding that the other craft was the *Scotian*, and he was especially glad that the officer of that vessel had hailed him in this particular form. The single word spoken through that trumpet was the key to the entire enigma. Every possible doubt was removed by it. He was now assured, as he had not been before, that he had fallen in with one of the two vessels of which his father had given him information, and which his sealed orders required him to seek, even if he was detained a week or more. Christy spent no time in congratulating himself on the situation, but the tremendous idea passed through his whole being in an instant.

"We are disabled!" shouted the officer on board of the *Scotian* through his trumpet. "Please send your engineer on board."

"All right!" replied Christy. "Go ahead a little

faster, Mr. Sampson. We are very near the steamer."

The young commander cast his eyes over the deck of his vessel to assure himself that everything was ready for the important moment, though the situation did not indicate that a very sharp battle was to be fought. Everything was in order, and the first lieutenant was planking the deck, looking as though he felt quite at home, for he was as cool as a Jersey cucumber. Farther aft was Lillyworth, as uneasy as a caged tiger, for no doubt he realized that the *Scotian* was to fall a victim to the circumstances that beset her, rather than as the result of a spirited chase or a sharply fought battle. He looked about him for a moment, and the instant he turned his head, Mulgrum came out from behind the mast and passed quite near him.

The captain could not tell whether the second lieutenant had spoken to the deaf mute or not, but the latter hastened to the engine hatch and descended to the engine room. The *Bronx* was within less than a cable's length of the *Scotian*, whose name could now be read on her stern, when Mulgrum, apparently ordered by Lillyworth to do so, had hastened to the engine hatch. Even on the bridge the noise of a scuffle could be heard in the engine room, and the captain was sure that Sampson

had been obedient to his orders. Another minute
or two would determine in what manner the *Scotian*
was to be captured, and Christy hastened down the
ladder to the deck.

As soon as his foot pressed the planks, he
hastened to the engine hatch. Calling to the
engineer, he learned that the deaf mute had been
knocked senseless by Sampson, and lay on the sofa.
He waited to hear no more, but went forward where
there were bell pulls on the deck and rang two bells
to stop her. Then he gave some orders to the
quartermaster and rang three bells to back her. The
Bronx came alongside of the *Scotian* as handsomely
as though she had been a river steamer making one
of her usual landings. The hands who had been
stationed for the purpose immediately used their
grappling irons, and the two vessels were fast to
each other.

"Boarders!—" the first lieutenant shouted at a
sign from the captain, but before he could complete
the order, Pawcett, for we may now call him by his
right name, leaped on the bulwarks of the *Bronx*.

"This is a United States—" he began to say, but
he was allowed to proceed no farther, for the first
lieutenant raised the revolver he carried in his left
hand, doubtless for this very purpose, and fired.

Pawcett did not utter another word, but fell back upon the deck of the *Bronx*, where no one took any further notice of him.

"Boarders, away!" shouted the first lieutenant.

This time the sentence was finished, and the order was promptly executed. Hardly a half minute had been lost by the attempt of Pawcett to prepare the officers of the *Scotian* to do their duty, but he had said enough to enable the ship's company to understand what he would have said if he had finished his announcement. The officers and seamen were both surprised, and there was a panic among the latter, though the former rallied them in a moment. But they had lost all their chances, and after an insignificant struggle, the deck of the steamer was in possession of the boarders. The crew were driven forward by the victorious *"Bronxies,"* as Giblock called them. "Do you surrender?" said Mr. Baskirk to the officer he took for the captain.

"I do not see that I have any other alternative," replied the commander of the *Scotian*, politely enough, but it was evident that he was sorely afflicted, and even ashamed of himself. "I understand now that I am the victim of a Yankee trick."

"Allow me to introduce you to Captain Passford, commander of the United States steamer *Bronx*," continued Mr. Baskirk, as Christy came on board of the prize.

The captain of the *Scotian* retreated a pace as Christy stepped up in front of him and gracefully lifted his cap to the unfortunate commander.

"I beg your pardon, sir, but did I understand you to say that this young gentleman is the commander of the steamer alongside?" demanded the captain, looking at Christy from head to foot.

"He is the commander, sir; Captain Passford," added Baskirk.

"May I be allowed to ask whom I have the honor to address?" Christy began, lifting his cap again, as did the other also.

"Captain Dinsmore, at your service."

"I sincerely regret your personal misfortune while I rejoice at the result of this action, as a loyal citizen of the United States," replied Christy.

Then he invited the captain to his cabin.

Chapter XV

The *Scotian* Becomes the *Ocklockonee*

As he went to the deck of the *Bronx*, the young commander sent the first lieutenant on board of the prize to superintend the arrangements for disposing of the ship's company. Captain Dinsmore was requested to produce his papers, and Christy conducted him to his cabin. As his father had advised him always to be on such occasions, he was studiously polite, as in fact he was at all times. Whether the other captain was usually so or not, he was certainly courteous in every respect, though, with the heavy misfortune which had befallen him, it was vastly more difficult for him to control his feelings and conduct himself in a gentlemanly manner. Captain Passford desired to understand in what capacity the *Scotian* was approaching the American coast before he made his final arrangements. After giving his guest, as he regarded him, or rather treated him, a chair in his cabin, Christy called Dave, who had followed him below.

"Will you excuse me a moment or two while I attend to a necessary duty?" said he, turning to Captain Dinsmore, as he seated himself at the table.

"Certainly, Captain; I am not so much in a hurry as I have been at other times," replied the other with a rather sickly smile.

"Keep a sharp lookout for the *Arran*," Christy wrote on a piece of paper, and handed it to the steward. "Give that to Mr. Flint."

Captain Passford had observed when he visited the deck of the *Scotian* that she was well armed, and he had no doubt that her consort was similarly provided for the business of war. It was therefore of the highest importance that the *Arran* should not come unexpectedly upon the *Bronx* at a time when she was hardly in condition to meet an enemy.

"Now, Captain Dinsmore, may I trouble you for your papers?" he continued, turning to his guest, as he preferred to regard him.

"I admit your right to examine them under present circumstances," replied Captain Dinsmore, as he delivered the package to him.

"Perhaps we may simplify and abbreviate this

examination to some extent, sir, if you are so disposed," added Christy, as he looked the other full in the face.

"I shall be happy to have you do so, Captain Passford," replied the visitor in the cabin with something like eagerness in his manner. "You conduct yourself like a gentleman, sir, and I am not at all disposed to embarrass you unnecessarily."

"Thank you, sir; I appreciate your courtesy."

"I am afraid it is not so much courtesy as it is desperation, for if I should act in accordance with my feelings, I should blow my brains out without any delay," said Captain Dinsmore. "I should not say as much as this to any but a generous enemy, but I feel that I am ruined, and that there is nothing more in the future for me."

Christy really sympathized with him, and could not help thinking how he should feel if the situations were reversed. He realized that the commander of the *Scotian* had been very careless in the discharge of his duty in permitting any vessel to come alongside of her without considering that she might be an enemy. This inefficiency was doubtless the cause of his distress. Christy had kept uppermost in his mind the advice of his father at the last moment before he sailed, and he asked himself if, while the prisoner was thus exciting his sympathy and compassion, the latter was not expecting the *Arran* would appear and reverse the fortunes of war.

"I am sorry you take such a severe view of your situation," added the captain of the *Bronx*. "But my first duty is to ascertain the character of the vessel which you surrender."

"You shall have no doubt in regard to that, Captain Passford," answered the commander of the *Scotian* proudly. "I am not a dickering merchant trying to make money out of the situation of my country. The *Scotian*, as you call her, is the Confederate steamer *Ocklockonee*, and here is my commission as a lieutenant in the Confederate Navy," he added as he took the document from his pocket and tendered it to his captor.

Christy looked at the paper, and then examined the other papers in the packet. They left no doubt in his mind as to the character of the *Ocklockonee*, if he had had any before. He folded up the commission and politely returned it to the owner. The examination was completed so far as he was concerned, but Captain Dinsmore did not seem to be satisfied, though he made no complaint that anything was wrong in the proceedings. He was evidently a very proud and high-strung man, and appeared to be unable to reconcile himself to the situation.

"I am a ruined man!" he exclaimed several times, and when he looked at the commander of the *Bronx*, measuring him from head to foot, as he had already done several times, it seemed to increase his distress of mind and make him more nervous than before.

"While I regret that a brave man like yourself, Captain, should be at war with the government which I honor and love, I hope that personally your future will be as bright as I am sure your merit deserves," said Christy.

"If it had been a square and well-fought action, I should not feel as I do about it. You will pardon me, and understand that I mean no disrespect to you, Captain, but I look upon myself as the victim of a Yankee trick," said Captain Dinsmore bitterly. "But please to consider that I do not charge any blame or treachery upon you, sir."

"I think I can understand your feelings, sir, but I cannot see that in resorting to strategy to save my men, my conduct has been in any manner dishonorable," replied Christy, holding his head a little higher than usual. "I should hold that I had been guilty of misconduct if I had failed to take advantage of the circumstances under which I have captured the *Ocklockonee*."

"I quite agree with you, Captain Passford. I should have done the same thing myself if the opportunity had been presented to me," the guest hastened to say. "But that does not in the least degree relieve me from the consequences of my own negligence. When you are more at leisure, I hope you will permit me to make an explanation of the situation in which I was placed."

"I shall be happy to listen to anything you may desire to say to me when I have the leisure to hear you."

"Thank you, sir."

Christy hastened on deck to attend to the many duties required of him. The first sight that presented itself when he reached the head of the companionway was the form of the second lieutenant, which remained as it had fallen from the rail. He sent for Dr. Spokely and directed him to ascertain whether or not Pawcett was dead. While the surgeon was examining him, Mr. Sampson came up from below with a bolt in his hand and touched his cap to the commander.

"You are at work on the engine of the *Ocklockonee*, are you?" asked Christy, and this inquiry was one of the duties which had been on his mind before he left the cabin.

"Yes, sir, and I have already examined her engine; I suppose you mean the *Scotian*, for that is the name on her stern, they tell me," replied the chief engineer.

"Her new name is the *Ocklockonee*."

"I have examined the engine," replied Sampson.

"Is the damage very serious?" asked the captain anxiously.

"Far from it; she has broken a bolt which disables her, and she ought to have had one to replace it without more than five minutes' delay, but it appears that they have not one on board; at least none could be found when it was wanted, and they were at work forging one when the *Bronx* came alongside."

"All right; repair the damage as soon as possible. I heard a scuffle in the engine room just as we were running alongside the *Ocklockonee*," said the captain, looking inquiringly at the engineer.

"Yes, sir; there was a scuffle there. Pink Mulgrum was rushing down the ladder when I stopped him. He tried to push by me when I made signs to him to return to the deck. Then he gave a spring at my throat, and as I saw that he had a revolver in his hand, I did not hesitate to hit him on the head with a bar of iron I had in my hand. He dropped on the deck. I put his revolver in my pocket and stretched him out on the sofa. He did not move, and I left him there."

"I will send the surgeon to him," added the captain, as he went on board of the prize, followed by Sampson.

The first lieutenant had been busy on the deck of the vessel, but he had been able to accomplish but little in the absence of definite instructions from the captain. All the seamen were held in the forward part of the deck, and there were twenty-four of them, including the petty officers, but not the stokers, as the firemen were called. The engineers and all connected with their department remained below so far as could be learned. Two officers remained seated on the quarterdeck, but they did not appear to be so thoroughly cast down as the captain, doubtless because they were not called upon to bear the responsibility of the capture.

"Have you set a sharp lookout, Mr. Flint?" asked the captain.

"The lookout remains the same on board of the *Bronx*, though I have cautioned the quartermaster on the foreyard to keep his eyes wide open, and I have stationed four men on board of the *Scotian*."

"Very well; we are all right so far, but if the other vessel is as well armed as this one, she is capable of giving us a great deal of trouble," replied the captain.

"I only hope we may find her," added Flint heartily.

"We shall look for her at any rate. But we must get things regulated on board of both vessels at once, for I judge that the *Arran* cannot be far off, for the officers hailed us as the *Arran* when we were approaching, which shows that they were confident in regard to her identity, or they would not have given themselves away so readily."

"We have made a lucky hit, and I hope we shall be able to reap the full benefit of it," added Flint.

"We must provide for the immediate future without any delay," continued Christy. "Our first duty will be to search for the *Arran*, and we can use the *Ocklockonee*, which the captain says is her present name, to assist in the chase, for we have force enough to man both vessels, though we are not oversupplied with officers."

"There are two more quartermasters who are nearly as good men as Baskirk," replied the first lieutenant.

"I ask no better officer than Baskirk has proved himself to be. I shall retain him on board of the *Bronx*, and for the present I shall ask you to take command of the *Ocklockonee*, and you may select your own officers. The probability is that, if we find the *Arran*, we shall have a fight with her."

"Then I shall make McSpindle my first lieutenant, and Luffard my second," added Flint, evidently pleased with the idea of having even a temporary command.

"I shall appoint Baskirk in your place on board of the *Bronx*, but I need one more."

"I recommend Amblen, though he is not as well qualified as the others I have named."

"Send for these men at once," added the captain.

One of them was on the topsail yard of the *Bronx*, but all of them soon appeared in the waist of the prize. They were informed of the honor which had been conferred upon them, and were immediately assigned to duty. The crew of the *Ocklockonee* were divided between the two steamers and were put under guard below.

Chapter XVI

Captain Passford's Final Orders

A tolerable state of order and regularity had been brought out of the confusion that prevailed on board of the *Ocklockonee*, and the newly appointed officers went to the stations where they belonged. Sampson reported the engine of the steamer as in good order and ready for service.

"Who is the chief engineer of the *Ocklockonee*, Mr. Sampson?" asked Captain Passford after he had listened to the report.

"His name is Bockburn; he is a Scotchman and appears to be a very good fellow," replied the engineer of the *Bronx*.

"Does he talk at all about what has just happened on board of his steamer?" asked the captain, deeply interested, for he had some difficulty in arranging the engineer's department on board of the prize, as he considered the new order of things.

"Yes sir; he talks at the rate of twenty knots an hour, and if his steamer can get ahead as well as his tongue, she is a fast one," replied Sampson, laughing.

"Well, what does he say? I want to know how he stands affected by the present condition of affairs," continued the captain rather impatiently, for he was too busy to enjoy the humor of the engineer.

"He is a thrifty Scotchman, and I don't believe he has any interest in anything under the sun except his wages, and he is a little sour on that account to find that his cruise is finished, as he puts it."

"Send for him and his assistants, Mr. Sampson."

The engineer went to the engine hatch and called the men below.

"Now send for Mr. Gawl," added the captain. "He is your first assistant; is he a competent man to run an engine?"

"As competent as I am myself, and the engine of this steamer is exactly like that of the *Bronx*, so that he can have no trouble with it, if you think of retaining him on board of the *Ocklockonee*," replied Sampson.

"I propose to make him chief engineer of her."

"You could not find a better man," said Sampson, as he went to summon Gawl.

The three engineers of the prize came on deck, and the captain took the chief aside.

"Mr. Bockburn, I believe, the chief engineer of the *Ocklockonee*?" said Christy.

"Of the *Scotian*, sir, for I know nothing of the jaw-cracking names that the officers in the cabin have given her," replied the engineer, shrugging his shoulders and presenting a dissatisfied air.

"Are you an engineer in the Confederate navy, sir?" asked Christy, bringing the business to a head at once.

"No, sir, I am not," answered the engineer very decidedly. "You see, Captain, that the *Scotian* was sold to come across the water, and I was out of a job, with a family to support. They did not say anything about the service in which the *Scotian* was to be engaged, but I understood it. When they spoke to me about it, I was glad to keep my place as long as she did not make war on the United Kingdom. In truth, I may say that I did not care a fig about the quarrel in the States, and was as ready to run an engine on one side as the other as long as I got my wages and was able to support my family handsomely, as, thank God, I have always done. I am not a student of politics, and I only read enough in the newspapers to know what is going on in the world. I always find that I get ahead better when I mind my own business, and it can't be said that Andy Bockburn ever—"

"Precisely so, Mr. Bockburn, but I will hear the rest of your story at another time," interposed the captain when he found that the man was faithful to the description Sampson had given of his talking powers.

"You understand perfectly what has transpired on board of the *Scotian* as you choose still to call her; in a word, that she is a prize to the United States steamer *Bronx*?"

"I understand it all as clearly as though I read it in a book, and it was all on account of the want of a bolt that I was sure I put on board of the vessel before she sailed, and I am just as sure of it now as I ever was. But then, you see, Captain, a man can't always be sure of the men under him, though he may be sure of himself. I have no doubt—"

"Short yarns, if you please, Mr. Bockburn. You understand the situation, and I will add that I intend to use this vessel as well as the *Bronx* in the service of my government. Are you willing to do duty on board of her in any capacity in which I may place you in the engineer department, provided you receive the same wages as before?"

"I am, sir, and I was paid a month in advance, so that I shall not lose anything," chuckled the careful Scotchman.

"If you are regularly appointed, though I can only give you a temporary position, in addition to your wages, you will be entitled to your share in any prize we may hereafter capture."

"Then I will take any position you will please to give me," answered the engineer, apparently delighted with the prospect thus held out to him.

"I shall appoint you first assistant engineer of the *Bronx*," continued the captain, not a little to the astonishment of Flint, who wondered that he was not assigned to the *Ocklockonee*.

"I am quite satisfied, Captain," replied Bockburn, bowing and smiling, for wages were more than rank to him. "I will bring up my kit at once, sir. You see, Captain, when a man has a family he—"

"Precisely as you say, Mr. Bockburn," interrupted the captain. "You will report to Mr. Sampson in the engine room of the *Bronx* for further orders."

"Thank you, sir; I supposed I was out of a job from this out, and I was feeling—"

"Feel your way to the engine room of the *Bronx*. Mr. Gawl," the captain proceeded.

"On duty, sir," replied the first assistant engineer of the *Bronx*, touching his cap as respectfully as though the commander had been forty years old.

"You are appointed temporarily as chief engineer of the *Ocklockonee*, and you will take your place in the engine room as soon as possible," said the captain, as brusquely as though favors cost nothing.

Mr. Gawl was taken to the engine room and introduced to the first and second assistants, Rowe and Leeds, and was kindly received by them, for, like their late chief, the question of wages was the only one that affected them. They promised to be faithful to the government they were to serve, and to discharge their duties faithfully under the direction of the new chief. The two officers on the quarterdeck had watched all these proceedings with interest. They were the only persons remaining on board who had not been disposed of in some manner.

Christy approached them while Captain Flint, as he was now to be called by courtesy, was making his final arrangements with the crew that had been assigned to the prize. Both of the officers bowed civilly to the commander as he presented himself on the quarterdeck. They were older men than Captain Dinsmore, though neither was over forty-five. Christy suspected that they were not

Confederate officers as soon as he had a chance to look them over.

"May I ask, gentlemen, if you are officers of the Confederate navy?" asked Christy, as he looked from one to the other of the men.

"We are not, sir," replied the senior of them.

"Of course, you are aware that you are serving in a Confederate man-of-war?" added Christy

"I should say that was hardly true up to date. The captain holds a commission in the Confederate navy, but the ship has never been into a Confederate port, Captain Passford," replied the senior, who had learned the commander's name.

"As you call me by name, perhaps you will enable me to do as much with you," added Christy.

"My name is Farley Lippard; I shipped as first officer of the *Scotian*," replied the senior.

"And mine is Edward Sangston, and I shipped as second officer of the steamer."

"We shipped only for the voyage, and were told that we could not retain our situations after the ship's company was fully organized," added Mr. Lippard.

"Then I hope you were paid in advance, as the engineers were," said Christy with a smile.

"We were, sir, thank you," added the first officer. "Though we were told that we could not obtain any rank in the navy because there were more officers than ships, the agent said we should find plenty of employment on board of blockade runners coming out with cotton."

"I suppose you are Englishmen?" said the captain.

"Scotchmen, sir, but British subjects."

"I cannot put you on shore, and I may not have an opportunity to ship you to your homes by another vessel. I shall leave you on board of the *Ocklockonee*, and the acting commander will assign to you such quarters in the cabin as may be at his command," continued Christy. "It is only necessary that I should say I expect you to remain neutral, whatever occurs on board of the steamer."

"That is understood," replied Mr. Lippard.

"You will be regarded as passengers, but, of course, if you commit any act hostile to the government of the United States, you will be considered as enemies and treated as prisoners of war," Christy proceeded. "I hope the situation is clearly understood."

"Certainly, sir; we have no interest in the quarrel in the States, and we are not in the pay of the Confederacy, as they call it," replied Mr. Lippard.

"Then there will be no trouble. Captain Flint," called the commander.

Flint, who had been very busy appointing petty officers and organizing the new crew, came at the call and was introduced to the late officers of the prize. The understanding which had just been reached in regard to them was repeated for the benefit of the new captain. He was quite as pliable as his superior had always been, and there was no indication that any friction would result from their presence on board of the prize, now temporarily put into the service of the navy.

"Have you made all your arrangements, Captain Flint?" asked Christy when he was all ready to return to the *Bronx*.

"I have very nearly completed them, Captain Passford, and I can easily finish them after we get under way," replied Flint. "All I need before we part is my orders."

"From all that I can learn, the *Arran* must be to the eastward of the *Ocklockonee*," said Christy, who had given this subject all the thought his time would permit. "The officers of the prize hailed the *Bronx* coming from that direction, and that indicates that she was expected from that quarter. Our coming from that way seems to have made Captain Dinsmore confident that the *Bronx* was the *Arran*. I shall lay the course of my ship to the northeast, while you will proceed to the southwest. After you have gone fifty miles in that direction, you will make a course due east, as I shall also after I have made the same distance. Having run due east twenty miles, you will run to the northeast, as I shall to the southwest. If you discover the *Arran,* fire your midship gun, and I will do the same."

Christy shook hands with Flint and went on board of the *Bronx.* The order was given on board of both vessels to cast off the grapnels; the gong bell sounded in each engine room, and both vessels went ahead, the *Bronx* coming about to her new course.

CHAPTER XVII

A COUPLE OF ASTONISHED CONSPIRATORS

The fog had been very variable in its density, and had been lifting and settling at times during the day of the capture. By the time the two vessels were ready to get under way, it had become more solid than before. The night had come, and the darkness with it, at about the same time. The lookouts were still in their places, but so far as seeing anything was concerned they might as well have been in the hold. If the *Arran* was still in the vicinity, as no doubt she was, the *Bronx* might run into her. Wherever she was, it was well assured that her officers knew nothing of the capture of the *Ocklockonee*, for not a great gun had been discharged, and the combat had been so quickly decided that there had been very little noise of any kind.

Everything worked without friction on board of the *Bronx*, and Captain Passford felt even more elastic than usual. Doubtless the capture he had just made afforded him a good deal of inspiration, but the fact that the mystery of the deaf mute and the second lieutenant had been solved, and the unfathomable catastrophe which their presence on board threatened had been escaped was a great source of relief.

The two conspirators were disabled and confined to the sick bay, and they were not likely to make any trouble at present. If they had had any definite plan on which they intended to act, they had certainly lost their opportunities, for the visit of Hungerford to the engine room of the *Bronx*, no doubt for the purpose of disabling the machinery, and the effort of Pawcett to warn the officers of the prize, had been simply acts of desperation, adopted after they had evidently failed in every other direction.

Pawcett was not really a loyal officer, and his expression and manners had attracted the attention of both the captain and the first lieutenant. The deaf mute had been brought on board in order to obtain information, and he had been very diligent in carrying out his part of the program. As Christy thought the matter over, seated at his supper in his cabin, he thought he owed more to the advice of his father at their parting than to anything else. He had kept his own counsel in spite of the difficulties, and had done more to blind the actors in the conspiracy than to enlighten them. He had hoped before he parted with the prize for the present to obtain some information in regard to the *Arran*, but he had too much self-respect to ask the officers of the *Ocklockonee* in regard to such matters.

The seamen who had been spotted as adherents of the late second lieutenant had done nothing, for there had been nothing that they could do under the circumstances. Spoors and two others of them had been drafted into the other vessel, while the other three remained on board of the *Bronx*. They were not regarded as very dangerous enemies, and they were not in condition to undertake anything in the absence of their leaders.

Christy had inquired in regard to the condition of Pawcett and Hungerford before he went to his cabin, and Dr. Spokeley informed him that neither of them would be in condition to do duty on either side for a considerable period. They were in no danger under careful treatment, but both of them were too seriously injured to trouble their heads with any exciting subjects.

"Good evening, Captain Dinsmore," Christy said, when he went into his cabin, after he had attended to all the duties that required present attention. "I hope you are feeling better this evening."

"Hardly better, Captain Passford, though I am trying to reconcile myself to my situation," replied the late captain of the *Ocklockonee*.

"Supper is all ready, sir," interposed Dave, as he passed by the captain, after he had brought in the dishes from the galley.

"Take a seat at the table, Captain Dinsmore," continued Christy, placing a chair for him and looking over the table to see what cheer he had to offer to his guest.

It looked as though the cook, aware that the commander had a guest, or thinking that he deserved a better supper than usual after the capture of a prize, had done his best in honor of the occasion. The broiled chickens looked especially inviting, and other dishes were quite tempting to a man who was two hours late at the meal.

"Thank you, Captain," replied the guest, as he took the seat assigned to him. "I can't say that I have a very fierce appetite after the misfortune that has befallen me, but I am none the less indebted to you for your courtesy and kindness."

"I acknowledge that I am in condition to be very happy this evening, Captain Dinsmore, and I can hardly expect to be an agreeable companion to one with a burden on his mind, but I can assure you of my personal sympathy."

"You are very kind, Captain. I should like to ask if many of the officers of the old navy are young gentlemen like yourself?" inquired the guest, looking at his host very curiously.

"There are a great many young officers in the navy at the present time, for the exigency has pushed forward the older ones, and there are not enough of them to take all the positions. But we shall all of us grow older," replied Christy good naturedly, as he helped the officer to a piece of the chicken, which had just come from the galley fire.

"Perhaps you are older than you appear to be," suggested the guest. "I should judge that you were not over twenty, or at least not much more."

"I am eighteen, sir, though, unlike a lady, I try to make myself as old as I can."

"Eighteen!" exclaimed Captain Dinsmore.

But Christy told something of his experience on board of the *Bellevite* which had prepared him for his duties, and his case was rather exceptional.

"You have physique enough for a man of

twenty-five," added the guest. "And you have been more fortunate than I have."

"And I have been as unfortunate as you are, for I have seen the inside of a Confederate prison, though I concluded not to remain there for any length of time," added Christy, laughing.

"You are a fortunate young man, and I do not belong to that class," said Captain Dinsmore, shaking his head. "I have lost my steamer, and I suppose that will finish my career."

"Perhaps not," but Christy was satisfied that he had lost his vessel by a want of care, and he could not waste any compliments upon him, though he had profited by the other's carelessness.

"I was confident when the *Bronx* approached the *Ocklockonee* that she was another vessel," continued the guest.

"What vessel did you take her to be?"

"You will excuse me if I decline to go into particulars. I can only say that I was sure your steamer was another, and I had no suspicion that I was wrong till that man mounted the rail of the *Bronx* and began to tell us to the contrary," replied Captain Dinsmore. "A bolt in the engine was broken, and the engineer could not find another on board. We expected to obtain one when the *Bronx* approached us. I was deceived, and that is the reason why I am here instead of in the cabin of my own ship."

The guest seemed to feel a little better after he had made this explanation, though it contained nothing new to the commander of the *Bronx*. Possibly the excellent supper, of which he had partaken heartily in spite of his want of appetite, had influenced his mind through the body. He had certainly become more cheerful, though his burden was no lighter than when he came on board of the *Bronx*. Christy was also lighthearted, not alone because he had been so successful, but because he felt that he was no longer compelled to watch the conspirators.

"I am sorry to be obliged to impose any restrictions upon you, Captain Dinsmore," said Christy, as he rose from the supper table. "The circumstances compel me to request you to remain in my cabin."

"Of course, I am subject to your will and pleasure, Captain Passford," replied the guest.

"You are a gentleman, sir, and if you will simply give me your word to remain here, there will be no occasion for any unpleasantness. It is possible that we may go into action at any time, and, in that case, you can remain where you please below."

"I give you my word that I will remain below until I notify you of my intention to do otherwise," replied the prisoner, though Christy preferred to regard him as his guest.

"I am entirely satisfied. I shall be obliged to berth you in the wardroom, and you are at liberty to pass your time as you please in these two apartments. I shall be happy to introduce you to the first lieutenant," added the captain, as he led the way to the wardroom.

Mr. Baskirk received the prisoner very politely, a berth was assigned to him, and Christy went on deck. It was as dark as Egypt there, but Mr. Amblen, the new acting second lieutenant on the bridge, said the wind was hauling to the westward, and he thought there would be a change of weather before morning. Mr. Baskirk had made all his appointments of petty officers rendered necessary by sending a portion of the seamen to the *Ocklockonee*. Everything was in good order on deck, and Christy next went down to the sick bay, where Hungerford and Pawcett were the only occupants. He found Dr. Spokeley there, and inquired in regard to the condition of the wounded men. The surgeon described the wounds of his patients and pointed them out to the captain.

"Does Mr. Hungerford talk any now?" asked Christy.

"Who is Mr. Hungerford?" asked the doctor.

"He is the deaf mute. He was the first officer of the Confederate steamer *Yazoo* when we captured her in the *Bellevite* last year," replied the captain, upon whom the eyes of the wounded man were fixed all the time.

"He has not spoken yet in my hearing, though I have thought that he could hear."

"His duty on board of the *Bronx* was to obtain information, and he procured a good deal of it, though not all of it was as reliable as it might have been."

"Indeed! Then he was a traitor," added the surgeon.

"He is a gentleman in spite of the role he has been playing, and I am sorry he has been injured, though Mr. Sampson obeyed my order when he struck him down in the engine room."

"Struck me from behind like an assassin," added Hungerford feebly.

"Did you expect to arrange a duel with him at such a time, Mr. Hungerford?" asked Christy. "You went into the engine room to disable the machine when you found you could do nothing else. If you had returned to the deck when the engineer told you to do so, he would not have disabled you. You crowded past him, and then he did his duty."

"I have been in the habit of serving with men who were square and above board," muttered Hungerford.

"Was that where you learned to listen at my cabin door, and to conceal yourself under the berth in my stateroom?" asked Christy, rather sharply for him. "Is that the reason why Mr. Pawcett wished to have you do the copying of my papers?"

"I can only say that I tried to do my duty to my country and I have failed," added Hungerford, as he turned over in his berth and showed his back to the captain.

"May I ask, Captain Passford, who told you my name?" asked the late second lieutenant, who seemed to be confounded by what he had heard.

"You called Mr. Hungerford by his real name, and he called you by yours, in the interview you had with him the first night out from New York. I have known you from the first," replied Christy.

Pawcett was as disgusted as the other had been, and he turned his face to the ceiling of his berth.

Christy was satisfied that these men would give him no more trouble at present.

Chapter XVIII

A Triangular Action With Great Guns

When Mr. Baskirk went on deck to take his watch at midnight, the fog had disappeared, and a fresh breeze was blowing from the westward. This change was reported to the captain, and he went on deck. No sail had been seen since the fog cleared off, and Christy returned to his stateroom, where he was soon asleep again. He was called, as he had directed, at four in the morning, but no change in the weather was reported, and no sail had been seen.

At four bells in the morning watch two sails were reported to him, one dead ahead, and the other on the port beam. He hastened to the deck, and found Mr. Amblen using his spyglass and trying to make out the distant sails. The one at the southeast of the *Bronx* was making a long streak of black smoke on the sky, and there was no such appearance over the other. Both were steamers.

"The one ahead of us is the *Ocklockonee*," said Captain Passford after he had used the spyglass. "I have no doubt the other is the *Arran*. Probably she has a new name by this time, but I have not heard it yet. Pass the word for Mr. Ambleton."

This was the gunner, and he was directed to fire a single shot, blank, from the midship gun. This was immediately done, and was the signal agreed upon with Flint if either discovered the *Arran*. It was promptly answered by a similar discharge on board of the *Ocklockonee*, indicating that she had seen the steamer in question.

"Now, make her course southeast, Mr. Amblen," said Christy after the two signals had been made.

"Southeast, sir," responded the second lieutenant, giving the course to the quartermaster at the wheel.

The commander of the *Ocklockonee* changed his course as soon as the *Bronx* had done so. Both steamers were headed directly towards the sail in the southeast, and both were running for the apex of the triangle where the third steamer was located.

The captain visited every part of the vessel and gave orders to have breakfast served at once, for he expected there would be lively times before many hours. Everything was overhauled and put in order. At eight bells, when Mr. Baskirk took the deck, the captain did not care how soon the battle began. Everything was ready and waiting, and he went below for his breakfast.

From delicacy or some other motive Captain Dinsmore spent most of his time in the wardroom, but he was called to breakfast with the commander. Both captains were as polite to each other as they had been the evening before, but it was evident to Christy that his guest was quite uneasy, as though he had discovered what had transpired on deck, and the movements there were quite enough to inform him without a word from anyone. He had not asked a question of any person on board, and it was impossible for him to know that a sail supposed to be the *Arran* was in sight.

"I have heard some firing this morning, Captain Passford," said he, as he seated himself at the table, and watched the expression of his host's countenance.

"Merely a couple of signals; the distant shot came from the *Ocklockonee*," replied Christy lightly.

"I thought it possible that you had fallen in with another steamer," added the guest.

"I have considered it more than possible, and within the limits of probability, that we should fall in with another steamer ever since we ran so opportunely upon the *Scotian*, as she was formerly called."

"Opportunely for you, but very inopportunely for me," added Captain Dinsmore with a faint smile.

"I am happy to inform you that we have passed beyond both possibility and probability, and come into the region of fact," continued Christy.

"Then you have made out a sail?" asked the guest anxiously.

"We have; a steamer on our port beam, and I am reasonably confident it is the vessel you supposed was coming alongside the *Ocklockonee* last evening."

"Indeed?" added the guest, as though he did not know just what to say and did not mean to commit himself.

"In other words, I am almost sure this steamer is the *Arran*, though doubtless you have changed her name," said Christy, as he helped the other from the choicest dish on the table.

"The *Arran*?" repeated Captain Dinsmore, manifesting, but not expressing, his surprise that his companion in a different service from his own knew this name.

"Perhaps you can give me her later name, as I have no doubt she is or will be called after some southern river, which is quite proper and entirely patriotic. Perhaps she is called the *Perdido*, which is not very far from perdition, where I shall do my best to send her unless she surrenders within a reasonable time, or runs away from me," said Captain Passford lightly. "Is your coffee quite right, Captain Dinsmore?"

"It is very good indeed, Captain, thank you."

"Perhaps it is too strong for you, like the United States Navy, and you would prefer it weaker," suggested Christy.

"It is quite right as it is, and, like the United States Navy of which you speak, it will be used up in a short time," replied the guest as pleasantly as the captain of the *Bronx*.

"That is yet to be settled," laughed Christy.

"Well, Captain, the coffee is settled, and that is more than can be said of our navy, which will be as clear as this in due time."

"I thought it best to inform you that we might be in action in the course of a couple of hours, and you were to notify me in case you wished to change your status on board," added Christy more seriously.

"I am much obliged to you, Captain Passford, for your courtesy and kindness, but I see no reason to change my position. I will still confine myself to the cabin and wardroom. I cannot wish you success in the action in which you are about to engage, for it would break my heart to have the *Arran*, as you call her, captured," added the guest.

"I think you may fairly count upon such a result," replied Christy confidently.

"You must excuse me, Captain Passford, but I think you are reckoning without your host, and therein your youth makes its only manifestation," said the guest, shaking his head. "I can only say that, when you are a prisoner on board of the *Escambia*, I shall do my best to have you as handsomely treated as I have been in your cabin."

"Thank you, Captain; I assure you I shall appreciate any courtesy and kindness extended to me. The *Escambia* is her name then. That is not so near perdition as the word I suggested, and I am glad it is not so long as the name you gave the *Scotian*. I shall expect to come across an *Apalachicola* in due time. They are all very good names, but we shall be compelled to change them when they fall into our hands," said Christy.

"I have plenty of spare time on my hands just now, and perhaps I had better think up a new name for the *Bronx*, and *Apalachicola* would be as good as any other. I wonder you did not call her the *Nutcracker*, for her present name rather suggests that idea."

"I have heard a similar remark before, but she is not big enough for such a long name as the one you suggest, and you would have to begin to pronounce it before breakfast in order to get it out before the dog watches," said Christy, as he rose from the table and went on deck.

The first thing he noticed when he came on the bridge was that the *Ocklockonee* was headed to intercept the *Bronx*. Captain Flint signaled that he wished to speak to him, and he changed his course to comply with the request. At the end of another hour they came together, the *Arran* being still at least four miles distant, going very slowly if she was moving at all.

Christy had written out his orders for Captain Flint in full. So far as he had been able to judge of the speed of the other steamer, it appeared to be about the same as that of the *Bronx*. He had directed the *Ocklockonee* to get to the southward of the *Arran*. A boat was sent to her with the orders, and Flint immediately proceeded to obey them. The *Bronx* slowed down her engines to enable the other to gain her position, but the *Arran* did not seem to be willing to permit her to do this and gave chase to her at once.

The commander of the *Bronx* met this change

by one on his own part, and went ahead with all
the speed he could get out of her. The Confederate
steamer was farther to the eastward than either of
the other two, and after the changes of position
which Christy had brought about in speaking the
Ocklockonee, the *Arran* was nearly southeast of
both of the others. Flint went directly to the south,
and Christy ran for the enemy.

All hands had been beaten to quarters on board
of the *Bronx*, and the captain was on the bridge,
watching with the most intense interest the progress
of the other two vessels. It was soon apparent to
him that the *Ocklockonee* could not get into the
position to which she had been ordered under
present circumstances, for the enemy was giving his
whole attention to her.

"There goes a gun from the enemy!" exclaimed
Mr. Amblen, as a puff of smoke rose from the forward
deck of the *Arran*.

"The shot struck in the water," added Christy a
moment later, "but the two vessels are within range.
There is the first shot from the *Ocklockonee*!
Captain Flint is not asleep."

The firing was done on both vessels with the
heavy midship guns, and doubtless the caliber of
the pieces was the same, but Flint was the more

fortunate of the two, for his shot struck the smokestack of the enemy, or partly upset it. Christy thought it was time for him to take a hand in the game, and he ordered the midship gun to be fired, charged as it was with a solid shot. The gunner aimed the piece himself, and the shot was seen to tear up the water alongside of the enemy. He discharged the piece four times more with no better result. Evidently he had not got the hang of the gun, though he was improving at every trial.

The three steamers were rushing towards each other with all the fury steam could give them, for the overthrow of the funnel of the enemy did not disable her, though it probably diminished the draught of her furnaces. Through the glass it could be seen that they were making an effort to restore the fallen smokestack to its position. All three of the steamers were delivering the fire of their midship guns very regularly, though with little effect, the distance was so great. The gunner of the *Bronx* was evidently greatly nettled at the number of solid shots he had wasted, though the gun of the *Ocklockonee* had done little better so far as could be seen. The three vessels were not much more than half a mile from each other, and the enemy had begun to use his broadside guns.

"Good!" shouted Mr. Amblen suddenly after the gunner had just let off the great gun. "That shot overturned the mid-ship piece of the *Arran*! Ambleton has fully redeemed himself." The announcement of the effect of this last shot sent up a volley of cheers from the crew.

The *Bronx* and her consort had set the American flag at the beginning of the action, and the Confederate had promptly displayed her ensign, as though she scorned to go into action without having it fully understood what she was. She did not claim to be a blockade runner, and do her best to escape, but "faced the music," even when she realized that she had two enemies instead of one.

Christy had evidently inherited some of the naval blood on his mother's side, and he was not satisfied with the slow progress of the action, for the shots from the broadside guns of the enemy were beginning to tell upon the *Bronx*, though she had received no serious injury. He caused the signal to prepare to board to be set as agreed upon with Captain Flint. The orders already given were to be carried out, and both vessels bore down on the *Arran* with all speed.

Chapter XIX

On the Deck of the *Arran*

Captain Passford had carried out the program agreed upon with Captain Flint, and the latter had been working to the southward since the *Bronx* came into the action, and as soon as the order to get ready to board was given, the *Ocklockonee* went ahead at full speed, headed in that direction. She had reached a position dead ahead of the *Arran*, so that she no longer suffered from the shots of the latter's broadside guns, and the *Bronx* was getting the entire benefit of them.

Both vessels had kept up a full head of steam, and the coal passers were kept very busy at just this time. The *Arran*'s midship gun had been disabled so that she could not make any very telling shots, but her crew had succeeded in righting her funnel, which had not gone entirely over, but had been held by the stays. Yet it could be seen that there was a big opening near the deck, for the smoke did not all pass through the smokestack.

The broadside guns of the *Arran* were well served, and they were doing considerable mischief on board of the *Bronx*. Christy was obliged to hold back until her consort was in position to board the *Arran* on the port hand, and he maneuvered the steamer so as to receive as little damage as possible from her guns. He was to board on the starboard hand of the enemy, and he was working nearer to her all the time. Mr. Ambleton, the gunner, had greatly improved his practice, and the commander was obliged to check his enthusiasm, or there would have been nothing left of the *Arran* in half an hour more. Christy considered the final result as fully assured, for he did not believe the present enemy was any more heavily manned than her consort had been, and he could throw double her force upon her deck as soon as the two steamers were in position to do so.

"Are you doing all you can in the engine room, Mr. Sampson?" asked Christy, pausing at the engine hatch.

"Everything, Captain Passford, and I think we must be making sixteen knots," replied the chief engineer.

"Is Mr. Bockburn on duty?"

"He is, sir, and if he were a Connecticut Yankee he could not do any better, or appear to be any more interested."

"He seems to be entirely impartial; all he wants is his pay, and he is as willing to be on one side as the other if he only gets it," said Christy. "Has any damage been done to the engine?"

"None at all, sir; a shot from one of those broadside guns went through the side and passed just over the top of one of the boilers," replied the engineer. "Bockburn plugged the shot hole very skillfully, and said it would not be possible for a shot to come in low enough to hit the boilers. He knows all about the other two vessels, and has served as an engineer on board of the *Arran* on the other side of the Atlantic."

Just at that moment a shot from the *Arran* struck the bridge, and a splinter from the structure knocked two men over. One of them picked himself up, but said he was not much hurt and refused to be sent below. The other man was Veering; he seemed to be unable to get up, and was carried down by order of the boatswain. This man was one of the adherents of Hungerford and Pawcett, though so far he had been of no service to them.

Christy hastened forward to ascertain the extent of the damage done to the bridge. It was completely wrecked, and was no longer in condition to be occupied by an officer. But the pilothouse was still in serviceable repair, and the quartermaster had not been disturbed. By this time, the *Ocklockonee* had obtained a position on the port bow of the *Arran*, and the commander directed the quartermaster at the wheel to run directly for the other side of the enemy.

The time for decisive and final action had come. Mr. Baskirk placed the boarders in position to be thrown on board of the *Arran*. He was to command the first division himself, and Mr. Amblen the second. The *Ocklockonee* was rushing at all the speed she could command to the work before her.

For some reason not apparent, the *Arran* had stopped her screw, though she had kept in motion till now, doing her best to secure the most favorable position for action. Possibly her commander believed a collision between the vessels at a high rate of speed would be more fatal to him than anything that could result from being boarded. It was soon discovered that she was backing, and it was evident then that her captain had some maneuver of his own in mind, though it was possible that he was only doing something to counteract the effect of a collision. Doubtless he thought the two vessels approaching him at such a rapid rate intended to crush the *Arran* between them, and that they desired only to sink him.

He was not allowed many minutes more to carry out his policy, whatever it was, for the *Ocklockonee* came up alongside of the *Arran*, the grapnels were thrown out, and the whole boarding force of the steamer was hurled upon her decks. But the commander was a plucky man, however he regarded the chances for or against him, and his crew proceeded vigorously to repel boarders. Christy had timed the movements of the *Bronx* very carefully, and the *Ocklockonee* had hardly fastened to the *Arran* on one side before he had his steamer grappled on the other.

"Boarders, away!" he shouted at the top of his lungs and flourishing his sword over his head, not however with the intention of going into the fight himself, but as a demonstration to inspire the men.

Baskirk and Amblen rushed forward with cutlasses in their hands, leaping upon the deck of the enemy. The crew was found to equal in numbers about the force that the *Ocklockonee* had brought to bear upon them. The boarders from the *Bronx* attacked them in the rear while they were fully occupied with the boarders in front of them. The officers of the enemy behaved with distinguished gallantry and urged their men forward with the most desperate enthusiasm. They struck hard blows, and several of the boarders belonging to the consort had fallen, to say nothing of wounds that did not entirely disable others. Some of the men belonging to the *Arran*, doubtless shipped on the other side of the ocean or at the Bermudas, were disposed to shirk their duty, though their officers held them well up to the work.

One of the brave officers who had done the boarders a good deal of mischief fell at a pistol shot from Mr. Amblen; this loss of his leadership caused a sensible giving way on the part of his division, and his men began to fall back. The other officers, including the captain, who fought with a heavy cutlass, held out for a short time longer, but Christy saw that it was slaughter.

The captain of the *Arran* was the next to go down, though he was not killed. This event practically ended the contest for the deck of the steamer. The boarders crowded upon the crew and drove them to the bow of the vessel, where they yielded the deck and submitted to the excess of numbers.

"Don't butcher my men!" cried the captain of the *Arran*, raising himself partially from his place where he had fallen. "I surrender, for we are outnumbered two to one."

But the fighting had ceased forward. Mr. Baskirk was as earnest to save any further slaughter as he had been to win the fight. Christy came on board of the prize, not greatly elated at the victory, for it had been a very unequal affair as to numbers. The *Arran* was captured; that was all that could be said of it. She had been bravely defended, and the "honors were even," though the fortunes of the day were against the *Arran* and her ship's company.

"Allow me to introduce myself as the commander of the United States steamer *Bronx*," said Christy, approaching the fallen captain of the *Arran*. "I sincerely hope that you are not seriously injured, sir."

"Who under the canopy are you?" demanded the commander of the prize, as he looked at the young officer with something like contempt in his expression.

"I have just informed you who under the canopy I am," replied Christy, not pleased with the manner of the other. "To be a little more definite, I am Captain Christopher Passford, commander of the United States steamer *Bronx*, of which the *Arran* appears to be a prize."

The Captain of the Arran

"The captain!" exclaimed the fallen man. "You are nothing but a boy!"

"But I am old enough to try to be a gentleman. You are evidently old enough to be my father, though I have no comments to make," added Christy.

"I beg your pardon, Captain Passford," said the captain of the *Arran*, attempting to rise from the deck, in which he was assisted by Christy and by Mr. Baskirk, who had just come aft. "I beg your pardon, Captain Passford, for I did not understand what you said at first, and I did not suspect that you were the captain."

"I hope you are not seriously injured, sir," added Christy.

"I don't know how seriously, but I have a cut on the hip, for which I exchanged one on the head, parrying the stroke so that it took me below the belt."

"Have you a surgeon on board, Captain—I have not the pleasure of knowing your name, sir."

"Captain Richfield, lieutenant in the Confederate navy. We have a surgeon on board, and he is below attending to the wounded," replied the captain.

"Allow me to assist you to your cabin, Captain Richfield," continued Christy, as he and Baskirk each took one of the wounded officer's arms.

"Thank you, sir. I see that you have been doubly fortunate, Captain Passford, and you have both the *Escambia* and the *Ocklockonee*. I did the best I could to save my ship, but the day has gone against me."

"And no one could have done any more than you have done. Your ship has been ably and bravely defended, but it was my good fortune to be able to outnumber you both in ships and in men."

Captain Richfield was taken to his stateroom and assisted into his berth. A steward was sent for the surgeon, and Christy and his first lieutenant retired from the cabin. The captured seamen of the *Arran* were all sent below, and everything was done that the occasion required.

Christy asked Captain Flint to meet him in the cabin of the *Bronx* for a consultation over the situation, for the sealed orders of the commander had been carried out to the letter so far as the two expected steamers were concerned, and it only remained to report to the flag officer of the eastern Gulf squadron. But with two prizes, and a considerable number of prisoners, the situation was not without its difficulties.

"I hope you are quite comfortable, Captain Dinsmore," said Christy as he entered his cabin and found his guest reading at the table.

"Quite so, Captain Passford. I have heard a great deal of firing in the last hour, and I am rather surprised to find that you are not a prisoner on board of the *Escambia*, or perhaps you have come to your cabin for your clothes," replied the guest cheerfully.

"I have not come on any such mission, and I have the pleasure of informing you that the Confederate steamer *Escambia* is a prize to the *Bronx*," replied Christy quite as cheerfully. "I am sorry to add that Captain Richfield was wounded in the hip and that Mr. Berwick, the first lieutenant, was killed."

The Confederate officer leaped out of his chair astonished at the news. He declared that he had confidently expected to be released by the capture of the *Bronx*. Christy gave a brief review of the action, and Captain Dinsmore was not surprised at the result when informed that the *Ocklockonee* had taken part in the capture. The commander then requested him to retire to the wardroom, and Flint came in. They seated themselves at the table, and proceeded to figure up their resources and consider what was to be done. Mr. Baskirk was then sent for to assist in the conference.

CHAPTER XX

"Captain Flint, the first question to be settled is in regard to the engineer force," said Christy, as the three officers seated themselves at the table.

"I think we shall have no difficulty on that score, Captain Passford, for I have already sounded those on board of the *Arran*, or the *Escambia*, as her officers call her. As long as their wages are paid, they don't care which side they serve. Mr. Pivotte is the chief, and he is as willing to go one way as the other."

"Very well; then he shall retain his present position, and Bockburn shall be restored to the *Ocklockonee*. Of course, the arrangements made after the capture of the first vessel were only temporary, and I propose to report to the flag officer with everything as nearly as possible in the condition in which we left New York," continued Christy.

"Of course, I expected to resume my former position on board of the *Bronx* as soon as we had disposed of the two steamers, and I can say that I shall not be sorry to do so," said Flint with a pleasant smile, as though he did not intend to grieve over the loss of his command.

"In a few days more, we shall move down a peg, and I shall cease to have a command as well as yourself," added Christy.

"And I suppose I shall be relegated to my position as a quartermaster," said Baskirk, "but I shall be satisfied. I don't care to wear any spurs that I have not won, though I shall be glad to have a higher rank when I deserve it."

"You deserve it now, Mr. Baskirk, and if you don't receive it, it will not be on account of any weakness in my report of the events of the last twenty-four hours," added Christy heartily.

"Thank you, Captain; I suppose I could have procured a better position than that of able seaman, but I preferred to work my way up."

"It was wise not to begin too high up, and you have already won your spurs. Now, Mr. Baskirk, I shall ask you to take the deck, relieving Mr. Amblen," added Christy, who wished to talk with Flint alone.

"I shall be really glad to get back into the *Bronx*,

for I feel at home here with you, Captain," said Flint.

"You will be back to your berth here very soon. Now we have to send these two steamers to New York. They are fine vessels, and will be needed. We want two prize masters, and we must have able men. Have you any suggestion to make, Mr. Flint? I first thought of sending you as the principal one, but I cannot spare you, and the service in the Gulf needs you."

"I am entirely willing to go where my duty calls me, without regard to personal preferences," replied Flint. "I have a suggestion to make, which is that Baskirk take one of the steamers."

"That is exactly my own idea; from what I have seen of him, there is no more devoted officer in the service."

"I have known him for many years, and I believe in him. McSpindle is almost as good, and has had a better education than Baskirk. I don't think you could find two better men in the navy for this duty."

"Very well; then I will appoint them both."

Flint was instructed to communicate their appointment to Baskirk and McSpindle, and make all the preparations for the departure of the *Escambia* and the *Ocklockonee*. Christy went to his stateroom and wrote his report of the capture of the two steamers, in which he commended the two officers who were to go as prize masters, and then wrote a letter to his father, with a strong appeal in their favor. Then he wrote very careful instructions for the government of the officers to be sent away, in which he directed them to use all necessary precautions in regard to the prisoners. In a couple of hours after the capture of the *Escambia*, the two prizes sailed for New York. Captain Dinsmore expressed his thanks very warmly to Captain Passford for his courtesy and kindness at parting.

Christy had visited every part of the two steamers and talked with the officers and men, and especially with the engineers, and he discovered no elements of discord on board of either. Hungerford and Pawcett were transferred to the *Escambia* and committed to the care of the surgeon of the ship. Both of them were suffering from fever, and they were not likely to give the prize master any trouble during the passage, which could only be three or four days in duration. Baskirk and McSpindle were required to make all the speed they could consistent with safety, though Christy hardly thought they would encounter any Confederate rover on the voyage, for they were not very plentiful at this stage of the war.

It seemed a little lonesome on board of the *Bronx* after the two steamers had disappeared in the distance, and the number of the crew had been so largely reduced by the drafts for the prizes. The steamer was hardly in condition to engage an enemy of any considerable force, and Sampson was directed to hurry as much as possible. Christy had heard of the *Bellevite* twice since he left her off Pensacola Bay. She had been sent to other stations on duty, and had captured two schooners loaded with cotton as prizes, but at the last accounts she had returned to the station where the *Bronx* had left her.

Christy was not so anxious as he had been before the recent captures to fall in with an enemy, for with less than twenty seamen it would not be prudent to attack such a steamer as either of those he had captured, though he would not have objected to chase a blockade runner if he had discovered one pursued by the gunboats.

It was a quiet time on board of the *Bronx* compared with the excitement of the earlier days of the voyage. In the very beginning of the trip, he had discovered the deaf mute at the cabin door, and his thought, his inquiries, and his action in defeating the treachery of the second lieutenant had kept him busy night and day. Now the weather was fine most of the time, and he had little to do beyond his routine duties. But he did a great deal of thinking in his cabin, though most of it was in relation to the events which had transpired on board of the *Bronx*.

He had captured two valuable prizes, but he could not feel that he was entitled to any great credit for the achievements of his vessel, since he had been warned in the beginning to look out for the *Scotian* and the *Arran*. He had taken the first by surprise, and the result was due to the carelessness of her commander rather than to any great merit on his own part. The second he had taken with double the force of the enemy in ships and men, and the latter was not precisely the kind of a victory he was ambitious to win.

At the same time, his self-respect assured him that he had done his duty faithfully, and that it had been possible for him to throw away his advantage by carelessness. If he had fallen in with both the *Scotian* and the *Arran* at the same time, the result might have been different, though he was sure that he should have fought his ship as long as there was anything left of her. In that case there would have been more room for maneuvering and strategy, for he did not admit to himself that he should have been beaten.

Amblen continued to hold his place as second lieutenant, and McLinn was appointed acting third lieutenant. The carpenter repaired the bridge, though Christy would not have been very sorry if it had been so thoroughly smashed as to be beyond restoration, for it was hardly a naval institution. The men who had been only slightly wounded in the action with the *Escambia* were progressing finely under the care of Dr. Spokeley, and when the *Bronx* was off the southern cape of Florida, they were able to return to duty. The latest information located the flag officer off Pensacola, and in due time Christy reported to him. The *Bellevite* was still there, and the commander went on board of her, where he received an ovation from the former officers and seamen with whom he had sailed. He did not take any pains to recite his experience, but it was soon known throughout the fleet.

"Christy, I shall hardly dare to sail in command of a ship of which you are the executive officer," said Lieutenant Blowitt, who was to command the *Bronx*, with a laugh.

"Why not? Is my reputation so bad as that?" asked Christy.

"Bad! No, it is so good. The fact of it is, you are such a tremendous fellow, there will be no room for any other officer to shine in the same sky."

"I have been in command for a few days, hardly more than a week, but I assure you that I can and shall obey the orders of my commander to the very letter," added Christy.

"But you took two steamers, each of them of nearly twice the tonnage of your own ship, in mid-ocean."

"But I took them one at a time. If I had fallen in with both at the same time, the affair might have gone the other way. We captured the first one by accident, as it were, and the second with double the force of the enemy. I don't take much credit to myself for that sort of thing. I don't think it was half as much of an affair as bringing out the *Teaser*, for we had to use some science on that occasion," replied Christy quietly.

"Science, is it?" laughed Mr. Blowitt. "Perhaps you can assist me to some of your science, when it is required."

"I shall obey my superior officer and not presume to advise him unless he asks me to do so."

"Well, Christy, I think you are the most audacious young fellow I ever met," added the future commander of the *Bronx*.

"I haven't anything about me that I call audacity,

so far as I understand myself. When I am told to do any duty, I do it if it is possible, and whether it is possible often depends upon whether you think it is or not."

"I should say that it was audacious for you to think of capturing two steamers, fitted out for war purposes and twice the size of your own ship, with the *Bronx*," added Mr. Blowitt, still laughing, to take off the edge of his criticism.

"Why did the Navy Department instruct me in my sealed orders to look out for these steamers, if I was to do so in a Pickwickian sense?" demanded Christy earnestly. "What would you have done, Mr. Blowitt?"

"Perhaps I should have been as audacious as you were, Christy, if such had been my orders."

This conversation took place on the deck of the *Bellevite* where Christy had come to see his friends, and it was interrupted by a boat from the flagship which brought a big envelope for Mr. Blowitt. It instructed him to go on board of the *Bronx*, to the command of which he had been appointed. Another order required him to proceed to a point on the western coast of Florida, where the enemy were supposed to be loading vessels with cotton, and break up the depot established for the purpose, where it could be supplied by the Florida Railroad.

The new commander packed his clothing, and he was sent with Christy in one of the *Bellevite*'s boats to the *Bronx*. They went on board, where the late acting commander had already removed his own property to the wardroom, and Captain Blowitt was conducted to his cabin and stateroom, of which he took formal possession. He seemed to be very much pleased with his accommodations since the government had put the vessel in order, though he had been on board of her, and fought a battle on her deck, while she was still the *Teaser*.

"I am sure I could not ask for anything better than this cabin," said he, after he had invited his first lieutenant to come in.

"I found it very comfortable," added Christy. "Flint is second lieutenant, and Sampson chief engineer, and that is all there are of those who were in the *Bellevite*. I will introduce you to the acting third lieutenant, Mr. Amblen, and you can retain him or not as you please."

Mr. Amblen was called in and presented to the captain, and then Flint was ordered to get under way.

CHAPTER XXI

AN EXPEDITION IN THE GULF

The *Bronx* had been three days on the station. Christy had made his report in full on her arrival, and the flag officer had visited the vessel in person in order to ascertain her fitness for several enterprises he had in view. The Confederates were not sleepy or inactive, and resorted to every expedient within their means to counteract both morally and materially the efficiency of the blockade.

The *Bronx* was admirably adapted to service in the shoal waters where the heavier vessels of the investing squadron could not go, and her arrival solved several problems then under consideration. Captain Blowitt and Christy had been sent for, and the late commander of the *Bronx* was questioned in regard to the steamer, her draught, her speed, and her ship's company. The damage done to her in the conflict with the *Escambia* had been fully repaired by the carpenter and his gang, and the steamer was in as good condition as when she sailed from New York.

"In regard to the present officers, Mr. Passford, excepting present company, of course, they are excellent," said Captain McKeon, the flag officer. "For the service in which the *Bronx* is to be engaged, its success will depend upon the officers, though it is hardly exceptional in this respect. I understand that you sailed from New York rather short handed abaft the mainmast."

"Yes, sir, we did, but fortunately we had most excellent material of which to make officers, and we made them," replied Christy.

"I should like to know something about them; I mean apart from Captain Blowitt and yourself, for you have already made your record, and yours, Mr. Passford, is rather a dazzling reputation for one so young."

"I am willing to apologize for it, sir," replied Christy, blushing like a maiden, as he was in duty bound to do, for he could not control the crimson that rose to his browned cheeks.

"Quite unnecessary," replied Captain McKeon, smiling. "As long as you do your duty nobody will be jealous of you, and you will be a fit officer for all our young men to emulate. You were the acting commander on the voyage of the *Bronx* from New York. Your executive officer is the present second lieutenant. Is he qualified for the peculiar duty before you?"

"No one could be more so, sir," replied Christy with proper enthusiasm.

"I can fully endorse this opinion of Mr. Passford," added Captain Blowitt. "In the capture and bringing out of the *Teaser*, Mr. Flint was the right hand man of the leader of the enterprise."

"And I gave him the command of the *Ocklockonee*, after her capture, and she took an active part in the affair with the *Escambia*, sir," said Christy.

"Then we will consider him the right man in the right place," replied the flag officer. "Who is the present third lieutenant?"

"Mr. Amblen is acting in that capacity at present, and he is a very good officer, though he holds no rank," answered Christy.

"Then I can hardly confirm him as second lieutenant," added Captain McKeon.

"In my report of the affairs with the *Ocklockonee* and the *Escambia*, I have strongly recommended him and three other officers for promotion, for all of them are fitted by education and experience at sea to do duty on board of such vessels as the *Bronx*."

"Have you any officer in mind who would acceptably fill the vacant place, Captain Blowitt?"

"I know of no one at present who holds the rank to entitle him to such a position, and I shall appeal to Mr. Passford," replied the new commander.

"You have named Mr. Amblen, Mr. Passford; is he just the officer you would select if the matter were left to you?" asked the flag officer.

"No, sir, though he would do very well. Mr. Baskirk, who served as executive officer while Mr. Flint was away in the *Ocklockonee*, is better adapted for the place," said Christy. "He commanded the first division of boarders on board of the *Escambia*, and he fought like a hero and is a man of excellent judgment. I am confident that he will make his mark as an officer. I am willing to admit that I wrote a letter to my father especially requesting him to do what he could for the immediate promotion of Mr. Baskirk."

"Then he will be immediately promoted," added Captain McKeon with an expressive smile.

"I may add also that I was presumptive enough to suggest his appointment as third lieutenant of the *Bronx*," continued Christy.

"Then he will be the third lieutenant of the *Bronx*, and what you say would have settled the matter in the first place as well as now," said the flag officer, as much pleased with the reticence of the young officer as with his modesty. "Amblen may remain on board till his commission comes, and you can retain him as third lieutenant, Captain Blowitt, if you are so disposed. I have ordered a draft of twelve seamen to the *Bronx*, which will give you a crew of thirty, and I cannot spare any more until more men are sent down. I may add that I have taken some of them from the *Bellevite*."

"I am quite satisfied, sir, with the number, though ten more would be acceptable," replied the commander of the *Bronx*.

The two officers were then dismissed and ordered on board of their ship. A little later the draft of seamen was sent on board, and among them Christy was not sorry to see Boxie, the old sheet-anchor man of the *Bellevite*, who had made him a sort of pet and had done a great deal to instruct him in matters of seamanship, naval customs, and traditions not found in any books.

The commander and the executive officer paid their final visit to the *Bellevite* the next day, and the order was given to weigh anchor. When all hands were called, Christy thought he had never seen a better set of men except on board of the *Bellevite*, and the expedition, whatever it was, commenced under the most favorable auspices.

The *Bronx* sailed in the middle of the forenoon, and the flag officer was careful not to reveal the destination of the steamer to anyone, for with the aid of the telegraph, the object of the expedition might reach the scene of operations in advance of the arrival of the force. At four o'clock in the afternoon Captain Blowitt opened his envelope in presence of the executive officer. He looked the paper through before he spoke and then handed it to Christy, who read it with quite as much interest as the commander had.

"Cedar Keys," said the captain, glancing at his associate.

"That is not a long run from the station," added Christy. "We are very likely to be there before tomorrow morning."

"It is about two hundred and eighty statute miles. I had occasion to ascertain a week ago when something was said about Cedar Keys," replied Captain Blowitt. "We have been making about fifteen knots, for the *Bronx* is a flyer, and we ought to be near our destination at about midnight. That would be an excellent time to arrive if we only had a pilot."

"Perhaps we have one," added Christy with a smile.

"Are you a pilot on this coast, Mr. Passford?" asked the commander, mistaking the smile.

"No, sir, I am not, but I remember a conversation Mr. Flint and I had with Mr. Amblen, who was engaged in some sort of a speculation in Florida when the war came on. He was so provoked at the treatment he received that he shipped in the navy at once. I only know that he had a small steamer in these waters."

"Send for Mr. Amblen at once!" exclaimed the commander, who appeared to have become suddenly excited. "There will be no moon tonight in these parts, and we may be able to hurry this matter up if we have a competent pilot."

Christy called Dave and sent him for the acting third lieutenant, for he knew that Mr. Flint had had the watch since four o'clock. Mr. Amblen was sunning himself on the quarterdeck, and he promptly obeyed the summons.

"I am glad to see you, Mr. Amblen, and I hope you will prove to be as useful a person as I have been led to believe you may be," said the captain.

"I shall endeavor to do my duty, sir," replied the third lieutenant, who was always very ambitious to earn the good opinion of his superiors. "I mean to do the best I can to make myself useful, Captain Blowitt."

"I know that very well, but the question now is what you know rather than what you can do as an officer. Mr. Passford informs me that you were formerly engaged in some kind of a speculation on the west coast of Florida."

"Hardly a speculation, sir, for I was engaged in the fish business," replied Mr. Amblen, laughing at the name which had been given to his calling. "When I sold a small coaster that belonged to me, I got in exchange a tugboat. I had been out of health a few years before; I spent six months at Cedar Keys and Tampa and got well. Fish were plenty here, and of a kind that bring a good price farther north. I loaded my tug with ice and came down here in her. I did a first-rate business buying from boats and in catching fish myself, and for a time I made money, though ice was so dear that I had to sell in the South."

"Did you have a pilot on board of your tug?" asked the captain.

"No, sir. I was my own pilot. I had the charts, and I studied out the bottom, so that I knew where I was in the darkest night."

"Then you are just the person we want if you were a pilot in these waters."

"What waters, sir? We are now off Cape St. Blas and Apalachicola Bay. I have been into the bay, but I am not a pilot in those waters, as you suggest."

"I have just opened my orders, and I find we are ordered to Cedar Keys," interposed the commander.

"That is quite another thing, sir, and there isn't a foot of bottom within five miles of the Keys to which I have not been personally introduced. When I was down here for my health, I was on the water more than half of the time, and I learned all about the bay and coast, and I have been up the Suwanee River, which flows into the Gulf eighteen miles north of the Keys."

"I am exceedingly glad to find that we have such an excellent pilot on board. I am informed in my orders that schooners load with cotton at this place and make an easy thing of getting to sea," added Captain Blowitt.

"I should say that it was a capital port for the Confederates to use for that sort of business. Small steamers can bring cotton down the Suwanee River, the railroad from Fernandina terminates at the Key, and this road connects with that to Jacksonville and the whole of western Florida as far as Tallahassee."

"We may find a steamer or two there."

"You may, though not one any larger than the *Bronx*, for there is only eleven feet of water on the bar. Probably no blockaders have yet been stationed off the port, and it is a good place to run out cotton."

"I am much obliged to you, Mr. Amblen, for the information you have given me, and your services will probably be in demand this very night," added the commander, rising from his chair.

"I am ready for duty at all times, sir," replied Mr. Amblen, as he retired from the cabin.

The charts were then consulted, and sundry calculations were made. At one o'clock that night the *Bronx* was off Cedar Keys.

CHAPTER XXII

A NIGHT EXPEDITION IN THE BOATS

During the evening Captain Blowitt had consulted his officers and arranged his plans for operations, or at least for obtaining information in regard to the situation inside of North Key, where the landing place is situated. He had already arranged to give the command of the boat expedition to Christy, with the second lieutenant in another boat, Mr. Amblen being with the executive officer in the first.

"Now, Mr. Passford, I do not expect you to capture the whole state of Florida, and if you should return without accomplishing anything at all, I shall not be disappointed, but I shall feel that you have done everything that could be done," said the captain with a very cheerful smile when all had been arranged.

"I shall endeavor to obey my orders, Captain Blowitt, if I can do so in the exercise of a reasonable prudence," replied Christy, who took in all that his superior looked, as well as all that he said.

"A reasonable prudence is decidedly good, coming from you, Mr. Passford," said the captain, laughing outright.

"Why is it decidedly good from me rather than from anybody else?" asked Christy, somewhat nettled by the remark.

"You objected once on board of the *Bellevite* when I mildly hinted that you might sometimes, under some circumstances, with a strong temptation before you, be just a little audacious," said the captain, still laughing, as though he were engaged in a mere joke.

"That statement is certainly qualified in almost all directions, if you will excuse me for saying so, Captain," replied Christy, who was fully determined not to take offence at anything his superior might say, for he had always regarded him as one of his best friends. "If I remember rightly the mild suggestion of a criticism which you gently and tenderly applied to me was after we had brought out the *Teaser* from Pensacola Bay."

"That was the time. Captain Breaker sent you

to ascertain, if you could, where the *Teaser* was, and you reported by bringing her out, which certainly no one expected you would do, and I believe this part of the program carried out on that excursion was not mentioned in your orders."

"It was not, but if I had a good chance to capture the steamer, was it my duty to pass over that chance, and run the risk of letting the vessel get out?"

"On the contrary, it was your duty, if you got a good chance, to capture the steamer."

"And that is precisely what I did. I did not lose a man or have one wounded in the expedition, and I have only to be penitent for being audacious," laughed Christy, and he was laughing very earnestly, as though the extra cachinnation was assumed for a purpose. "I suppose I ought to dress myself in ash cloth and sashes, shut myself up in my stateroom always when off duty, and shed penitential tears from the rising of the sun to the going down of the same, and during the lone watches of the night, and in fortifying my soul against the monstrous sin of audacity. I will think of it."

"I hope you have no feeling about this matter, Mr. Passford," said the captain, rising from his chair and taking Christy by the hand.

"Not a particle, Captain Blowitt. I am absolutely sure that you would have done precisely what I did, if you had been in my situation," protested Christy. "About the last thing my father talked about to me when we parted in this cabin in New York Harbor was the necessity of prudence and discretion in the discharge of my duties, and I am sure his advice saved me from falling into the traps set for me by Hungerford and Pawcett and enabled me to capture two of the enemy's crack steamers."

"I will never use the word audacity or the adjective audacious to you again, Christy. I see that it nettles you, to say the least," added the captain, pressing his hand with more earnestness.

"I am perfectly willing you should apply both words to me when I deserve it. Audacity means boldness, impudence, according to Stormonth. Audacious means very bold, daring, impudent. It may have been bold to run out the *Teaser*, and the enemy would even call it impudent, for the meaning of a word sometimes depends upon which side you belong to. My father was quite as impudent as I was when he ran the *Bellevite* out of Mobile Bay, under the guns of Fort Morgan. He was audacious, wasn't he?"

"We should hardly apply that word to him."

"Why not? Simply because my father was forty-five years old when he told Captain Breaker to do it. If I were only thirty years old I should not be audacious. I am a boy, and therefore anything that I do is daring, audacious, impudent, imprudent."

"I rather think you are right, Mr. Passford, and it is your age more than the results of your actions that is the basis of our judgment," said Captain Blowitt.

"I wish to add seriously, Captain, as a friend and not as an officer, I do not claim that the command of this expedition should be given to me because I am first lieutenant of the *Bronx*, or for any other reason," added Christy with an earnest expression. "Perhaps it would be better to give the command to the second lieutenant, and if you do so, I assure you, upon my honor, that it will not produce a particle of feeling in my mind. I shall honor, respect, and love you as I have always, Captain Blowitt."

"My dear fellow, you are entirely misunderstanding me," protested the commander as earnestly as his subordinate had spoken. "I give you the command of this expedition because I honestly and sincerely believe you are the very best person on board to whom I can commit such a responsibility."

"That is enough, Captain, and a great deal more than you were under any obligations to say to me, and I shall obey my orders with all the prudence and discretion I can bring to bear upon them," said Christy, taking the captain's offered hand. "If I fail, it will not be because I do not try to be prudent."

"There is such a thing as being too prudent, and I hope that nothing which has been said to you by your father or by me will drive you to the other extreme."

Though this conversation had, at times, been very animated, Christy was glad that it had taken place, for it gave him a better insight into his own standing than he had before. He did not look upon it as a very great affair to command a couple of boats, in a night expedition, for he had recently commanded two steamers and brought them off victorious. He had it in mind to ask the captain to send Flint in command of the expedition, though it would compel him, on account of his rank, to remain inactive on board of the *Bronx*, but he could not do this, after what had been said, without leaving some evidence that he was disaffected by what the commander had said to him about audacity.

It was found after a calculation of the run, very carefully made, that the *Bronx* would arrive too soon at her destination, and she was slowed down as the evening came on. In the wardroom, of which Christy was now the occupant of the forward berth on the starboard side, he studied the chart with Amblen a good part of the waiting hours, and the executive officer obtained all the information he could from the third lieutenant. There were three principal keys, or cays, one of which, called the North Key, was the nearest to the mainland and was set in the mouth of a bay. This was the nearest to the peninsula at the end of which the railroad terminates. About southwest of it is the Seahorse Key, on which there is a light in peaceful times. To the south of the point is the Snake Key, and between the last two is the main channel to the port, which twists about like the track of a snake. There is a town, or rather a village, near the landing.

Six bells, struck on deck, and all the officers, including the captain, adjourned to the bridge, which was a useful institution on such occasions as the present. A sharp watch had been kept by Lieutenant Flint in charge, but though the night was clear, nothing had been made out in the direction of the shore. All lights on board had been put out, and the *Bronx* went along in the smooth sea as quietly as a lady on a fashionable promenade, and it was not believed that anything could be seen of her from the shore.

About midnight the lookout man aloft reported that he could see a twinkling light. It was promptly investigated by Mr. Amblen, who went aloft for the purpose. He was satisfied that it was a light in some house in the village, probably in the upper story. It soon disappeared, and it was thought to be occasioned by the late retiring of some person.

"I should say, Captain Blowitt, that we are not more than five miles outside of Seahorse Key," said Mr. Amblen, after he had interpreted the meaning of the light. "It is after midnight, and these people are not in the habit of sitting up so late."

"If they are shipping much cotton from this port, it is not improbable that there is a force here to protect the vessels, whatever they are," added the commander.

"Of that, of course, I can know nothing, but I shall expect to find a Confederate battery somewhere on the point, and I know about where to look for it."

"The place has never been of any great importance, and you can hardly expect to find a very strong force in it," added the captain.

"It has since become a place of more note, both as a resort for invalids and pleasure seekers, and as the termination of the railroad from Fernandina and Jacksonville, and steamers have run regularly from the port to Havana and New Orleans."

"If you will excuse me, Captain Blowitt, I should say that it was not advisable to take the *Bronx* nearer than within about four miles of the Seahorse Key," suggested Mr. Amblen.

"I was just thinking that we had gone as far as it is prudent to go. Do you think you could take the *Bronx* up to the landing?" added the captain.

"I am very sure that I could, for I have been in many a time on a darker night than this."

"We will not go in tonight, but perhaps we may have occasion to do so tomorrow. We shall know better what to do when we get a report of the state of things in the place," replied the captain, as he gave the word through the speaking tube to stop the steamer.

Christy had been given full powers to make all preparations for the boat expedition, and was allowed ten men to each of the quarter boats. He had selected the ones for his own boat, and had required Flint to pick his own crew for the other. The oars had been carefully muffled by the coxswains, for it was desirable that no alarm should be given in the place. The starboard quarter boat was the first cutter, pulled by six oars, and this was for Christy and Mr. Amblen, with the regular coxswain and three hands in the bow. The second cutter was in charge of Mr. Flint and followed the other boat, keeping near enough to obtain her course in the twists of the channel.

It was a long pull to the Seahorse Key, and a moderate stroke was taken as well not to tire the men as to avoid all possible noise. When the first cutter was abreast of the key, the pilot pointed out the dark outline of the peninsula, which was less than a mile distant. No vessel could be seen, but the pilot thought they might be concealed by the railroad buildings on the point. Christy asked where the battery was which the pilot thought he could locate, and the spot was indicated to him. Christy wanted a nearer view of it, and the cutter was headed in that direction.

Chapter XXIII

The Visit to a Shore Battery

The first cutter reached the Seahorse Key closely followed by the second. It was within an hour of high tide, the ordinary rise and fall of which was two and a half feet. On the key was a lighthouse and a cottage for the keeper of it, but the former was no longer illuminated, and the house was as dark as the head of the tower. So far as could be discovered, there was no one on the key, though the boats did not stop to investigate this matter. The crews still pulled a moderate stroke with their muffled oars, the men were not allowed to talk, and everything was as silent as the inside of a tomb.

The pilot stood up in the stern sheets of the cutter, gazing intently in the direction of the point, nearly a mile ahead. The outlines of the buildings could be discerned, and Amblen soon declared that he could make out the tops of the masts of several vessels to the westward of the point with which the peninsula terminated. This looked hopeful and indicated that the information upon which the expedition had been sent out was correct. Christy began to think he should have a busy night before him when Amblen said there were at least three vessels at the port.

The battery was first to be visited and cared for if there was one, and it was not probable that a place so open to the operations of the blockading force would be without one, especially if the people were actually engaged in loading cotton, as the masts of the vessels indicated, though the hulls could not yet be seen. As the first cutter approached nearer to the place, the outlines became more distinct and soon embodied themselves into definite objects. Both officers in the stern sheets watched with the most anxious vigilance for any moving object denoting the presence of life and intelligence.

As the boats came nearer to the shore, a breeze sprang up and cooled the air, for early as it was in the season, the weather was very warm, and it was not uncommon for the thermometer to rise above ninety. These breezes were usually present to cool the nights, and doubtless the inhabitants slept the sounder for the one which had just begun to fan the cheeks of the officers and seamen of the expedition.

"There is a battery there, Mr. Passford," said the pilot in a very low tone. "I can make it out now, and it is just where I supposed it would be."

"I can see something that seems like an earthwork at the right of the buildings," added Christy. "Can you make out anything that looks like a sentinel?"

"I can see nothing that denotes the presence of a man. If there were a sentinel there, he would be on the top of the earthwork, or on the highest ground about it, so that he could see out into the bay, for there can be no danger from the land side of the place," added Amblen.

"I can hardly imagine such a thing as a battery without a sentinel to give warning if anybody should try to carry it off. There must be a sentry somewhere in the vicinity."

"I can't say there isn't, though I can't make out a man, or anything that looks like one," replied the pilot.

"Very likely we shall soon wake him up, Mr. Amblen, and in that case it will be necessary for us to find a safer place than in front of the guns of the battery, for I do not feel at liberty to expose the men to the fire of the works, whatever they are."

"All you have to do is to pull around to the other side of the point into the bay, where the vessels are. I am confident there is no battery on that side, and there can hardly be any need of one, for this one commands the channel, the only approach to the place for a vessel larger than a cutter."

"I fancy this battery does not amount to much, and is probably nothing more than an earthwork with a few field guns behind it. Suppose we should wake it up and have to make for the bay, can we get out of it without putting the boats under the guns of the battery?"

"Without any difficulty at all, sir. We have only to pull around the north key and pass out to the Gulf, beyond the reach of any field gun that can be brought to bear on us," replied Mr. Amblen.

"If they have one or two field batteries here, they may hitch on the horses and follow us," suggested Christy, who, in spite of the audacity with which he had been mildly charged, was not inclined to run into any trap from which he could not readily withdraw his force.

"We shall have the short line, and if they pursue us with the guns, we can retire by the way of the channel, which they will leave uncovered."

"We are getting quite near the shore," continued Christy. "How is the water under us?"

"The bottom is sandy, and we shall take the ground before we reach the shore if we don't manage properly. But we can tell something by the mangroves that fringe the land," replied the pilot, "and I will go into the bow of the cutter and look out for them."

Mr. Amblen made his way to the fore sheets and asked Boxie, who was there, for the boathook, with which he proceeded to sound. When he had done so, he raised both his hands to a level with his shoulders, which was the signal to go ahead and the men pulled a very slow stroke. He continued to sound, after he had selected the point for landing.

When the first cutter was within three lengths of the shore, he elevated both his hands above his head, which was the signal to cease rowing, though the two bow oarsmen kept their oars in the water instead of boating them as the others did. Mr. Amblen continued to feel the way, and in a few minutes more, aided by the shoving of the two bow oarsmen, he brought the boat to the shore.

Then he gave his attention to the second cutter, bringing it to the land alongside of the first.

Stepping out on the sand himself, he was followed by all the crew, with cutlass in hand and revolvers in readiness for use. The men were placed in order for an advance, and then required to lie down on the sand, so that they could not readily be seen if any stroller appeared on the ground.

Leaving the force in charge of Mr. Flint, Christy and Amblen walked towards the battery, crouching behind such objects as they could find that would conceal them in whole or in part. The earthwork was semicircular in form, and was hardly more than a rifle pit. No sentinel could be discovered, and getting down upon the sand, the two officers crept cautiously towards the heaps of sand which formed the fort.

Christy climbed up the slope with some difficulty, for the dry sand afforded a very weak foothold. On the top of it, which was about six feet wide, they found a solid path which had evidently been a promenade for sentinels or other persons. Behind it, on a wooden platform, were four field guns with depressions in the earthwork in front of the muzzles.

Christy led the way down the slope on the inside to the pieces, which were twelve-pounders. At a little distance from the platform was a sort of casemate, which might have been constructed for a magazine, or for a place of resort for the gunners if the fort should be bombarded. Not a man could be seen, and if there was any garrison for the place, they were certainly taking things very comfortably, for they must have been asleep at this unseemly hour for any ordinary occupation.

Not far from the battery was a rude structure, hardly better than a shanty, which Christy concluded must be the barracks of the soldiers if there were any there. He walked over to it, but there was not a human being to be seen in the vicinity. It was half past one at night, when honest people ought to be abed and asleep, and the first lieutenant of the *Bronx* concluded that the garrison, if this shanty was their quarters, must be honest people.

Christy walked very cautiously to the side of the building, for the entrance was at the end nearest to the fort, and found several windows there, from which the sashes seemed to have been removed, if there had ever been any. The bottom of each opening was no higher than his head, and he went to one of them and looked in.

Extending along the middle of the interior was a row of berths. It was very dark inside, and he could not make out whether or not these bunks were occupied. The windows on the other side of the shanty enabled him to see that there were two rows of berths, each backing against the other. There were two in each tier, and he judged that the barrack would accommodate forty-eight men.

He retained his place at the window in order to discover any movement made by a sleeper that would inform him whether or not the berths were occupied. If there were any soldiers there, they were as quiet as statues, but while he was watching for a movement, he heard a decided snore. There was at least one man there, and he continued to hear his sonorous breathing as long as he remained at the window, which was the first on the side of the shanty.

Christy decided to push the investigation still farther, and he went to a window in the middle of the building. He regarded the berths with attention for a few minutes, but he could perceive no movement. He could hear two snorers who seemed to be competing with each other to see who could make the most noise.

If the berths were all occupied, three snorers were not a very great proportion in forty-eight. He was very anxious to ascertain if this was the number of soldiers in the place, but it was too dark in the shanty for him to determine whether or not the bunks were all in use. It was too many for him to encounter with his force of twenty men and three officers in the open field.

Christy returned to the end of the building and tried the door. It was not locked, and he decided to make use of a little of the audacity of which he was accused of having a good deal. Taking off his shoes and passing his sword to Mr. Amblen, he entered the barrack on tiptoe.

The boards of the floor began to creak under his weight; he stooped down and felt till he found the nail holes; then he knew that he was on a timber, and he walked the whole length of the shanty, returning on the opposite side, counting the occupied berths, for he passed within three feet of all of them. The count gave seventeen men as the number of sleepers, though this might not be all the force at the place.

He had ascertained all he wished to know, and he walked back to the shore where the men were concealed. Apart from the men, he had a conference with Flint and Amblen, giving them the details of what he had discovered. Then he stated his plan, and the men were marched silently to the battery, and were posted behind the breastwork. Not a man was allowed to move, and Christy and Flint went to the casemate, which looked like a mound of sand.

CHRISTY WALKED THE WHOLE LENGTH OF THE SHANTY

It was locked, but taking a bar of iron they found with some tools for digging, they tore off the padlock. A lantern had been brought from the steamer, which was lighted. The structure was found to be for the protection of the artillerists in the first instance, but the apartment was connected with the magazine, the lock of which was removed.

Amblen was sent for ten men, and all the ammunition they could carry was removed. The rest of it was thrown into a pool of water made by recent rains. The powder, solid shot, and shells were carried to the boats. The rest of the men drew the four guns to the shore, where one was placed, with its carriage, in each of the cutters, and the other two put where they could be carried to the *Bronx* or thrown overboard in deep water, as occasion might require.

The seventeen soldiers, reinforced by any that might be in the town, were thus deprived of the power to do any mischief except in a hand-to-hand fight. If the place was not actually captured, it was practically lost to the enemy. The next business of the expedition was to examine the bay and ascertain what vessels were at the landing place. The boats shoved off and pulled around the point.

Chapter XXIV

The two twelve-pounders in each boat were believed to weigh about six hundred pounds each, while the ordinary bronze boat gun of the same caliber weighs seven hundred and sixty pounds. The four guns, therefore, were rather too heavy a burden for the size of the cutters. But Christy was unwilling to throw the two without carriages overboard, for the water in this locality was so clear that they could have been seen at a depth of two or three fathoms. They were useless for the duty in which the expedition was engaged, and the commander of the expedition decided to land them on the Seahorse Key till he had completed his operations in the bay, when they could be taken off and transported to the *Bronx* as trophies, if for nothing better.

Mr. Flint was disposed to object to this plan, on account of the time it would require, but he yielded the point when Christy informed him that it was only half past two, as he learned from the repeater he carried for its usefulness on just such duty as the present expedition.

The guns and all that belonged to them were landed on the key, and the boats shoved off, the lieutenants happy in the thought that they were no longer embarrassed by their weight, while they could not be brought to bear upon them.

The boats had hardly left the little island behind them when the noise of paddle wheels ahead was reported by one of the trio in the bow of the first cutter. Christy listened with all his ears, and immediately heard the peculiar sounds caused by the slapping of the paddle wheels of a steamer upon the water.

"We are in for something," said he to the pilot, as he listened to the sounds. "What might that be?"

"It is a steamer, without any doubt, coming around the point, and she will be in sight in a moment or two," replied Mr. Amblen. "It may be a river steamer that has brought a load of cotton down the Suwanee, and is going out on this tide."

"Then we may need those guns we have left on

the key," suggested Christy.

"If she is a river steamer, there is not much of a force on board of her," replied the pilot.

"We might return to the island and use the two guns with carriages there."

"If she is a river steamer, we shall not need great guns to capture her."

Christy had ordered the men to cease rowing, and the two cutters lay motionless on the full sea, for the tide was at its height by this time. Even in the darkness they could make out whether the approaching vessel was a river or a sea steamer as soon as she could be seen.

"Whatever she is, we must capture her," said Christy very decidedly.

"If she is a river steamer, she will be of no use to the government," added Mr. Amblen.

"Of none at all," replied Christy. "In that case, I shall burn her, for it would not be safe to send good men in such a craft to a port where she could be condemned. The next question is, shall we take her here or nearer to the shore."

"The farther from the shore the better, I should say, Mr. Passford. After she passes the Seahorse Key, she will be in deep water for a vessel coming out of that port, and until she gets to the key, she will move very slowly, and we can board her better than when she is going at full speed," said Mr. Amblen.

"You are doubtless quite right, Mr. Amblen, and I shall adopt your suggestion," replied Christy. "There she comes, and she is no river steamer."

She had not the two tall funnels carried by river steamers, and that point was enough to settle her character. There could be no doubt she would have been a blockade runner, if there had been any blockade to run at the entrance to the port. Christy decided to board the steamer between the two keys, the channel passing between Snake and Seahorse. The first cutter fell back so that Christy could communicate with Mr. Flint, and he instructed him to take a position off the Snake Key, where his boat could not be discovered too soon, and board the steamer on the port side, though he did not expect any resistance. Each cutter took its position and awaited in silence the approach of the blockade runner. The only thing Christy feared was that she would come about and run back to the port, though this could only delay her capture.

The steamer, as well as the officers could judge her in the distance, was hardly larger than the *Bronx*. They concluded that she must be loaded with cotton, and at this time it was about as valuable a cargo as could be put on board of her. She would be a rich prize, and the masts of the schooners were still to be seen over the tops of the buildings. She must have chosen this hour of the night to go out, not only on account of the tide, but because the darkness would enable her to get off the coast where a blockader occasionally wandered before the blockade was fully established. Her paddle wheels indicated that she had not been built very recently, for very nearly all sea steamers, including those of the United States, were propelled by the screw.

As Mr. Amblen had predicted, the steamer moved very slowly, and it was all of a quarter of an hour before she came to the Seahorse Key. At the right time Christy gave the word to the crew to "Give way lively!" and the first cutter shot out from the concealment of the little island, while Flint did the same on the other side of the channel. Almost in the twinkling of an eye the two boats had made fast to her, and seven men from each boat leaped on the deck of the steamer, cutlass in hand. No guns were to be seen, and the watch of not more than half a dozen men were on the forecastle, and perhaps this was the entire force of the sailing department.

"What does all this mean?" demanded a man coming from the after part of the vessel, in a voice which Christy recognized as soon as he had heard half of the sentence.

"Good morning, Captain Lonley," said Christy in the pleasantest of tones. "You are up early, my friend, but I think we are a little ahead of you on this occasion."

"Who are you, sir?" demanded Lonley, and Christy had at once jumped to the conclusion that he was the captain of the steamer. "I have heard your voice before, but I cannot place you, sir."

"Fortunately for me, it is not necessary that you should place me this time," replied Christy. "It is equally fortunate that I am not compelled to place you again, as I felt obliged to do, on board of the *Judith* in Mobile Bay."

"Passford!" exclaimed Captain Lonley, stepping back a pace in his astonishment.

"Passford, late of the *Bellevite*, and now executive officer of the United States steamer *Bronx*, formerly the *Teaser*, privateer," answered Christy in his usual cheerful tones. "May I inquire the name of this steamer?"

"This steamer is the *Havana*," replied Captain Lonley. "May I ask you, Mr. Passford, in regard to your business on board of her?"

"I have a little affair on board of her, and my duty

compels me to demand her surrender as a prize to the *Bronx*."

"Caught again'" exclaimed Captain Lonley, stamping violently on the deck in his disgust at his misfortune, and it was the third time that Christy had thrown him "out of a job."

"The way of the transgressor is hard, Captain Lonley," added the commander of the expedition.

"Transgressor, sir!" exclaimed the captain of the *Havana*. "What do you mean by that, Mr. Passford?"

"Well, Captain, you are in arms against the best government that the good God ever permitted to exist for eighty odd years, and that is the greatest transgression of which one can be guilty in a patriotic sense."

"I hold no allegiance to that government."

"So much the worse for you, Captain Lonley, but we will not talk politics. Do you surrender?"

"This is not an armed steamer, and I have no force to resist; I am compelled to surrender," replied the captain as he glanced at the cutlasses of the men from the *Bronx*.

"That is a correct, though not a cheerful view of the question on your part. I am very happy to relieve you from any further care of the *Havana*, and you may retire to your cabin, where I shall have the honor to wait upon you later."

"One word, Mr. Passford, if you please," said Captain Lonley, taking Christy by the arm and leading him away from the rest of the boarding party. "This steamer and the cotton with which she is loaded are the property of your uncle, Homer Passford."

"Indeed?" was all that Christy thought it necessary to say in reply.

"You have already taken from him one valuable cargo of cotton, and it would be magnanimous in you, as well as very kind of a near relative, to allow me to pass on my way with the property of your uncle."

"Would it have been kind on the part of a near relative to allow his own brother to pass out of Mobile Bay in the *Bellevite*?"

"That would have been quite another thing, for the *Bellevite* was intended for the federal navy," protested the Confederate captain. "It would have been sacrificing his country to his fraternal feelings. This is not a Confederate vessel, and is not intended as a war steamer," argued Lonley.

"Every pound of cotton my uncle sells is so much strength added to the cause he advocates, and I hope, with no unkind thoughts or feelings in regard to him, I shall be able to capture every vessel he sends out. That is my view of the matter, and I am just as strong on my side of the question as Uncle Homer is on his side. I would cut off my right hand before I would allow your vessel or any other to escape, for I have sworn allegiance to my government, and when I fail to do my duty at any sacrifice of personal feeling, it will be when I have lost my mind, and my uncle would do as much for his fractional government. We need not discuss such a subject as you suggest, Captain."

Captain Lonley said no more and retired to his cabin. Christy was ready for the next question in order. Accompanied by Mr. Flint, he looked the steamer over. The mate had lighted his pipe and seated himself on a water cask, and he seemed to be the only officer besides the captain on board. The engineers were next visited. There were two of them, but they were red hot for the Confederacy, and nothing was said to them except to order them on deck, where they were placed with the crew and a guard of seamen set over them. The firemen were Negroes, and they were willing to serve under the new master, and doubtless were pleased with the change. The crew of the *Bronx* on board of the

Havana were canvassed to find a man who had run an engine, but not one of them had any experience.

"That's bad," said Flint, when they had finished the inquiry. "We have not an engineer on board, and we shall have to send off to the *Bronx* for one."

"Not so bad as that, Mr. Flint," replied Christy. "There is one loyal engineer on board, and I am the one. You will take the deck, and Mr. Amblen will go into the pilothouse. I am not quite ready to go off to the *Bronx* yet, for there are two or three cotton schooners in this port, and we are so fortunate as to have a steamer now to tow them out."

"Very likely those soldiers have waked up by this time," said Flint.

"Let them fire those guns at us, if they can find them," laughed Christy.

Then he took Mr. Amblen into the engine room with him.

Chapter XXV

The New Engineer of the Prize Steamer

While enthusiastically pursuing his studies as an engineer, Christy had visited a great many steamers with Paul Vapoor for the purpose of examining the engines, so that he could hardly expect to find one with whose construction he was not familiar, whether it was an American or a foreign built machine. At the first glance after he entered the engine room of the *Havana*, he knew the engine and was ready to run it without spending any time in studying it. He had brought the pilot with him in order to come to an understanding in regard to the bells, for in the navy the signals differ from those in the commercial marine.

"This steamer is provided with a gong and a jingling bell," said Christy, as he pointed them out to his companion.

"My little steamer on this coast was run with just such bells," replied Mr. Amblen.

"And so was the *Bellevite*, so that I am quite accustomed to the system of signals, but it is well to be sure that we understand each other perfectly if we expect to get this vessel out of the bay after we go up to the port," added Christy.

"I agree with you entirely, sir. A single strong stroke on the gong is to start or to stop her according to the circumstances," said the pilot.

"Precisely so, and two strokes are to back her," continued Christy. "Going at full speed, the jingler brings the engine down to half speed, or at half speed carries it up to full speed."

"That is my understanding of the matter," replied Mr. Amblen.

"Then we understand each other to a charm," continued the temporary engineer. "Report to Mr. Flint that we are ready to go ahead."

Christy found a colored man who was on duty as an oiler, and four others in the fire room, who seemed to be engaged in an earnest discussion of the situation, for the capture of the *Havana* was a momentous event to all of them. The oiler was at work and had thoroughly lubricated the machinery, as though he intended that any failure of the steamer should not be from any fault on his part.

The new official set two of the firemen at work, though the boilers had a good head of steam. The gong bell gave one sharp stroke, and Christy started the engine.

The *Havana* was headed out to sea when she was captured, and in the slack water she had not drifted at all. He went ahead slowly, and soon had the bell to stop her, but he expected this, for the channel was narrow, and it required considerable maneuvering to get the steamer about. Then he happened to think of the guns on the Seahorse Key, and through the speaking tube he passed the word to Mr. Flint to have him land there in order to take the guns and ammunition on board.

After a great deal of backing and going ahead, the *Havana* was headed for the key, where she was stopped as near to it as the depth of water would permit. The guns and other material were brought off, two of the firemen, the oiler, and other colored men of the crew of the *Havana* assisting in the work. The two guns that were provided with carriages were mounted and placed on the forecastle. They were loaded and prepared for service by the trained gunners of the crew. Christy had directed all this to be done on account of the delay which had attended the good fortune of the expedition, for he might not get out of the bay before the daylight came to reveal the presence of the force he commanded to the people on the shore.

The gong rang again when all these preparations had been made, and the *Havana* steamed slowly up the channel towards the bay. The oiler appeared to have finished his work for the present. He was a more intelligent man than the others in the engine room and seemed to understand his duties. Christy spoke to him, for he said nothing unless he was spoken to, and he had learned that the commander of the expedition was doing duty as engineer in the absence of any other competent person.

"How many schooners are there at the landing place at the keys?" asked Christy.

"Only two schooners, sir," replied the man very respectfully.

"Are they loaded—what is your name?" asked the engineer.

"My name is Dolly, sir."

"Dolly? That is a girl's name."

"My whole name is Adolphus, sir, but everybody calls me Dolly, and I can't help myself," replied the oiler soberly, as though he had a real grievance on account of the femininity of his nickname. "The two schooners are not quite loaded, sir, but they are very nearly full. They had some trouble here, among the hands."

"Had some trouble, did they? I should think there were soldiers enough here to keep everything straight. How many artillerists or soldiers do they keep here?" added Christy.

"They had about forty, but they don't have half that number now."

"What has become of them?"

"They were sent away to look for the hands that took to the woods. One of the officers and about half of the men were sent off yesterday," replied Dolly, who seemed willing to tell all he knew.

"Why did the men run off?" asked Christy curiously.

"They brought about fifty hands, all slaves, down here to load the steamer and the schooners. They set them at work yesterday morning, and they had nearly put all the cotton into the schooners at dinner time. To make the slaves work harder, they gave them apple jack."

"What is that?" asked the engineer, who never heard the name before.

"It is liquor made out of apples, and it is very strong," answered Dolly, and he might have added that it was the vilest intoxicant to be found in the whole world, not even excepting Russian vodka.

"And this liquor made the hands drunk, I suppose."

"They did not give them enough for that, sir, but it made them kind of crazy, and they wanted more of it. That made the trouble; the hands struck for liquor before dinner, and when they didn't get it, they took to the woods, about fifty of them. The soldiers had to get their dinner before they would start out after them, and that is the reason the schooners are not full now, sir, and not a bale had been put into this steamer."

"But she seems to be fully loaded now."

"Yes, sir; Captain Lonley paid the soldiers that were left to load the *Havana*. They worked till eleven in the evening; they were not used to that kind of work, and they got mighty tired, I can tell you," said Dolly, with the first smile Christy had seen on his yellow face, for he appeared to enjoy the idea of a squad of white men doing Negroes' work.

"That was what made them sleep so soundly and leave the battery on the point to take care of itself," said Christy. "Where were the officers?"

"Two of them have gone on the hunt for the hands, and I reckon the captain is on a visit to a planter who has a daughter, about forty miles from here."

"The soldiers were sleeping very soundly in the barrack about two this morning, and perhaps they were also stimulated with apple jack," added Christy. "Did you drink any of it, Dolly?"

"No, sir, I never drink any liquor, for I am a preacher," replied the oiler with a very serious and solemn expression on his face.

"How do you happen to be a greaser on a steamer if you are a preacher?"

"I worked on a steamer on the Alabama River before I became a preacher, and I took it up again. I was raised in a preacher's family and worked in the house."

He talked as though he had been educated, but he could neither read nor write, and had picked up all his learning by the assistance of his ears alone. But Christy had ascertained all he wished to know in regard to the schooners, and he was prepared to carry out his mission in the bay. At the fort, it appeared that all the commissioned officers were absent from the post, and the men, after exhausting themselves at work to which they were unaccustomed, had taken to their bunks and were sleeping off the fatigue, and perhaps the effects of the apple jack. While he was thinking of the matter, the gong struck, and Christy stopped the engine.

"Do you know anything about an engine, Dolly?" he asked, turning to the oiler.

"Yes, sir; I run the engine of the *Havana* over here from Mobile," replied Dolly. "I can do it as well as anyone, if they will only trust me."

"Then stand by the machine and obey the bells if they are struck," added Christy, as he went on deck.

He found the second and third lieutenants standing on the rail engaged in examining the surroundings. The day was just beginning to show itself in the east, though it was not yet light enough to enable them to see clearly on shore. By the side of the railroad building was a pier, at which the two schooners lay. They could hear the sounds of some kind of a stir on shore, but were unable to make out what it meant.

"We are losing time," said Christy, as he took in at a glance all he deemed it necessary to know in regard to the situation.

"I was about to report to you, Mr. Passford, but Mr. Amblen wished to ascertain whether or not there is a battery on this side of the point," said Flint.

"Do you find anything, Mr. Amblen?"

"No, sir; I can see nothing that looks like a battery," replied the pilot.

"Then run in, and we will make fast to these schooners and haul them out," added Christy in hurried tones.

The pilot went to the wheel and rang one bell on the gong. Dolly started the engine before Christy could reach the machine. He said nothing to the oiler, but seated himself on the sofa and observed his movements. A few minutes later came the bell to stop her, and then two bells to back her. Dolly managed the machine properly and promptly, and seemed to be at home in the engine room. The color of his skin was a sufficient guarantee of his loyalty, but Christy remained below long enough to satisfy himself that Dolly knew what he was about, and then went on deck.

By this time the noise on shore had become more pronounced, and he saw the dark forms of several persons on the wharf. Flint and Amblen were making fast to the nearest schooner, and a couple of seamen had been sent on shore to cast off the fasts which held her to the wharf. This was the work of but a moment, and the two men returned to the steamer, but they were closely followed by two men, one of whom stepped on the deck of the schooner.

"What are you about here?" demanded the foremost of the men in a rude and impertinent manner.

"About our business," replied Christy with cool indifference.

"Who are you, young man?" demanded the one on the deck.

"I am yours truly; who are you?"

"None of your business who I am! I asked you a question, and you will answer it if you know when you are well off," blustered the man, who was rather too fat to be dangerous, and by this time, Christy discovered that he wore something like a uniform.

"I will try to find out when I am well off, and then I will answer you," replied Christy.

"All fast, sir," reported Flint.

The commander of the expedition, turning his back to the fat man, went forward to the pilothouse.

Chapter XXVI

The Battle with the Soldiers

Mr. Amblen went to the pilothouse and rang two bells. Dolly responded properly by starting the engine on the reverse, and the schooner alongside began to move away from the wharf, for the stern of the *Havana* pointed out into the bay.

"Stop, there! What are you about?" shouted the fat man on the deck of the schooner.

"About going," replied Christy.

"These vessels are the property of a citizen of the Confederate states, and I command you to stop," yelled the fat man with all the voice he could muster.

"All right," replied Christy, as the gong sounded to stop her. "Now, Mr. Flint, cast off the fasts and let the schooner go astern," he added to the second lieutenant.

"All clear, sir," replied Flint a moment later, and

after the steamer lost her headway, the vessel continued to back, though the *Havana* was checked by the engine.

The fat man went adrift in the schooner, but Christy gave no further attention to him. The steamer was started ahead again; her bow was run alongside of the other vessel at the wharf, and Flint proceeded in the same manner as with the first one.

"Orderly!" shouted the fat man, evidently addressing the man who had come to the schooner with him, and had retreated to the wharf when the vessel began to move.

"Captain Rowly!" replied the man, who was doubtless the orderly sergeant of the company.

"Go to the barracks and have the men haul the four field pieces over to the wharf," yelled the fat captain.

"All right, little one! Have them hauled over by all means," said Christy, as the men made fast to the other schooner and cast off the fasts.

But it was soon evident that the sleepy soldiers had been roused from their slumbers by some other agency than the orderly, though it was not quite possible for them to haul over the four guns, as they happened to be on the forward deck of the *Havana*. But the men were armed with muskets, and were capable of doing a great deal of mischief with them. Christy hurried up the men at the fasts, but they had about finished their task.

"All clear, Mr. Passford," called Mr. Flint as the soldiers double-quicked across the railroad to the wharf, upon which there was still a huge pile of bales of cotton.

"Back her, Mr. Amblen," said Christy, as he hastened aft to avoid a collision with the other schooner.

But the tide had begun to recede, and had carried the first vessel to a safe distance from the wharf.

The soldiers reached the edge of the wharf, and were probably under the command of the orderly by this time. At any rate, they marched farther down the pier, where they could be nearer to the *Havana* as she backed away. Then the troops fired a volley at the steamer, but in the darkness they did no serious injury to the party, though two seamen were slightly wounded.

"Cast off the fasts!" shouted Christy when he realized that some of his men were in a fair way to be shot down before they could get the two schooners alongside and properly secured for the trip to the *Bronx*, and the order was promptly obeyed. "Now, check her, Mr. Amblen," and two bells were sounded on the gong, after one to stop her.

The second schooner kept on her course out into the bay to join the first one cast loose, but Christy feared that they might get aground, and give them trouble. The seventeen soldiers whom he had counted in their bunks appeared to have been reinforced either by the return of the absent party, or by the civilians in the place, for they presented a more formidable front than the smaller number could make. Whatever the number of the defenders of the place, they could harass the expedition while the men were preparing for the final departure.

"With what were those two guns charged, Mr. Flint?" asked Christy.

"With solid shot, sir," replied the second lieutenant.

"Open fire on the wharf, and then load with the shrapnel," added Christy.

The two guns, which had been placed in proper position for use on the top-gallant forecastle, were aimed by Flint himself and discharged. The report shook the steamer, and Christy, who retained his position on the quarterdeck, heard a scream of terror, coming from a female, issue from the companionway, at the head of which a seaman had been placed as a sentinel over the officers below.

"What was that, Neal?" asked the commander of the expedition.

"It was the scream of a lady, sir, and that is all I know about it," replied the man. "I haven't seen any lady, sir, and I think she must have been asleep so far. The captain tried to come on deck a while ago, but I sent him back, sir."

By this time the two field pieces had been loaded again, and they were discharged. Christy watched the effect, and he had the pleasure of seeing the whole troop on the wharf retire behind the great pile of bales of cotton. A random fire was kept up from this defense, but the soldiers were safe behind their impenetrable breastwork. Flint continued to fire into it.

At the report of the guns, nearly together which made the *Havana* shake and everything on board of her rattle, for she was not built to carry a battery of guns, another scream came forth from the companionway. A moment later, Christy saw a female form ascending the stairs. The sentinel placed his cutlass across the passage, but the lieutenant told him to let her come on deck if she desired to do so.

It was light enough for the gallant young officer to see that she was young and fair, though she had evidently dressed herself in great haste. She looked around her with astonishment, perhaps to find that the steamer was no longer at the wharf. The guns on the forecastle were again discharged, and she shrunk back at the sound.

"Do not be alarmed, Miss," said Christy, in his gentlest tones. "But I must say that you will be safer in the cabin than on deck."

"Will you please to tell me what has happened, sir, or what is going to happen?" asked the lady, and the listener thought he had never heard a sweeter voice, though he might not have thought so if he had heard it at Bonnydale, or anywhere else except in the midst of the din of pealing guns and the rattling of musketry.

"I can tell you what has happened, but as I am not a prophet, I cannot so accurately inform you in regard to what is going to happen," he replied.

"But what has occurred on board of the *Havana*?" she interposed, rather impatiently.

"The *Havana* has been captured by an expedition, of which I have the honor to be in command, from the United States gunboat *Bronx*. Just now we are defending ourselves from an attack of the soldiers in the place. As to the future, Miss, I have no reasonable doubt that we shall be able to get the steamer and two schooners we have also captured alongside the *Bronx*, where all the prizes will be subject to the order of her commander. Permit me to advise you to retire to the cabin, Miss, and later, I shall be happy to give you all the information in my power," said Christy, touching his cap to her and pointing to the companionway.

She accepted the advice and went down the steps. The young officer had no time then to wonder who and what she was, for he realized that there was little hope of stopping the desultory firing, from behind the cotton pile, and perhaps by this time the soldiers realized what had become of their four field pieces, for they knew that the *Havana* had not been armed when they loaded her with cotton.

Christy went forward to set the officers at work in picking up the two prizes, and as he stopped to look down into the engine room, he felt his cap knocked off his head and heard the whizzing of a bullet unpleasantly near his ears. He picked up his cap and found a bullet hole through the top of it. If it had gone an inch or two lower, Mr. Flint would have succeeded to the command of the expedition without any ceremonies. Though there was no reason for it, this incident seemed to provoke him, for it assured him that he could not pick up his prizes without exposing his men to this nasty firing for some time longer.

It was now light enough for him to make out the situation of the breastwork of cotton, and he saw that it was a long and narrow pile, probably near a siding of the railroad where the bales had been unloaded from the cars. Another glance at the surroundings in regard to the point enabled him to make up his mind what to do, and he did not lose a moment in putting his plan into execution. The firing of shot and shrapnel at the cotton pile seemed to produce no adequate effect, and he ordered Flint to cease his operations.

"Back her, Mr. Amblen," he added to the pilot. "Back her at full speed."

The schooners were doing very well; instead of wandering off into the bay, they had fallen into the channel and were drifting with the tide. Several persons appeared on the deck of each of them, and it was plain that a portion of the crews had been asleep on board of them. While he was observing them, he discovered two boats coming out from behind the point, and making for the two vessels. This movement indicated an attempt to recapture the prizes.

"Port the helm, Mr. Amblen, and circle around till the bow points in the direction of those boats coming out from beyond the point," said Christy.

"Mr. Flint, man your guns again at once, and drop some solid shot into those boats."

The *Havana* continued to back till the guns would bear on the boats, and then Flint delivered his fire. The headmost of the boats was smashed, and was a wreck on the bay. The other hastened to pick up the crew, and then pulled for the shore with all possible speed, though not till two other boats, apparently filled with soldiers, were discovered approaching the retreating boat.

Christy did not wait to dispose of these, but mounted the topgallant forecastle and ordered the guns to be loaded with shells. Then he waited till the steamer reached a point off the end of the peninsula, when he gave the order to stop and back her. Sighting the first gun himself, he directed the man at the lockstring to fire. He waited a moment for the smoke to clear away, and then, with his glass, he saw several forms lying on the wharf by the side of the cotton pile. He had fired so as to rake the rear of this breastwork and before the soldiers there understood what he was doing. Those who had not dropped before the fire were picking up their wounded companions and retreating with all practicable haste.

It was not necessary to discharge the other gun, and it was swung round and brought to bear on the two boats advancing towards the prizes, the men in which were pulling with the most desperate haste. Flint took careful aim this time, and the gun was discharged. The shrapnel with which it was charged did not knock the boat to pieces as a solid shot might have done, but two of the oars were seen to drop into the water, and both boats began to retreat, which was quite a proper thing for them to do in face of such a destructive fire.

There was nothing more to detain the expedition at the place, and the two prizes were picked up, made fast, one on each side of the *Havana*, and then the bell to go ahead was sounded. The pilot then informed Christy that he had made out the *Bronx* approaching at a distance of not more than three miles beyond the Seahorse Key. Probably, Captain Blowitt had heard the guns and was coming in to assist in the fight.

Chapter XXVII

The Innocent Captain of the Garrison

The firing of the musketry was continued from the end of the point by a small squad of soldiers, though the most of them seemed to have gone over to the other side of the peninsula to take part in the attempt to recapture the schooners with boats, which had utterly failed. It was now fairly light, the battle had been fought, and the boat expedition had done all and more than all it had been expected to accomplish.

Christy had hardly expected to do anything more than obtain information that would enable the *Bronx* to capture the schooners, and nothing had been said about the steamer that had been found there. It appeared from the statement of Captain Lonley that the *Havana* was the property of his uncle, Homer Passford, and doubtless he had chosen Cedar Keys as a safer place, at this stage of the war, to send out his cotton than the vicinity of his plantation.

Christy certainly had no desire to capture the property of his father's brother rather than that of any other Confederate planter, for he had had no knowledge of his operations in Florida. But he was quite as patriotic on his own side as his uncle was on the other side, and as it was his duty to take or destroy the goods of the enemy, he was not sorry he had been so fortunate, though he did regret that Homer Passford had been the principal sufferer from the visit of the *Bronx* to this coast.

The planter had now lost three schooners and one steamer loaded with cotton, but Christy was satisfied that this would not abate by one jot or tittle his interest in the cause he had espoused. The young man did not think of such a thing as punishing him for taking part in the rebellion, for he knew that Homer would be all the more earnest in his faith because he had been a financial martyr on account of his devotion to it.

The *Havana*, with one of the schooners on each side of her, was steaming slowly down the channel, and the *Bronx* was approaching at a distance of not more than three miles. For the first time since he obtained possession of the prizes, he had an opportunity to look them over and collect his thoughts. From the very beginning of the enterprise he had been extremely anxious in regard to the result.

His orders had been to obtain all the information he could in regard to the position of the vessels that were reported to be at this port, and to do anything the circumstances would permit without incurring too much risk. The adventure had been full of surprises from first to last. Something new and sometimes something strange had been continually exposed to him, and it looked to him just as though all the preparations to accomplish the result he had achieved had been made for his coming.

Before the boats went around into the bay, he had been satisfied with the finding and carrying off of the twelve-pounders. He had hardly expected to do anything more, and he knew that Captain Blowitt would be amused as well as pleased at this rather singular feat. The removal of the four field pieces had rendered the capture of the schooners possible and even easy, as it would not have been if the order of Captain Rowly to drag them over to the wharf could have been carried out.

The taking of the *Havana* had been rather a side incident, hardly connected with the rest of the affair.

Everything had favored the young commander of the expedition, and he had made good use of his opportunities, though he had embraced some of them blindly, without being able to foresee the consequences of his action at the time it was taken. He had time now to review the events of the morning, and the result was in the highest degree pleasing to him.

On board of the two schooners the crew had put in an appearance, but when he inquired of the Negroes, he learned that the captains of the vessels were not on board. The mate of each was on deck, and they were the only white men. On the rail of the one on the port side sat the fat captain of the garrison of the place. Thus far he had said nothing, and he appeared to be sitting figuratively on the stool of repentance, for he had not been faithful to the trust reposed in him.

Dolly had said he had gone to visit a planter who had a daughter, but this statement did not appear to be true, for he had put in an appearance early, as the *Havana* was making fast to the first prize. He had left his men in the barrack to sleep off their fatigue and apple jack after their unaccustomed labor in loading the steamer. He had not so much as posted a sentinel, who might have enabled him to defeat the invaders of the port, even with his diminished force. If Homer Passford had been on the spot, his faith in the Providence that watched over his holy cause might have been shaken.

"Good morning, Captain Rowly," said Christy cheerfully, as he walked up to the disconsolate captain. "I hope you are feeling quite well."

"Not very well; things are mixed," replied the fat officer, looking down upon the planks of the deck.

"Mixed, are they?" added Christy.

"I can't see how it all happened," mused the military gentleman.

"How what happened, Captain Rowly?" inquired Christy.

"All the vessels in the place captured and carried off," exclaimed the late commander of the garrison.

"I don't discover the least difficulty in explaining how it all happened. You were so very obliging as to allow your men to go to sleep in the barrack without even posting a sentinel at the battery. That made the whole thing as easy as tumbling off a sawhorse," replied the leader of the expedition, without trying to irritate the repentant captain of the forces.

"And, like an infernal thieving Yankee, you went into the fort and stole the guns!" exclaimed Captain

Rowly, beginning to boil with rage as he thought of his misfortune.

"Well, it did not occur to me that I ought to have waked you and told you what I was about before taking the guns."

"It was a nasty Yankee trick!" roared the soldier.

"I suppose it was, Captain, but we Yankees cannot very well help what was born in our blood, and I have heard that some of your honest and high-toned people have made bigger steals than this one. While I have carried off only four twelve-pounders, your folks have taken entire forts, including scores of guns of all calibers," replied Christy, amused at the view the fat gentleman took of his operations.

"Our people took nothing that did not belong to them, for the forts were within our territory," retorted the soldier.

"That was just my case. I have the honor to be an officer of the United States Navy, and as these guns happened to be within the territory of our government, of course it was all right that I should take them."

"You stole the vessels after I ordered you to stop," muttered Captain Rowly.

"Precisely so, but, being in a hurry just then, I hadn't time to stop," laughed Christy.

"Where are you going now? You knew I was on the deck of this schooner, and you have brought me off here where I didn't want to come. I am not used to the water, and I am afraid I shall get sea sick," continued the fat officer.

"Perhaps we may be able to provide a nurse for you if you are very sick."

"Why don't you answer my question and tell me where you are going?" demanded the soldier.

"We are going out here a mile or two farther, just to take the air and get up an appetite for breakfast."

"But I object!"

"Do you indeed?"

"And I protest!"

"Against what?"

"Against being carried off in this way. You knew I was on board of the schooner."

"I confess that I did know you were on board, though I must add that it was your own fault."

"I had a right on board of the vessel."

"I don't deny it. You have a sword at your side, but as you neglected to use it, you will excuse me if I ask you to give it to me," added Christy, reaching out for the weapon.

"Give you my sword!" exclaimed Captain Rowly.

CAPTAIN ROWLY PROTESTS

"It is a formality rather insisted upon on such occasions as the present."

"I don't see it."

"You don't? Then I must say that I think you are rather obtuse, Captain Rowly, and I shall be under the painful necessity of helping you to see it. As a prisoner of war—"

"As what?" demanded the soldier.

"I regard you as a prisoner of war, and I must trouble you to give me your sword in token of your surrender."

"I was not taken in a battle."

"Very true; your men fought the battle after you had left them. I have no more time to argue the question. Will you surrender your sword, or will you have the battle now? Two or three of my men will accommodate you with a fight on a small scale if you insist upon it."

"Don't you intend to send me back to the keys?" asked the captain, whose military education appeared to have been neglected, so that his ideas of a state of war were very vague.

"I have not the remotest idea of doing anything of the sort. Your sword, if you please."

"This sword was presented to me by the citizens of my town—"

"Here, Boxie and Lanon, relieve this gentleman of his sword," added Christy, as he saw the young lady coming up the companionway.

"Oh, I will give it up, if you really say so, but this is a queer state of things when my sword, presented to me by my fellow citizens, is to be taken from me without any warrant of law," said Captain Rowly, as he handed the sword to Christy, who returned it when it had done its duty as a token of submission.

The prisoner was marched to the forecastle of the *Havana* and put under guard. Christy walked towards the young lady, who had evidently dressed herself for the occasion. She was not only young, but she was beautiful, and the young commander of the expedition was strongly impressed by her grace and loveliness. He had heard her speak in the gloom of the early morning, and she had a silvery voice. He could not but wonder what she was doing on board of a blockade runner.

"Good morning, Miss—I have not the pleasure of being able to call you by name," Christy began as he touched his cap to her and bowed his involuntary homage.

"Miss Pembroke," she added.

"I trust you are as comfortable as the circumstances will permit, Miss Pembroke. I hope you have ceased to be alarmed, as you were when I saw you before."

"I am not alarmed, but I am exceedingly anxious in regard to the future, Mr.—"

"Mr. Passford."

"I only wish to know what is to become of us, Mr. Passford."

"You speak in the plural, Miss Pembroke, as though you were not alone."

"I am not alone, sir; my father, who is an invalid, is in the cabin. The excitement of this morning has had a bad effect upon him."

"I am sorry to hear it. I suppose you embarked in this steamer with the desire to reach some other place?"

"We reside in the state of New York, and all that remain of our family are on board of this steamer, and all we desire is to get home. We have lived two years in southern Georgia for my father's health."

Christy thought they would be able to reach New York.

Chapter XXVIII

The Bearer of Dispatches

Christy had assured himself that the father of the beautiful young lady was a loyal citizen, and then he pointed out to her in what manner they might reach their home, which was at Newburgh on the Hudson. Mr. Pembroke was not a wealthy man, though he had the means of supporting what was left of his family comfortably. But Christy had to ask to be excused, as the *Bronx* was but a short distance from the *Havana*.

He directed Mr. Amblen to stop her, so as to permit the gunboat to come alongside of her. As the *Bronx* came within hailing distance of the steamer towing the schooners, a hearty cheer burst from the crew on the forecastle of the former, for the prizes alongside of the *Havana* indicated the success of the expedition. The sea was smooth, and the naval steamer came alongside of the port schooner, and Christy, who had put himself in position to do so as soon as he understood her intention, sprang lightly on board of her.

Captain Blowitt was on the quarterdeck, and the commander of the expedition hastened into his presence. Of course Christy could not help realizing that he had been successful, however the circumstances had aided him, and he felt sure of his welcome.

The commander of the *Bronx* was a man that weighed two hundred pounds, and his fat cheeks were immediately distended with laughter as soon as he saw his executive officer hastening towards him. He almost doubled himself up in his mirth as he looked into the young man's sober face, for Christy was struggling to appear as dignified as the importance of the occasion seemed to require of him. But the commander restrained himself as much as he could and extended his hand to the first lieutenant, which the young man accepted, and received a pressure that was almost enough to crush his feebler paw. In spite of himself, he could not help laughing in sympathy with his superior.

"I am sorry you did not bring it all off with you,

Mr. Passford," said Captain Blowitt as soon as he was able to speak, for his risibility seemed to have obtained complete control of him.

"I have brought it all off with me, Captain," replied Christy, though he had not yet got at the point of the joke and spoke at a venture.

"What, the whole state of Florida!" exclaimed the commander.

"No, sir; I did not bring it all off with me, for I did not think it would be quite safe to do this, for it might set the Gulf Stream to running in a new course and derange navigation by making all our charts useless," replied Christy, smoothing down the muscles of his face so that he looked as sober as before.

"I thought from the appearance that you had brought it all off," added Captain Blowitt. "Did I instruct you to bring it off?"

"No, sir; you were considerate enough to say that you did not expect me to capture the whole state, and therefore I have not done it."

"But we heard heavy guns this morning," continued the commander, putting on his sober face, for he could be as serious as a judge, though his adipose structure compelled him to be a great joker at suitable times. "You had no boat guns."

"No, sir, but we picked up four twelve-pounder field pieces, which you see, two of them on carriages, on the forecastle of that steamer. We found the garrison asleep, and we carried off the four guns with which the battery was mounted. We put them on the Seahorse Key and went into the bay to see what was there, sir. We found two schooners, and on the way we took the steamer. When we were hauling out the two schooners, the garrison woke up and attempted to drive us off with musketry. We beat them off and sunk two boats with the field pieces. This is my report in brief."

"And a very good report it is, Mr. Passford. I did not expect you to do anything more than bring off full information in regard to the situation at the port," added Captain Blowitt.

"But you ordered me to do anything I could to prepare the way for a visit from the *Bronx*," suggested Christy.

"And you have prepared the way by bringing off everything at the port, so that there is nothing for the *Bronx* to do there," said the commander with a smile.

"When I found that the garrison were all asleep, I thought it was my duty not to lose the opportunity that was thus presented to me. Everything was in our favor, and I was led to do one thing after another till there was nothing more to do. I found that Captain Lonley, the worthy gentleman who had made prisoners of Mr. Flint and myself on Santa Rosa Island, was in command of the steamer. He was not glad to see me, and from him I learned that the *Havana*, which is her name, belonged to my Uncle Homer, and so did the schooners."

"Then your uncle has a heavy charge against you, for you have now taken four of his vessels."

"Possibly the Confederate government is behind him in this operation. I don't know, but I am sure that the loss of every dollar he has in the world would not change his views in regard to the justice of his cause. But, Captain Blowitt, there are on board of the *Havana* a gentleman and his daughter, who reside in Newburgh. He is an invalid and a loyal citizen," continued Christy, as he happened to see Miss Pembroke on the quarterdeck of the steamer.

"They wish to go home, I suppose, and there will soon be an opportunity for them to do so," replied the captain, as he went with his lieutenant to take a look at the prizes.

He gave particular attention to the *Havana*, which it was said had been built to run between Cedar Keys and the port for which she had been named, in connection with the railroad. She appeared to be a good vessel of about four hundred tons, which was as large as the navigation of the channel to the port would permit. She was not fit for war purposes in her present condition, and Captain Blowitt decided to send her to New York. Most of the hands on board of the three prizes were Negroes, who were too happy to go to the North.

"Sail, ho!" shouted the lookout on board of the *Bronx*, while the commander was still discussing his plans with Christy.

"Where away?" demanded the captain.

"Coming down from the northwest," reported a quartermaster.

Captain Blowitt hastened on board of the *Bronx*, for it did not yet appear whether the vessel was a friend or an enemy. She was a steamer, and she left a thin streak of black smoke in the sky, which indicated that her coal came from British territory.

The *Havana* and the schooners were left in charge of Mr. Amblen, after the prisoners had been properly disposed of in safe places. Mr. Spinnet, the second assistant engineer, was sent on board of her, for the commander had not full confidence in Dolly, though he permitted him to remain as assistant. The boats used by the expedition were hoisted up to the davits, and the first and second lieutenants were ordered to return to the *Bronx*, and only six seamen were left on board to guard the prisoners, of whom Lonley was the only dangerous one at all likely to make trouble.

The *Bronx* steamed off at her best speed in the direction of the approaching steamer, which appeared to be fast, and to be of that peculiarly rakish class of vessels of which there were so many engaged in the business of blockade running. She was examined by the officers with their glasses, but they were unable to make her out. Her ensign was set on a stern pole, but they could not see whether it was the American or the Confederate flag.

"What do you make of her, Mr. Passford?" asked the captain, as they watched her advance over the smooth sea.

"She is or has been a blockade runner, and that is all I can make out of her," replied Christy.

"She may have run the blockade, fitted in Mobile or some other port as a cruiser, and come out to do what mischief she can. We may have to fight for our prizes, but the splinters will fly before she gets them away from us," said Captain Blowitt, who watched the steamer with an anxious look on his face, resolute as he was in the discharge of his duty. "She is considerably larger than the *Bronx*."

"As I make her out, she looks something like the *Ocklockonee* and the *Escambia*, which we sent to New York, though they had but one smokestack each while this one has two. They were about five hundred tons, and I should think this vessel was of very nearly the same size," added Christy.

"Flies the American flag, sir," reported a quartermaster who had been sent into the main rigging to observe her.

"That may be a trick," said the captain, "though I hardly think it is, for she is larger than the *Bronx*, and need not resort to tricks."

A little later, she began to hoist her signals on the foremast where they could be plainly seen. Mr. Flint made them out to the effect that the steamer had orders for the *Bronx*. This settled the question, and there was no more anxiety in regard to her, and there was to be no sea fight for the possession of the prizes.

In less than half an hour the two steamers were within hailing distance of each other, and the stranger sent off a boat with an officer as soon as both vessels had stopped their screws and lost their headway. As Christy watched the approaching boat, he recognized the chief engineer of the *Bellevite* in the stern sheets. It was Paul Vapoor, his old friend and crony, who waved his cap as soon as he discovered the first lieutenant. The boat came to the side, and Paul mounted the accommodation ladder. He was a demonstrative young man, and he embraced Christy as though he had been a Frenchman, as soon as he reached the deck. He touched his cap to Captain Blowitt, and then delivered several huge envelopes to him, and also a dispatch bag.

"Bearer of dispatches, sir," said the chief engineer of the *Bellevite*.

"I see you are, Mr. Vapoor. If you will make yourself at home on board of the *Bronx*, I will read these papers in my cabin," said the captain, as he went below.

"I think Mr. Passford and I shall not waste any time while you are engaged, Captain," replied Mr. Vapoor.

Certain personal and social matters had to be spoken of, and Paul had to ask about Florry Passford first, and Christy's father and mother afterwards, though there was no news to tell.

"What are those vessels off there, Christy?" asked Paul, pointing to the *Havana* and the schooners.

"They are our prizes," replied the first lieutenant.

"Did you have to fight for them?"

"A little, not much. What steamer is that in which you came, Paul?"

"Our prize," replied Paul, with a smile as though he knew more than he was permitted to tell. "We had an awful fight to get her, but we got her all the same. Poor Mr. Dashington was badly wounded, and he may not get over it."

"I am sorry to hear that. Where was the fight?" asked Christy.

"About a hundred miles off the entrance to Mobile Bay. We were sent to look out for her on account of our speed. She came out, and seemed to think she was going to have her own way. We overhauled her and captured her by boarding."

"Captain Blowitt wishes to see Lieutenant Passford and Mr. Vapoor in his cabin," said Dave, coming up to them at this moment, and both of them hastened to obey the summons.

"Take seats, gentlemen," said the commander, as he pointed to chairs at the table at which he was seated. "I am ordered back to the *Bellevite* as first lieutenant, for poor Dashington has been seriously wounded. Mr. Passford is ordered to New York in the *Vixen*, which brings these dispatches, for she must be condemned. Mr. Flint is ordered to the temporary command of the *Bronx*, though I am unable to understand why it is made temporary. You are to convoy several vessels at Key West in the *Vixen*, which is fully armed and has a sufficient crew."

Christy was never more astonished in all his life.

Chapter XXIX

"Have I done anything to offend the flag officer, or has he no confidence in me?" asked Christy, who heard in utter surprise that he was ordered to New York in command of the *Vixen*.

"Certainly not, Mr. Passford," replied Captain Blowitt with a deprecatory smile which was almost enough to satisfy the young officer.

"What could have put such an idea as that into your head?"

"It looked to me just as though I was sent away simply as a prize-master because my services were not needed down here where there is fighting, and is likely to be a great deal more of it," added Christy, not yet quite satisfied. "Perhaps I am banished for the crime of audacity."

"That is a little too bad, Christy," said the

commander, shaking his head. "I promised not to use that word again and you ought not to twit me for it, for it was only a pleasantry on my part."

"It was the farthest thing in the world from my mind to twit you for the word; I was only afraid that they considered me an imprudent officer on board of the flagship. I beg your pardon, Captain Blowitt, and I will never again remind you of the conversation we had on the subject of audacity," answered Christy, rising from his chair and taking the commander by the hand.

"It is all right, Christy, my dear fellow," replied the captain, coming down from the dignified manner of the navy. "I think we understand each other perfectly, and I don't wish to part with the shadow of a shadow between us. We have sailed together too long to be anything but the best of friends, and the fate of poor Dashington reminds me that we may never meet again in this world."

"Whatever you say and whatever you do, Captain Blowitt, we can never be anything but the best of friends, and, so far as you are concerned, I never had an instant of doubt or suspicion."

"Now, Christy," interposed Paul Vapoor, "you entirely mistake the motive which has led to your appointment to the *Vixen*, for I happen to know something about it. You are not sent simply as a prize-master to New York, but you are put in temporary command of the *Vixen* because an able, vigilant, courageous officer was required."

"Then I wonder all the more that I was selected," added Christy.

"You wonder!" exclaimed Paul, looking intently into the brown face of the young officer, apparently to discover if there was not some affectation in this manifestation of modesty.

There was nothing like affectation in the composition of Christy Passford, and whatever he had done to distinguish himself, he had done strictly in the line of his duty and from the purest of patriotic motives. It was the most difficult thing in the world to make him believe that he had done "a big thing," though all others on board of his ship believed it with all their might. Paul Vapoor knew what everybody thought of his friend, and he was surprised that he should he so innocent and ignorant of the great reputation he had won.

"I do wonder," replied Christy, earnestly and honestly. "I believe I am about the youngest officer in the fleet, and if this service requires an able officer, it seems very strange to me that I should have been selected."

"Captain Breaker was consulted in regard to you, though he was not asked to name a commander, for the flag officer had thought of you himself, and no doubt he had just been reading your report of your voyage to the Gulf in the *Bronx*," said Paul, laughing. "I don't see how he could do otherwise than select you, Christy."

"You are chaffing me, Paul, as you do sometimes," said Christy with a smile.

"Then the expression of my honest opinion, which is also the opinion of every other officer in the ship, is chaffing you," retorted the engineer.

"I am satisfied, and I am sorry I said a word," added the subject of all these remarks.

"It is a very important and responsible situation to which you are ordered, Mr. Passford," said Captain Blowitt, putting on his dignity again. "Not a few steamers fitted up in part for service as Confederate men-of-war, in spite of neutrality treaties, are expected on the coast. You have diminished the number by two, and I hope you will be able to make a still further reduction of that fleet. We have three vessels to send on for condemnation, and your orders will inform you that there are several others, including another steamer, at Key West, and a Confederate armed steamer could easily recapture the whole of them. You will have to protect a fleet of at least seven vessels and this command ought to satisfy your ambition. You will also have charge of a dispatch bag to be forwarded to Washington at once, and this must not fall into the hands of the enemy. Sink or burn it if you are captured."

"I don't intend to be captured," added Christy with a smile.

"I remember that you were taken by the enemy on one occasion, and misfortunes may come to the best of officers. You must get ready to sail at once, but you must write your report of your expedition before you leave," added Captain Blowitt, as he rose from his chair, and the trio left the cabin.

Christy gaped several times during the latter part of the interview, for he had not slept a wink during the preceding night. He went to the wardroom and began to write his report, while the *Bronx* and the *Vixen* proceeded towards the three vessels which had been captured. It was well that they did so, for as they approached the *Havana* and her consorts they discovered quite a fleet of boats coming out from behind the Seahorse Key, evidently intending to recapture the prizes in the absence of the gunboat. They retired at once as she approached.

Christy was a rapid writer, and his report was

soon finished, for the subject was still very fresh in his mind, and he never attempted to do any "fine writing." He had packed his valises, and he took an affectionate farewell of the captain, Flint, and Sampson, as well as the ship's company in a more general way, though he said he expected to be back again in a few weeks. The *Vixen's* boat was waiting for him, and he embarked in it with Paul Vapoor. In a few minutes, he ascended to the deck of the steamer, and the side was manned at his appearance. He was presented to the officers of the ship by the engineer, and all three of them were older men than Christy, though he was their senior in rank, for his commission had been dated back to his enlistment in the navy.

Every one of the officers was a stranger to Christy, though there were a few men who had served in the *Bellevite*, but not in her original crew. With the customary proceedings he took command of the *Vixen*, and he found from sundry remarks made to him or dropped in his hearing that his reputation was already established on board. He directed the executive officer to follow the *Bronx*. In a short time the screw was stopped in the vicinity of the prizes. The *Bronx* reclaimed the men left on board of the *Havana*, and Captain

Lonley was sent on board of the *Vixen*.

Christy had been down into his cabin, and taken a hasty glance at the wardroom. In addition to his own apartments like those on board of the *Bronx*, though they were larger, he found a stateroom opening from the foot of the companionway, and another from the passage way leading to his principal cabin. These two rooms he appropriated to the use of Mr. Pembroke and his daughter, though they were very well provided for on board of the *Havana*. They were invited on board, and gratefully accepted the accommodations tendered to them.

Mr. Amblen was to retain the place assigned to him as prize-master, and two competent men were found to take charge of the schooners. All the arrangements were completed in a couple of hours, and the prizes of the *Bronx* were started at once. The Negroes were employed in transferring the deckload of the *Havana* to the holds of the schooners, which were not quite full.

The engineer of the *Bellevite* was to return to her in the *Bronx*, and he shook hands at parting with Christy, giving him a letter to Miss Florry Passford, and even her brother could not help seeing that he was greatly interested in her. Three rousing cheers went up from the *Bronx* as the screw of the

Vixen began to turn, and she started on her voyage.

The new commander, though he was very sleepy, gave his first moments to an examination of the vessel. The carpenter and his gang were still engaged in repairing the damage done to her in the engagement with the *Bellevite*. She was about the size of the two steamers captured by the *Bronx*, and coming out of the small steamer, she seemed quite large. She carried a midship gun of heavy caliber, and four broadside pieces. She had a crew of sixty men, besides those employed in the engineer's department, selected from the fleet, for the mission of the steamer was regarded as a very important one.

"Your machine looks well, Mr. Caulbolt," said Christy, as he went to the engine room in making his round with the executive officer.

"I fancy it is as good as can be built on the other side of the water," replied the chief engineer.

"Do you know anything in regard to the speed of the *Vixen*, for that may be a very important matter with us?" asked the commander.

"I do not know very much yet, sir, but I think she is a fast steamer. Mr. Vapoor told me that the *Bellevite* made twenty-two knots in chasing her, and that no other vessel in the navy could have

overhauled her. He gave me the figures," added Mr.
Caulbolt, taking a paper from his pocket. "I think
she is good for eighteen knots when driven hard."

"I dare say that will do," replied Christy, finishing
his examination and retiring to his cabin.

He found Mr. Pembroke and his daughter there.
The young lady presented him to her father, who
appeared to be about fifty years of age. He was very
gentlemanly in his manners and thanked the captain
heartily for the courtesy and kindness with which
he had been treated. Later in the voyage he learned
that Mr. Pembroke's wife and son had been killed
some years before in a railroad accident, and that
the money recovered from the corporation was about
his only fortune. Miss Bertha, as her father called
her, had been educated to become a teacher, but
when his health failed, she had devoted herself
wholly to him. They had gone to Georgia just before
the war, and had lived in the pine woods nearly two
years.

"My health is very much improved, and the genial
climate just suited my case, but in the present
situation, I had rather die at home than live in the
South," said the invalid in conclusion.

"Father is ever so much better than when we
came to Georgia," added Bertha.

Christy looked at her, and he had never seen a young lady before who made such a decided impression upon him. Of course the reason for this was that she was so dutiful and devoted to her sick father, for not every young and beautiful maiden would have been so entirely unselfish as she was. The commander could not help looking at her till he made her blush by the intensity of his gaze, and after all, it is possible that Christy was as human as other young men of his age. He had never been so affected before, and he hardly knew what to make of it, but he concluded that it was not because she was so pretty, but because she was so good and so devoted to her father.

In due time the *Vixen* and her convoy reached Key West. He found only two schooners and a steamer, all loaded with cotton, awaiting his coming, for two others had been sent with another steamer. Christy went on board of them, and as the sea was smooth, he arranged them as he had the others, though tow lines were ready in case of need, and the fleet sailed for the North.

CHAPTER XXX

THE ACTION WITH A PRIVATEER STEAMER

Christy had made up his lost sleep. On the first day out he had taken Captain Lonley's word that he would not interfere with anything on board, and had then given him a berth in the wardroom, where he messed with the officers. Captain Rowly had also been taken on board, and as he was a captain in the Confederate army, innocent as he was, he demanded similar accommodations. His request was granted, but Christy decided to leave him at Key West, for the wardroom was full.

The fleet continued on its voyage after the call at the Florida port and was soon in the Gulf Stream. It was an exceedingly quiet time in the little fleet of vessels, though the drill on board of the *Vixen* was closely followed up. On the second day they had a mild gale, and the schooners were cast off, and towed astern, one behind the other.

Then the weather was fine again, though the sea was still too rough for the *Havana* and the *Aleppo* to tow the prizes alongside. Christy observed the drill a great deal of the time, and Bertha Pembroke was often his companion. He told her all about vessels in the navy, explained actions at sea, but hoped she would not be permitted to see one.

Then he related to her the experience of the *Bellevite* as a yacht and as a naval vessel, and no one ever had a more attentive listener. He could not conceal it from himself that he was deeply interested in the young lady, and observers would have said that she was not less interested in him. On the fifth day out from Key West, while they were thus agreeably occupied, there was a hail from the fore rigging.

"Sail, ho!" shouted the lookout on the fore crosstrees, where the prudence of the commander required a hand to be stationed at all times, day and night.

"Where away?" called Scopfield, the third lieutenant, who was the officer of the deck.

"Broad on the starboard bow," replied the lookout.

"Can you make it out?"

"A steamer, sir; black smoke behind her," responded the lookout.

Mr. Fillbrook had joined the third lieutenant by this time, and the former reported to the captain. Christy had heard all that had passed, and he immediately began to feel a heavy anxiety in regard to the sail.

"What do you think of her, Mr. Fillbrook?" he asked, after the executive officer had reported to him.

"There are so many steamers coming over from British ports about this time, bound to Confederate ports, that it is not very difficult to guess what she is," replied the first lieutenant. "She is either a blockade runner or a steamer fitted out to prey upon the commerce of the United States."

"That seems to be plain enough, and from the position in which we find her, she has come out of the Bermudas, or is bound there," added the commander. "Bring my glass from my stateroom," he continued to his cabin steward, who was sunning himself on the deck.

When it was brought, the captain and the executive officer went forward and mounted the topgallant forecastle. Mr. Fillbrook procured a glass from the pilothouse, and both of them looked long and earnestly at the speck in the distance. The steamer was hull down, and they soon agreed that she was bound to the eastward.

"We have no business with her at present," said Christy, as he shut up his glass.

"But I have no doubt she has already run the blockade, and came out of Wilmington or Savannah. If that is the case, she must be loaded with cotton, which contains a fortune at the present time within a small compass," replied Mr. Fillbrook, who had not been as fortunate as some others in the matter of prizes.

"Very likely," replied Christy rather coldly, his companion thought. "I do not think I should be justified in giving chase to her, which could only be done by abandoning the convoy."

"Could we not pick up the convoy after we had captured the steamer?" asked the first lieutenant.

"Yes, if some Confederate cruiser does not pick it up in our absence," replied Christy with a significant smile.

Mr. Fillbrook was evidently very much disappointed, not to say disgusted, with the decision of Captain Passford, but he was too good an officer to make a complaint or utter a comment. The ship's company had become somewhat excited when it was

announced that a sail, with black smoke painting
a long streak on the blue sky, was made out. If it
was a blockade runner, with a cargo of cotton, it
meant a small fortune to each officer, seaman, and
others on board.

The new commander had a reputation as a daring
leader, and the hopes of the officers and men ran
high. They waited eagerly to have the steamer
headed to the eastward, but no such order was
given, and the chins of all hands began to drop down.

Christy had no interest in the money value of a
prize, and yet he could understand the feeling of
his ship's company. He was an heir of a millionaire,
and he had no occasion to trouble his head about
the profits of a capture. He looked at the question
from a purely patriotic point of view, and every prize
secured was so much taken from the resources of
the enemy.

He saw the disappointment painted on the face
of the first lieutenant, and he went to his cabin to
consider his duty again and review the reasoning
that had influenced him, but he came to the
conclusion he had reached in the beginning. He was
in charge of six vessels loaded with cotton, and the
ship's company of the *Bronx* and other vessels had
an interest in their cargoes. The *Vixen* was less

than a hundred and fifty miles from the coast, and a tugboat, with a bow gun and a crew of twenty-five, could come out and capture the whole fleet without the least difficulty. The risk was too great, and the commander was as firm as a rock.

The next morning, before it was daylight, Mr. Bangs, the second lieutenant, who had the mid watch, sent a messenger to the commander to inform him that a sail was made out, which appeared to be a steamer, on the starboard bow, very broad, nearly on the beam. Christy dressed himself in a great hurry and hastened on deck. It was beginning to be a little light, and the steamer appeared to be about five miles to the eastward of the *Vixen* and was headed towards her.

Christy at once concluded that the vessel meant mischief, and he promptly gave the order to beat to quarters. He thought it must be the steamer seen the day before, as she could hardly be a blockade runner for the reason that she was headed towards the fleet. If she desired to break through the blockading squadron, she would be likely to keep as far as possible from anything that might be an armed vessel.

Christy went to his stateroom to write an order for Mr. Amblen in the *Havana*, which was hardly

a cable's length from the *Vixen* on the port side,
the *Aleppo* being ahead of her. He had already given
his general orders to the prize masters. But this
was a special one. In the cabin he found Bertha,
who had been awakened by the tramping of the men
on deck.

"Pray what is the matter, Captain Passford?" she
asked, evidently somewhat alarmed.

"Nothing is the matter yet, Miss Pembroke, but
something may be the matter within an hour or two,
for there is a sail making for us," replied Christy
with the smile he always wore when she spoke to
him, or he to her. "In other words there may be
an action, for I must defend my convoy."

"Is there any danger?" she inquired.

"Of course there is, for a shot may come through
the side of the ship anywhere and at any time. But
I have thought of this matter, and I propose to put
you and your father on board of the *Havana* until
after the danger is passed. Be kind enough to get
ready as soon as possible."

Christy wrote his order and hastened on deck
with it. Hailing the *Havana*, he ordered the
prize-master to send a boat on board. When it came,
the two passengers were embarked in it and the
order sent. The commander did not wait a moment

to watch the receding form of the maiden, but immediately directed his attention to the steamer approaching the *Vixen*.

"Run for that steamer, Mr. Fillbrook," said he, after his first glance.

"Make the course east by north, Mr. Bangs," added the first lieutenant.

"East by north," repeated the quartermaster at the wheel when the order reached him.

"I have just been aloft, and she flies the Confederate flag, Captain Passford," said Mr. Fillbrook. "She is a large steamer, and she is by no means as jaunty as the *Vixen*."

Both steamers were going at full speed, and it required but a short time to bring them near enough together for something to happen. She was well down in the water, and appeared as though she might be loaded with something besides the appliances of a man-of-war. She looked as though she might be twice as large as the *Vixen*, and it was soon evident that her speed was nothing to boast of. She certainly was not one of the high-flyer yachts which had been bought up for service in the Confederate navy.

When the two vessels were not more than a mile apart, a column of smoke rose from her waist, as she swung around so that her great gun could be brought to bear, and a shot dropped into the water at least an eighth of a mile short of the *Vixen*.

"Thank you, sir," exclaimed Christy. "Half speed, if you please, Mr. Fillbrook."

The commander went to the long English gun in the waist, to which he had already given a great deal of study, and sighted along the heavy piece. He had not forgotten when he pointed the gun on board of the *Bellevite*, the shot from which had disabled the *Vampire*, and he had some confidence in his ability to put a shot where he wished it to go, for he had brought all his mathematics and all his physics to bear on the matter, though the best gunners must sometimes fail. When he was ready, he gave the word to fire. The ship was shaken by the heavy report, and every one waited with peculiar interest for the smoke to clear away, because the captain had pointed the gun.

Christy had ordered the screw to be stopped, and had waited till the steamer lost her headway. She rolled but slightly, and he had allowed for everything. Glasses were in demand, and, a moment later, a shout went up from the men at the gun, followed by another from the rest of the crew. The shot had upset the great gun on the deck of the enemy. She was swinging round and beginning to fire her broadside guns, but the shots came nowhere near the *Vixen*. Christy did not believe there was any naval officer on board of that steamer.

"Keep up the fire with the long gun, Mr. Fillbrook," said the commander in a low tone and with no excitement apparent in his manner, for he always studied and labored to appear cool and self-possessed, whether he was so or not, and there was nothing in the present situation to try him in the least.

For a full hour the long gun of the *Vixen* continued to pelt the enemy with solid shot, about every one of them bulling her or carrying away some of her spars. Her mainmast had gone by the board, and the resistance she was making was becoming very feeble.

"She is full of men, Captain Passford," said Mr. Fillbrook when the steamer seemed to be almost a wreck.

"I observed that she had a large crew some time ago, and it is better to knock her to pieces than to board her," replied Christy. "Keep her as far off as she is now."

The enemy tried to get nearer to the *Vixen*, but failed to do so.

CHAPTER XXXI

A SHORT VISIT TO BONNYDALE

The firing was continued from the long gun, though only at intervals that would permit any signals to be seen on board of the enemy. When it looked as though there would soon be nothing left of her, she hauled down the Confederate flag at her fore, where she had hoisted it when the mainmast went over. The order to go ahead was given, and in a short time the *Vixen* was alongside of her.

"Do you surrender?" asked Christy, mounting the rail of his ship.

"We do; there is not much left of the steamer, and I am not justified in throwing away the lives of my men," replied a very spruce looking officer.

"You will board her, Mr. Fillbrook, with the first division, and take possession of her," said Christy when he had received the captain's answer.

"Ascertain her condition as soon as possible."

The steamer proved to be the *Pedee*, formerly the *Carnfield*, commanded by Captain Linden. She had run the blockade with a valuable cargo, which more than paid the cost of the vessel, and was then loaded with cotton and armed for her own protection, as well as to capture anything that fell in her way.

She had a crew of eighty men to do her fighting, and the commander confidently expected to pick up a better steamer than the *Pedee*, to which the greater portion of the ship's company were to be transferred.

"I saw your steamer yesterday afternoon," said the captain, "but she had several other vessels near her, and I thought she might have a whole blockading squadron with her. I kept off and put about in the night. When I saw the *Vixen* early this morning, I thought she would just answer my purpose, and I wanted her. A nearer view of her assures me she is exactly the steamer I needed."

"For your sake, Captain, I am sorry I cannot accommodate you," replied Christy, laughing at the cheerful expressions of Captain Linden. "I presume you are an officer of the Confederate navy?"

"No, sir; I am not, but I am a Confederate to the

backbone. It was my intention to set up a navy on my own hook. The *Pedee* was the first vessel, and I intended that the *Vixen* should be the second and become my flagship."

"Then you came out as a privateer?"

"That's just the color of it. If you hadn't unhorsed my big gun, I should have been as polite to you about this time as you are to me. The fact of it is, Captain Passford, you did not manage your ship just right."

"Indeed? In what respect?" asked Christy.

"Well, you see, you knocked my big gun all to pieces, and then, instead of running down and boarding the *Pedee*, you stood off out of range of my side guns, and knocked the starch all out of us. If you had only boarded us, I could have whipped you out of your boots, for I have got the greatest crowd of fighting dogs that was ever hitched up together."

"Of course, I was not aware of your views in regard to the manner in which I ought to have managed the affair on my own part, and, therefore, I could not handle my ship just as you desired," replied Christy. "As it is, I am afraid you will have to start your navy over again."

Mr. Fillbrook had by this time driven the "fighting dogs" forward and taken full possession of the prize. On examination, Christy found that, though the *Pedee* had been terribly battered in her upper works, she was not materially injured below the water line. He sent for Mr. Caulbolt and required him to inspect the engine, which was not injured in any important part.

Captain Linden had three times attempted to get nearer to the *Vixen* with the intention of boarding her, but Christy preferred to fight the battle at long range under the circumstances, and he had preserved his distance from the enemy. He had discovered that she had a large crew, and he was vastly more prudent than most of his critics gave him the credit of being. He was surprised, after examining the *Pedee*, that the captain had hauled down his flag, for the steamer could have stood a good deal more pounding without being used up. He concluded that Captain Linden was full of fight, but, for the want of a naval education, he had not fully comprehended his situation.

It was deemed advisable to transfer one half of the *Pedee*'s crew of "fighting dogs" to the *Vixen*, as she was not encumbered with any prisoners to speak of, and this was effected without any delay. Mr. Scopfield, the third lieutenant, was appointed prize-master and instructed to keep as near as

practicable to the *Vixen* on the voyage. Captain
Linden and his principal officers were allowed to
remain on board. An assistant engineer and two
first-class firemen, on their way to New York for
examination and promotion, were sent on board of
the prize. The two steamers were soon under way,
and then it was ascertained that the *Pedee*'s ordinary
rate of sailing did not exceed ten knots, and it was
not probable that she would be bought into the navy.

The fleet of prize vessels had continued on its
course to the north, and was soon overhauled by
the *Vixen* and her capture. The progress of the
fleet was very slow, for the *Aleppo*, which was said
to have a speed of ten knots, did very badly towing
two schooners. Mr. Pembroke and Bertha were sent
on board of the *Vixen*, and the young lady blushed
beautifully when Christy welcomed her return.

Possibly she had feared he might be killed in the
action, and had worried about him till his return
in safety, with the prize alongside his ship. Her
father was very cordial in his congratulations to the
young commander, and even said that he and his
daughter had prayed that he might not be killed or
injured in the conflict, and Bertha blushed all the
more when he said it.

Mr. Scopfield was instructed to take one of the

schooners of the *Aleppo* in tow. Five men had been killed on board of the *Pedee*, and her surgeon had more than he could do with at least twenty wounded men. Dr. Appleton was sent on board of her to assist him. The fleet thus reorganized got under way, and it was found that the log gave better results after the change. Fortunately no enemy interfered with its progress, for Christy felt that his hands were already full.

In the early days of the month of May, he sailed into New York harbor with his fleet of eight vessels, though only three of them were the prizes of the *Bronx*. He had been absent hardly a month; though he had something to show for the time he had been employed. The vessels were delivered over to the authorities, and the young commander obtained leave of absence to visit his mother and sister at Bonnydale, for his father came on board of the *Vixen* as soon as he heard the news of her arrival in command of his son.

Captain Passford, Senior, was conducted to the cabin of Captain Passford, Junior, and the meeting of father and son was very affectionate and very demonstrative. Mr. Pembroke and his daughter were presented to the commander's father, and after they had talked over the incidents of the return voyage, the former owner of the *Bellevite* suspected that relations were altogether pleasant between Christy and Bertha.

He was greatly pleased with the young lady, and, whatever else he thought, he could not very well help endorsing his son's good taste. In the course of the subsequent conversation it appeared that Mr. Pembroke owned a small house at Newburgh, but that the occupant of it had a three years' lease of the premises. Captain Passford immediately extended an invitation to the invalid and his daughter to visit Bonnydale, which became so pressing that it was finally accepted. In the afternoon the entire party took the train for the home of the captain.

Christy's welcome was as hearty as though he had come home a commodore. The visitors were received with a sincere greeting, and Bertha and Florry were soon fast friends. Even if Christy's father had not dropped a hint to Mrs. Passford in regard to the fact that his son was at least tenderly inclined towards the lovely maiden from the South, she could not have failed to notice his attentions to her. Later at night his father and mother had a long talk over the matter.

"Christy, I have a couple of envelopes for you,"

said Captain Passford, as the party seated themselves in the drawing room after supper.

"Envelopes, Father?" asked the young officer curiously. "Baseball or boatclub business?"

"I should say neither; decidedly not," replied his father, taking the documents from his pocket and handing them to him. "They have an official look and bear the imprint of the Navy Department."

"What business can the Navy Department have with me now? I have the honor to be the executive officer of the gunboat *Bronx*, with the rank of master, on detached duty as prize-master," added Christy, as he looked at the ponderous envelopes.

"You can easily answer that question by reading the papers," replied his father.

"A commission!" exclaimed Christy, as he opened the first one. "I am promoted to the rank of lieutenant."

"And, though you are my son, I must say that you deserve the promotion," added Captain Passford. "I have read your report of the capture of the *Ocklockonee* and the *Escambia*, and you have won your spurs, my son. I did not ask for this promotion, or even suggest it to anyone."

"Well, I am astonished, confounded, overwhelmed," exclaimed the young lieutenant, as we are now permitted to call him. "And the commission is dated back far enough to put me over the heads of not a few others of the same rank."

"Perhaps it will please you quite as much when I inform you that the officers you recommended for appointment as masters have been promoted to that rank," added the captain.

"I am even more pleased at their promotion than at my own," replied Christy, opening the other envelope, in which he was addressed as "Lieutenant Christopher Passford." "Ah, ha!" he exclaimed, leaping out of his chair in his excitement, to which he gave way on such an occasion as the present.

"What in the world is the matter with you, Christy?" demanded his mother, astonished at such an unusual demonstration on the part of her son.

"I am appointed to the command of the *Bronx*, in place of Lieutenant Blowitt, transferred to the *Bellevite*!" almost shouted the young officer. "If I could have selected a position for myself, this is the very one I should have chosen."

"I heard you say as much as that when you were appointed to the temporary command of the *Bronx*, and I shall plead guilty of having inserted a hint where it would do the most good," added Captain Passford.

"I am much obliged to you, Father, for I don't object to that kind of influence, though I could have commanded the *Bronx* just as well as a master, which is the rank of her present temporary commander, Mr. Flint. I desire to win my own rank, and not get it by influence. I am ordered to proceed to the Gulf as soon as possible."

In three days he obtained passage in a storeship steamer, and he spent all this time at home, as perhaps he would not have done if Bertha Pembroke had not been there. Before he reported on board of the storeship, he visited the *Vixen*, which was undergoing alterations and repairs, and took leave of his officers. Before dark he was on board of the vessel and on his voyage to the scene of his future operations, where we hope to find him again, doing his best for his whole country, and true to his motto from the beginning, "*Stand by the Union.*"

GLOSSARY

———+———

abaft a-baft′ *preposition* behind *63, 64, 228*

abate a-bate′ *verb* to make less *290*

accommodation steps or ladder ac-com-mo-da′-tion steps or lad′-der *noun* temporary stairs on the side of a ship to allow people on and off the ship *33, 309*

adherents ad-her′-ents *noun* followers or supporters *185, 207*

adipose ad′-i-pose *adjective* fat *303*

adjourned ad-journed′ *verb* went from one place to another *243*

admonition ad-mo-ni′-tion *noun* a warning *32*

adroitly a-droit′-ly *adjective* skillfully or cleverly *77*

affectation af-fec-ta′-tion *noun* a manner that is artificial or not genuine *315*

aft aft *adverb* toward the rear of a ship *62, 213*

aground a-ground′ *adverb* onto land or a shoal *282*

amiable a′-mi-a-ble *adjective* good-natured or friendly *131*

amplifying am′-pli-fy-ing *verb* developing more fully by giving more details *31*

animated an′-i-mat-ed *adjective* lively *242*

anomalous a-nom′-a-lous *adjective* unusual or abnormal *136*

anthracite an′-thra-cite *noun or adjective* a hard coal which has little smoke or flame *143, 149*

apex a′-pex *noun* the highest point *66, 196*

appendage ap-pend′-age *noun* an attachment or something added *115*

appropriated ap-pro′-pri-at-ed *verb* set aside *319*

armament ar′-ma-ment *noun* guns and other weapons used for military defense *22, 23*

artillerists ar-til´-ler-ists *noun* gunners; those people who operate the artillery *273*

ascertain as-cer-tain´ *verb* to find out *63, 73, 133*

astern a-stern´ *adverb* backward *279*

audacity au-dac´-i-ty *noun* boldness or daring *24, 101, 224*

auditor au´-di-tor *noun* listener *69, 120, 132*

auspices aus´-pic-es *noun* protection *232*

barometer ba-rom´-e-ter *noun* an instrument used to predict changes in the weather *66*

battery bat´-ter-y *noun* a group of large guns and cannons *244, 246, 248*

beaten to quarters beat´-en to quar´-ters *phrase* sent to their stations *202*

bells bells *noun* the ringing of a bell on ship every half-hour to mark the time during a four-hour period (or watch); is measured from one to eight bells *34, 61, 74*

berth berth *noun* a built-in bed on a ship *25*

bight bight *noun* a section of rope *81*

bi-hourly bi´-hour-ly *adjective* twice an hour *59*

billeted bil´-let-ed *verb* assigned sailors to their living quarters *63*

billows bil´-lows *noun* large waves *115, 140*

blockade block-ade´ *noun* the shutting or closing of a port by the enemy to prevent ships from entering or leaving *106, 245, 263*

blockade runners block-ade´ run´-ners *noun* ships that try to get into a closed or blockaded port *21, 56, 125*

blockaded block-ad´-ed *adjective* prevented from having ships enter and leave a port *22*

blockader block-ad´-er *noun* those people and ships that are maintaining a blockade *263*

boarders board´-ers *noun* those who go on board an enemy ship to capture it *152, 154, 155*

boathook boat´-hook *noun* a long pole with a hook on the end used for moving boats around *251*

boating boat´-ing *noun* putting something in a boat *251*

boatswain boat´-swain *noun* the ship's officer in charge of the deck crew and the rigging anchors and other deck equipment *25, 34, 118*

bogus bo´-gus *adjective* not true *139*

bow bow *noun* the front of a ship *208, 210, 324*

brailed brailed *verb* tied up with ropes *77*

breastwork breast´-work *noun* low walls put up quickly for defense against enemy fire *283, 287*

bridge bridge *noun* the platform above the main deck of a ship from which the captain gives his orders *62, 65, 78*

broad broad *adjective* to the side *324, 328*

broadside guns broad´-side guns *noun* those guns or cannon on the side of a ship *152, 203, 206*

brusquely brusque´-ly *adverb* roughly or bluntly *178*

bulling bull´-ing *verb* making its way with force *332*

bulwarks bul´-warks *noun* the sides of a ship that rise above the deck *160*

burthen bur´-then *adjective* the weight of a ship when loaded *21*

by one jot or tittle by one jot or tit´-tle *phrase* not in the least *290*

cachinnation cach-in-na´-tion *noun* loud laughter *241*

canopy can´-o-py *noun* heavens or the sky *211*

canvassed can´-vassed *verb* to question a group of people *268*

capital cap´-i-tal *adjective* excellent *56, 235*

capstan cap´-stan *noun* the device around which the anchor chain is wound *34*

carriage car´-riage *noun* a structure with wheels that goes under a heavy load for the purpose of moving it *257, 259, 271*

casemate case´-mate *noun* a fortified area with openings through which guns may be fired *252, 255*

catted and fished cat´-ted and fished *verb phrase* hoisted and brought into view *35*

chaffing chaff´-ing *verb* teasing or mocking *316*

chartered char´-tered *verb* hired or paid money for the use of *30*

cipher ci´-pher *noun* a secret writing system or code *31*

coal passers coal pass´-ers *noun* crew members who shovel coal into the ship's furnace *205*

coaster coast´-er *noun* a ship that carries cargo along a coast going from port to port *106, 234*

collation col-la´-tion *noun* a light meal *129*

commended com-mend´-ed *verb* recommended or praised *220*

commodore com´-mo-dore *noun* the military rank above a captain but below a rear admiral *339*

companionway com-pan´-ion-way *noun* a ship's stairway going from one deck to another *20, 25, 45*

comprise com-prise´ *verb* contained or included *100*

Confederate Con-fed´-er-ate *noun or adjective* the Southern states which broke away from the Union during the Civil War; someone who fought on the side of the South in the Civil War *70, 103, 104*

confederate con-fed´-er-ate *noun* an accomplice or partner in a plot *94, 102, 109*

confidant con´-fi-dant *noun* a close friend with whom one discusses very personal or secret matters *83, 137*

confounded con-found´-ed *verb* confused or bewildered *120*

confounding con-found´-ing *verb* confusing or mixing up *78*

conjecture con-jec´-ture *noun* predictions or guesses *107*

consort con´-sort *noun* a ship that travels along with another ship *148, 164, 204*

constitutional con-sti-tu´-tion-al *noun* a walk that is taken to improve or maintain one's health *124*

contingency con-tin´-gen-cy *noun* unknown future conditions or circumstances *115*

convoy con´-voy *noun* a group of ships *329*

copyist cop´-y-ist *noun* a secretary *94, 112*

cordial cor´-dial *adjective* warm and hearty *337*

coveted cov´-et-ed *verb* longed for or wanted strongly *60*

coxswain cox´-swain *noun* the sailor in charge of steering a boat *245*

cronies cro´-nies *noun* close friends *18*

crosstrees cross´-trees *noun* the horizontal bars that extend out from the mast to hold the sails *324*

crowding crowd´-ing *verb* pressing or pushing *38*

cudgeled his brains cudg´-eled his brains *verb phrase* thought very hard *98, 151*

cutlass cut´-lass *noun* a short thick and curving sword used by sailors *152, 209, 252*

cutter cut´-ter *noun* a boat used for carrying passengers and supplies from the shore to a ship *246, 247, 257*

davits da´-vits *noun* devices on a ship used for raising and lowering a small boat *307*

deaf mute deaf mute *noun* a person who can neither hear nor speak *50, 53, 57*

deference def´-er-ence *noun* respect or honor *84*

deferential def-er-en´-tial *adjective* very respectful *112*

demonstrative de-mon´-stra-tive *adjective* showing one's feelings *309*

depot de´-pot *noun* a storage place *225*

deprecatory dep´-re-ca-to-ry *adjective* showing disapproval *313*

derange de-range´ *verb* to upset *140, 303*

desultory des´-ul-to-ry *adjective* random or without a definite plan *285*

disarm dis-arm´ *verb* to make harmless *58*

discerned dis-cerned´ *verb* perceived or made out clearly *247*

dispatches dis-patch´-es *noun* official messages *309, 310*

distended dis-tend´-ed *verb* swollen or puffed out *302*

divine di-vine´ *verb* to guess *149*

dog watch dog watch *noun* one of two duty periods from 4 to 6 P.M. or from 6 to 8 P.M. *35, 61, 141*

draft draft *noun* people chosen for some duty or task *231*

draught draught *noun* the depth of water a ship needs to stay afloat *155, 227*

dumb dumb *adjective* unable to speak *57, 63, 71*

earthwork earth´-work *noun* a wall of packed earth used as protection *249, 252*

elastic e-las´-tic *adjective* buoyed up or feeling like oneself again *184*

emulate em´-u-late *noun* to try to equal *229*

endeavored en-deav´-ored *verb* tried to do something *51, 234, 238*

enigma e-nig´-ma *noun* a mystery *31*

enjoined en-joined´ *verb* forbidden *122*

ensign en´-sign *noun* flag *204, 307*

epicure ep´-i-cure *noun* someone who takes a great deal of pleasure in dining *67*

etiquette et´-i-quette *noun* rules for behavior *25, 69*

exigency ex´-i-gen-cy *noun* a need or demand that must be met soon *187*

expedient ex-pe´-di-ent *adjective* useful or convenient *106, 227*

expeditiously ex-pe-di´-tious-ly *adverb* efficiently and speedily *114*

expletive ex´-ple-tive *noun* an exclamation or curse word *81*

fairing off fair´-ing off *verb phrase* becoming clear (used to describe the weather) *125*

fast fast *adjective* firmly fastened *277, 280*

fasts fasts *noun* ropes used to moor or hold a ship in place *277, 279, 280*

fathom fath´-om *noun* a measure of depth equal to six feet *259*

fathom fath´-om *verb* to thoroughly understand *97*

field pieces field pie´-ces *noun* small cannons used in battle *291*

figuratively fig´-ur-a-tive-ly *adverb* not in a literal sense but in a manner of speaking *292*

flag officer flag of´-fi-cer *noun* the officer in command of a fleet of ships *24, 25, 134*

forage for´-age *verb* to look for something *113*

fore rigging fore rig´-ging *noun* the sails and mast on the front of a ship *324*

fore sheets fore sheets *noun* an open space at the front of a boat *251*

foreyard fore´-yard *noun* the wooden crosspiece holding up the front sail on mast *70*

forecastle fore´-cas-tle *noun* the upper deck in front of the first mast *263, 271, 301*

formidable for´-mi-da-ble *adjective* inspiring awe or fear *31, 282*

fractional frac´-tion-al *adjective* forming a fraction or part of a whole *267*

Freemason Free´-ma-son *noun* a member of a secret society *68*

frigate frig´-ate *noun* a medium-sized war ship carrying 24 to 60 guns *91*

gallantry gal´-lan-try *noun* nobility and bravery *210*

galling gall´-ing *adjective* irritating or upsetting *84*

gangway gang´-way *noun* the opening in the ship's bulwarks that allows passage on and off the ship *25*

gaped gaped *verb* yawned *317*

garrison gar´-ri-son *noun* soldiers who are stationed in a place to defend it *253, 304*

genial gen´-i-al *adjective* healthful; warm *321*

gesticulating ges-tic´-u-lat-ing *verb* making gestures with one's hands and arms *77*

glass glass *noun* telescope *325, 331*

gone by the board gone by the board *phrase* fallen overboard *332*

grapnels grap´-nels *noun* small anchors or hooks with four or five arms used to hold a ship in place *182, 209*

grappling iron grap´-pling i´-ron *noun* a small anchor used to hold a ship in place *160*

head sea head sea *noun* waves on the ocean that are running directly head-on into a ship *89, 96*

heaving of the log heav´-ing of the log *noun phrase* the noting of the ship's movement in the written record or log *59*

heavy heav´-y *adjective* violent and rough *61*

hulls hulls *noun* bodies of ships *60, 326*

humbug hum´-bug *noun* someone who is pretending to be something he is not *55*

in train in train *phrase* in a state of being ready *140*

Indiaman In´-di-a-man *noun* a merchant ship that regularly sailed between England and India *105*

inert in-ert´ *adjective* inactive *61*

infirmity in-fir´-mi-ty *noun* a physical defect of weakness *81*

injunction in-junc´-tion *noun* a command or order *37*

intelligence in-tel´-li-gence *noun* information or news *22*

intercourse in´-ter-course *noun* a conversation or interaction *62*

intermitting in-ter-mit´-ting *verb* stopping or discontinuing *67*

interpolated in-ter´-po-lat-ed *verb* added to the meaning of what has been said *83*

interposed in-ter-posed´ *verb* interrupted *176, 284, 314*

jaw jaw *noun* a talk or scolding *83*

Jeff Davis Jeff Da´-vis *noun* President Jefferson Davis, the president of the Confederacy from 1861-1865 *70*

keel keel *noun* the main timber running underneath the boat from front to back *46*

keel to truck keel to truck *phrase* from the bottom of the ship to the smallest item on board, in other words everything on a ship *34*

keys keys *noun* low islands or reefs *243, 261, 271*

Knight of Pythagoras Knight of Py-thag´-o-ras *noun* a member of a secret society *68*

Knight of Pythias Knight of Pyth´-i-as *noun* also a member of a secret society *68*

knots knots *noun* unit of speed equal to about 6,076 feet (one nautical mile) an hour *38, 39, 155*

latitude lat´-i-tude *noun* the distance north or south from the equator measured in degrees *119, 125*

lee lee *noun* the direction or side away from the wind　*88*

lockstring lock´-string *noun* the string used to explode the charge of ammunition in a gun causing it to fire　*287*

longitude lon´-gi-tude *noun* the distance east or west from the prime meridian, which runs through Greenwich England, measured in degrees　*119*

magazine mag-a-zine´ *noun* a place where ammunition and guns are stored　*253, 257*

magnanimous mag-nan´-i-mous *adjective* generous; rising above meanness or pettiness　*266*

mangroves man´-groves *noun* a kind of tree that forms dense cover　*251*

manifest man´-i-fest *verb* to show or reveal　*26, 52, 139*

manifestation man´-i-fes-ta-tion *noun* a showing or proving　*200, 315*

manifestation of zeal man-i-fes-ta´-tion of zeal *noun phrase* showing of great enthusiasm　*92*

man-of-war man-of-war´ *noun* a warship　*115*

master mas´-ter *noun* the captain of a ship　*17, 19*

meridian me-rid´-i-an *noun* an imaginary line passing between the north and south poles and a point in between them　*85, 119*

messed messed *verb* regularly ate meals　*323*

midship gun mid´-ship gun *noun* the gun at the middle of a ship　*182, 196, 202*

midshipman mid´-ship-man *noun* someone who is being trained for the position of ensign, the lowest-ranking officer　*19*

midwatch mid´-watch *noun* the watch or period of guard duty that comes in the middle of the night　*96*

modesty mod´-es-ty *noun* not thinking too much of oneself or one's abilities　*231, 315*

mulatto mu-lat´-to *noun* a person of mixed race with a white (or Caucasian) and a black (or Negro) parent　*41*

nettled net´-tled *verb* irritated or annoyed　*203, 238*

neutral neu´-tral *adjective* not taking sides　*180*

obtuse ob-tuse´ *adjective* dull; slow to understand　*297*

oiler oil´-ler *noun* the person who oils the machinery on board a steamship　*270, 272, 275*

on the beam on the beam *phrase* at a right angle to the side of a ship *328*

ornamentation or-na-men-ta´-tion *noun* decoration *24*

orthodox or´-tho-dox *adjective* conventional or usual *24*

overhauled o-ver-hauled´ *verb* thoroughly checked; overtaken or caught up to *114, 196, 310*

pantry pan´-try *noun* place near the kitchen where food is stored *25*

parallel par´-al-lel *noun* an imaginary line running parallel to the equator used to measure latitude *126*

peak peak *noun* a pole extending from the mainmast from which the ensign or flag is flown *156*

peninsula pen-in´-su-la *noun* an area of land that extends out into the water *289*

penitent pen´-i-tent *adjective* feeling sorry and wanting to make amends *239*

perdition per-di´-tion *noun* hell or complete ruin *199, 200*

petty officers pet´-ty off´-i-cers *noun* noncommissioned enlisted officers of a lower rank than commissioned officers *181*

physique phy-sique´ *noun* appearance *187*

Pickwickian Pick-wick´-i-an *adjective* in an abstract manner not to be taken seriously (named after the kindly Samuel Pickwick in *The Pickwick Papers* by Charles Dickens) *225*

pier pier *noun* a dock or other structure that extends out over the water and which is used as a landing place for ships *276, 281*

planking the deck plank´-ing the deck *verb phrase* walking the deck forcefully *61, 141, 159*

pliable pli´-a-ble *adjective* easily persuaded or influenced *181*

poltroon pol-troon´ *noun* a coward *32*

port, port beam, or port hand port, port beam, port hand *adjective or noun* the left-hand side of a ship *198, 206, 208*

port the helm port the helm *phrase* turn the helm to the left *155, 286*

portières por-tières´ *noun* curtains *25, 37, 45*

post post *verb* to make aware *21, 107*

precepts pre´-cepts *noun* commands or orders *45*

pressing press´-ing *adjective* insistent or strong *339*

presumptive pre-sump´-tive *adjective* bold *230*

privateer pri-va-teer´ *noun* a privately owned warship paid by a government to attack the merchant ships which supply its enemy *264, 335*

procured pro-cured´ *verb* got or obtained *19, 110, 143*
prodigious pro-di´-gious *adjective* huge *76*
prognostics prog-nos´-tics *noun* a forecast *66*
promenade prom´-e-nade *noun* a walk or stroll; an area where people walk *243, 252*
prudence pru´-dence *noun* good judgment or carefulness *41, 238, 324*
prudent pru´-dent *adjective* wise *23, 70, 109*
purport pur-port´ *noun* intention or object *139*

quarterdeck quar´-ter-deck *noun* the rear of the upper deck *25, 115, 149*
quartering quar´-ter-ing *noun* sailing at an angle to the wind or waves *140*
quartermasters quar´-ter-mas-ters *noun* the officers on a ship who are responsible for steering the ship and plotting its course *90, 99, 105*
Quixotic Quix-ot´-ic *adjective* like Don Quixote, that is being overly or foolishly idealistic *24*

rake rake *verb* slightly slanted *287*
redback red´-back *noun* vermin; insect *42*
rendered ren´-dered *verb* gave or delivered *127*
repeater re-peat´-er *noun* a watch that will strike the time when a spring is pressed *260*
report re-port´ *noun* the noise made by an explosion *331*
repose re-pose´ *verb* to place or put *64*
reproved re-proved´ *verb* expressed disapproval *97*
restrained re-strained´ *verb* held back *302*
reticence ret´-i-cence *noun* an unwillingness to speak freely *231*
rigged rigged *verb* fitted with sails *34*
risibililty ris-i-bil´-i-ty *noun* the state of being inclined to laugh *303*
rover rov´-er *noun* a pirate ship *220*

schooners schoon´-ers *noun* ships with two or more masts *221, 235, 272*
screw screw *noun* the propeller that moves a ship *145, 147, 308*
scullion scul´-lion *noun* a kitchen helper *50, 51, 57*
sentinel sen´-ti-nel *noun* a guard *292, 293*
sextant sex´-tant *noun* an instrument used to determine the position or course of a ship by measuring the angle of the sun, moon or stars from the horizon *118*

shipped shipped *verb* signed up to serve on a ship *210, 233*

shoal shoal *adjective* shallow *227*

shrapnel shrap´-nel *noun* a shell filled with smaller pieces of metal designed to explode and spray over an area *282, 288*

singular sin´-gu-lar *adjective* unusual or strange *291*

slight slight *noun* being treated as unimportant *123*

smart smart *adjective* lively or brisk *140*

sonorous so-no´-rous *adjective* loud *254*

sound sound *verb* to measure the water's depth *251*

spars spars *noun* the poles on a ship such as the masts, yards, gaffs or booms used to suspend sails *332*

speaking speak´-ing *verb* act of communication between ships at sea *202*

speaking trumpet speak´-ing trum´-pet *noun* a device used to make one's voice louder *155, 158*

speculation spec-u-la´-tion *noun* hoping to make a financial profit by taking advantage of a possible future event *233*

spinning yarns spin´-ning yarns *verb phrase* telling stories or tales *77*

starboard star´-board *adjective* the right-hand side of a ship *25, 119, 157*

starboard bow star´-board bow *noun* the right-hand side of the front of a ship *144, 155*

stays stays *noun* ropes *206*

steerage steer´-age *noun* the area on a ship where the steering mechanism is located *25, 75, 126*

stern stern *noun or adjective* the rear end of a ship; at the rear of a ship *24, 279, 307*

stern sheets stern sheets *noun phrase* an open space at the rear of a boat *247, 248*

stool of repentance stool of re-pent´-ance *noun phrase* a seat where those who are sorry for their actions sit *292*

subordinate sub-or´-di-nate *noun* someone of a lesser rank or lower position *44, 241*

sundry sun´-dry *adjective* various *236, 318*

superfluous su-per´-flu-ous *adjective* excess or extra *24*

superintend su-per-in-tend´ *verb* to manage or supervise *163*

supernumerary su-per-nu´-mer-ar-y *noun* an extra person *75, 77, 82*

tendered ten´-dered *verb* offered *67, 166*

tonnage ton´-nage *noun* the carrying capacity of a ship measured in tons *224*

topgallant forecastle top-gal´-lant fore´-cas-tle *noun* the topmost upper deck in front of the mast *61, 77, 157*

topsail schooner top´-sail schoon´-er *noun* a ship with two masts and with two sails on the fore-mast *34*

topsail yard top´-sail yard *noun* the wooden spar that suspends the topsail from the mast *141, 155, 172*

transcendent tran-scend´-ent *adjective* superior or extraordinary *70*

transgressor trans-gres´-sor *noun* one who goes beyond a law or limit *265*

transpired tran-spired´ *verb* happened; took place *176*

treason trea´-son *noun* betraying one's country *97*

valises va-lis´-es *noun* traveling bags *318*

waist waist *noun* middle part of a ship *77, 172, 331*

wardroom ward´-room *noun* the living quarters for the ship's officers *25, 63, 64*

wear any spurs wear an´-y spurs *verb phrase* take the credit *218*

wharf wharf *noun* a wood or stone structure at the shore of a harbor where ships may be tied up *277, 284*

windward wind´-ward *adjective* the direction from which the wind is blowing *87*

without friction with-out´ fric´-tion *phrase* without problems *184*

yielded yield´-ed *verb* gave up or surrendered *210*

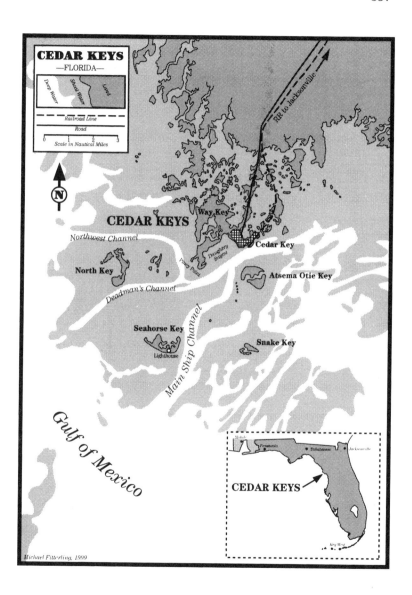

CEDAR KEYS
—FLORIDA—

Deep Water
Shoal Water
Land

- - - Railroad Line
—— Road

0 1 2 3
Scale in Nautical Miles

N

RR to Jacksonville

Way Key

CEDAR KEYS

Northwest Channel

Cedar Key

North Key

Pinery Point

Doughtry Bayou

Deadman's Channel

Atsema Otie Key

Seahorse Key

Main Ship Channel

Snake Key

Lighthouse

Gulf of Mexico

Michael Fitterling, 1999

CEDAR KEYS

Mobile
Pensacola
Tallahassee
Jacksonville

Key West

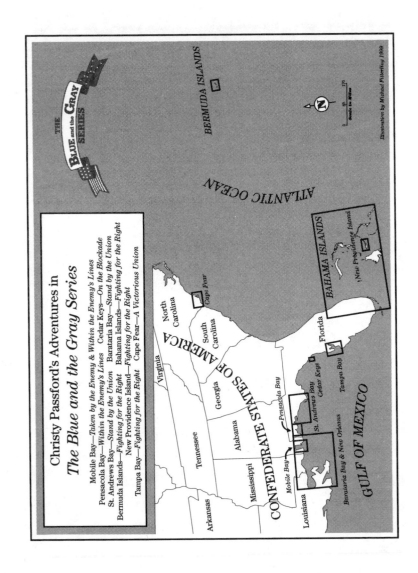

Books Available from
Lost Classics Book Company

American History
Stories of Great Americans for Little Americans ... Edward Eggleston
A First Book in American History .... Edward Eggleston
A History of the United States and Its People .... Edward Eggleston

Biography
The Life of Kit Carson .... Edward Ellis

English Grammar
Primary Language Lessons .... Emma Serl
Intermediate Language Lessons .... Emma Serl

Historical Fiction
With Lee in Virginia .... G. A. Henty
A Tale of the Western Plains .... G. A. Henty
The Young Carthaginian .... G. A. Henty
In the Heart of the Rockies .... G. A. Henty
For the Temple .... G. A. Henty
A Knight of the White Cross .... G. A. Henty
The Minute Boys of Lexington .... Edward Stratemeyer
The Minute Boys of Bunker Hill .... Edward Stratemeyer
Hope and Have .... Oliver Optic
Taken by the Enemy, First in *The Blue and the Gray Series* .... Oliver Optic
Within the Enemy's Lines, Second in *The Blue and the Gray Series* .... Oliver Optic
On the Blockade, Third in *The Blue and the Gray Series* .... Oliver Optic
Mary of Plymouth .... James Otis

To Place an Order or Request a Catalog

Telephone Orders: (888) 611-BOOK *(2665)*
Postal Requests: Lost Classics Book Company
　　　　　　　　P. O. Box 1756, Ft. Collins, CO 80522
Please send a catalog and order form to:

Company name: _____

Name: _____

Address:_____

City: _____

State:_____　　Zip:_____ - _____

Telephone: (　　　　) _____